AFTERNOON DELIGHT

Afternoon Delight

DANI COLLINS

SUGAR SHACK BOOKS
CHARLOTTETOWN

Sugar Shack Books is an imprint of Pownal Street Press. Requests for permission to make copies of any part of the work should be emailed to permissions at hello@pownalstreetpress.com. Our books may be purchased for promotional, educational, or business use. Please contact your local bookseller or Pownal Street Press to purchase.

pownalstreetpress.com • @sugarshackbooks

Cataloguing data available from Library Archives Canada:
ISBN 978-1-997918-10-3 • eBook ISBN 978-1-997918-11-0

Edited by Alison Strumberger. Proofread by Lara Hyde. Cover design by Erin Craig. Author photograph by Suzanne Le Stage Photography. Designed by Jordan Beaulieu.

Pownal Street Press gratefully acknowledges Mi'kma'ki, the ancestral and unceded territory of the Mi'kmaq First Nation on whose land our office is located.

Printed and bound in Canada.

1 2 3 4 5 26 27 28 29 30

CHAPTER ONE

MEG

I hadn't suffered this much gut-crunching anxiety and loin-tingling thrill since I'd been Meg Crutcher, lying to Mom about staying at Georgia's house on graduation night when I was actually meeting Joel at the Island Value Inn on Gorge Road.

I slowed my rented SUV, and the steering wheel grew slippery under my sweaty palms. My skin tightened with the pressure of holding in my lewd secret. My ears filled with a rushing noise. I kind of had to pee.

Screw parallel parking—I found a spot where I could nose in.

My conscience writhed with snakes that hissed, *You're being bad*, but I was a grown-ass woman. I could do what I wanted.

Which was exactly what I'd told myself twenty-one years ago, when I'd left my virginity in room twelve of the I.V. Inn.

That act of rebellion was supposed to turn me into an adult. It had. Except, I'd thought growing up meant making choices for myself, when in reality, cells had met and combined and divided without my permission. From there, one responsibility after another had appeared in front of me like stepping stones leading into a cave where a neon sign above the opening flashed, *Where did my life go?*

Now I was a few kilometres east of my youthful misconception. I had lied to my mother again, this time texting her that I was running an errand for Georgia.

It was kind of true. I had agreed to run Georgia's *store*. Actually, I'd agreed to open the doors and figure out if there was a way to keep it running—even if she couldn't come back right away. Or at all.

I cut the engine and sat there, listening to the February rain patter on the roof. Winter never really arrived in Victoria, BC. Not the way it did back in Toronto. Snow rarely stuck to these streets, but spring wasn't here yet, either. It was a messy, unpredictable shoulder season, and very much a metaphor for the state of my life.

This wasn't even *Victoria*. Not the downtown waterfront that looked so pretty on the postcards. No, this was Milestone—one of the oldest suburbs of the city. It was the name of the most popular streetcar stop back when those were a thing here. Locals called it Mild Stone. I'll give you three guesses why.

Milestone had had its rough years, but it was still where the broke creatives came together. Its commercial area was a colourful hodgepodge of brick storefronts and people running businesses out of their Victorian-style homes.

Georgia had picked this location because it was busy but affordable. And because they had said yes to an adult toy store. Sometimes people were picky about that sort of thing.

I studied the two-storey building through the drips that gathered and ran down the windshield. There were four windows on the second floor. Georgia had told me there were two apartments up there. She'd been cagey when I asked about the tenants, making me think she knew one of them. A man? I hadn't pressed her. She was either in pain or drowsy from painkillers these days. All I really needed to know was that she had asked me for help.

She'd shocked me by asking. Georgia was the poster girl for independent women—meaning she would kick the ass of anyone who dismissed her as a girl or tried to put her face on a poster without her permission.

She had recently called me out when I began moaning about how envious I was of my daughter. Shelby was living the university life I had never experienced because I'd had her straight out of high school.

"You just got divorced. It's the perfect time to reinvent," Georgia had said.

"I know, but I have to get Mom to move to Toronto first. Then get Roddie through high school and off to uni. *Then* I can start making changes to my life."

"Seriously, Meg? Do you hear these excuses you're making? Just jump."

I have responsibilities, I wanted to say, but this was Georgia. She'd always been able to throw herself off cliffs and then yell, *Just jump*. She'd always known how to keep her head above water.

Three weeks after grad, she'd been the one to say, *I'll go with you if you want an abortion*. She also had a healthy respect for leaps that were truly too big, but I had been convinced I was getting everything I wanted—independence, a husband, and a life off this damned island. I moved to Montreal with Joel, and Georgia went to California. She didn't get into the movies like she wanted, but she danced on cruise ships, sang backup in a studio, and had thousands of colourful stories that spoke of a life well lived.

I had two kids I loved beyond measure, a steady job as an accountant, and a Final Divorce Order.

"I'm scared," I had admitted to Georgia with a laugh that didn't disguise any of the painful truth in that statement. "What if I make a wrong choice? It's easier to blame Mom and Joel and work than accept that I've wound up with exactly what I settled for. Which is what will happen again unless I get it right this time."

"You never change. You know why? *Because you never change*." Georgia shook her scarf-covered head.

Her spinal tumors weren't cancerous, but she was in so much pain her hair had become more work than she wanted to fuss with. She'd shaved her head, and because it was still winter—and winter in southern BC brought a damp cold that settled into your bones—she had to keep her head covered. Her light brown complexion was wan, her mouth strained with tension and worry, but she still managed to make me feel like the pitiful one.

"There's no *getting it right*," she scolded. "Shake things up. You know what you should do? Quit your job and run my store for me."

"Can you imagine? Mom would shit a brick."

"I'm serious."

"Right," I scoffed. That store was her baby—still spanking new and something she'd worked hard to make happen.

"Meg. I actually am." Her expression sobered into pensive. Desperate. "I'm really worried about it. The landlord is calling about rent and…" Her eyes welled up.

"Hey." I reached out to squeeze her hand. "You know I'll do anything. I can cover rent for a few months if you need me to."

"It's not that. I need my business to *run*. To generate income. For bills and the bank loan. I put all my savings into this. If I lose it, I'm starting from nothing. At forty."

"You're not going to lose it. That's the pain pills talking." They cramped her mood, she'd told me.

"I'm high as a kite," Georgia agreed as she ran a thumb under her leaking eye. "Otherwise, I wouldn't ask for help. But I really don't want to lose my store, Meg."

"I know, but—" I bit back the protest that rose from sheer cowardice.

I thought of Roddie, who lived with Joel and kept insisting he was fine. And Mom, who was fighting me at every turn when it came to cleaning out the house. She wanted to keep everything the same. I didn't want to be Mom—stuck in the past. We both needed to start moving forward.

"You don't want to let me down, do you?" Georgia prodded.

I dropped my jaw in exaggerated outrage. "You ruthless bitch."

Georgia showed all her teeth in a slow, wide grin, knowing she had me.

So here I was, shaking things up.

Shaking.

Afraid.

Imagining I could hear Georgia yelling, *The water's fine!*

I studied the awnings on the brick building—one blue, the other pink—that sheltered the storefront windows and the stoop in between. Under the pink one, the building looked gloomy and dark. Below the blue one, a golden light beckoned.

No use waffling. I said I would do it, but I couldn't help wondering if this decision would leave me as screwed as last time.

Mom was going to *hate* it. Helping a friend meant dropping off a casserole or donating bone marrow. It didn't mean becoming the face of an adult toy shop. As for what Joel would say—

Ugh. No more Joel. No more spiralling through old choices, wishing I'd made different ones. No more sitting in a cubicle promising myself things would get better.

Get out of the car, dipshit. Make it better.

I threw open the door. A gust of wind caught it, nearly smashing it into the side of the SUV parked next to mine. I managed to hang on to it, then stepped into the puddle of water backed up from the clogged drain in the curb, swore, slammed the door, and trotted the half block until I was under the pink awning of the building.

I gasped against the frigid air filling my lungs. I *really* needed to start some cardio.

At the darkened window, I cupped my hands above the gold-stenciled *Afternoon Delight* on the glass. A translucent white curtain hid the window display, but there was nothing to see. The display was empty. A tall wooden shelf was strategically placed to limit the view of any stock it might hold. Sheets were draped over odd shapes on the table in the middle of the room. There was a cheerful area rug before the cash desk, open rafters in the ceiling, and a slatted wall at the back peppered with hooks. Bagged goods hung on either side of a door that presumably led to a stockroom and bathroom.

For me, it was Room Twelve all over again—filled with mysteries both titillating and intimidating. It was filled with *sex*.

I felt in my coat pocket for the key and moved to the door, glancing over my shoulder at the store behind me.

The two shops were mirrors of each other. *Twice Is Nice Emporium* was painted on their glass. Their open sign glowed extra bright on this gloomy Thursday.

Inside their window, a flowery ceramic basin and jug sat next to a small pendulum clock atop an ornate wooden dresser. A lazy Susan stood on a fancy coffee table with pretty china cups arranged on it. Old-timey tins were stacked on shelves lit beneath a lamp with a fringed shade.

The crowded display reminded me of the books my kids used to love—the ones with busy photos and rhyming lists of things to search for: five buttons, a dime, three yellow tins, and a thing that tells time.

Twice Is Nice had an additional selling feature hand-printed on a piece of paper taped to the inside of their door: "We specialize in wood revival."

Same, I snickered to myself as I unlocked the door to Afternoon Delight.

"It was the cheesiest name I could think of," Georgia had said of the store's name. The inside of the door displayed a handwritten sign that read "Closed for medical reasons."

I pushed in, and a sleigh bell tied to the door jangled. At the same time, the steady chime of the alarm system sounded from across the room. I hurried to the box on the wall and punched in the code Georgia had given me. It silenced, and I felt ridiculously proud of myself for not causing a SWAT team to descend on the street.

I slid the thermostat from frigid to survivable and hit the switches to illuminate the track lighting in the rafters. No harsh fluorescent office lights here. Intimate pools of gold landed on a rotating stand of books. A hammock-like contraption was suspended from the ceiling, and a variety of whips and crops were mounted on the wall. The shelf that formed a privacy wall held a selection of vibrators in a variety of shapes, colours, and sizes. Several were displayed out of their boxes.

One monster compelled me to pick it up to see how heavy it was. Honestly, even though my eight-pound children had come out of my vagina, I was intimidated by the breadth of this goliath.

I tried to close my fist around it, brushing away the dust from its silicone coating while thumbing the dial to check the different vibration speeds. I resisted the impulse to press it against the top of my inseam, but I was intrigued enough to consider it.

The sleigh bell clanged.

I threw the elephantine penis back onto the shelf in the most obvious "Nothing, Mother" in history. It knocked over two other vibrators and lay there buzzing, the sound amplified by the boxy shelf.

I scrambled to pick it up but couldn't figure out how to turn it off. I called out a high-pitched, "I'm not open!" while I turned the dial, accidentally increasing the vibration. Why hadn't I locked the door? Oh, right—because of the alarm. Note to self: Grab a brain, not a dildo.

"I'm from next door," a deep voice said as I finally silenced the vibrator. "I have a question."

Shit. The landlord Georgia had warned me about?

I set the vibrator back on the shelf and brushed my hands on the seat of my jeans, then slapped a compassionate smile on my face before stepping out where I could see him.

Double shit. Georgia had made it sound like the guy was a senior. How did a man in his mid-thirties have dementia? There were glints of gold in his beard, not silver. Same with his hair. His thick dark crew cut needed a trim, but it was kind of sexy, all dishevelled like that. He was tall and fit and had a smile that skewed left in a very charming way.

"Hi, Dale," I said gently, repeating what Georgia had told me to say. "I'm new here. I know this might feel confusing, but if we go back into your shop, your daughter can explain." How old was this guy's daughter anyway? Seven? And she was knee-capping Georgia for rent?

His face moved through a comical series of expressions, landing on bemusement. "Dale is my dad. I'm Zak. Are you not Georgia?"

"What? No. Ha." I wanted to die. "I'm Georgia's friend, Meg. Hi." I moved forward and offered my hand. "I'm helping Georgia for a couple of weeks." I kept it vague, since I didn't really know what I was doing.

"Nice to meet you." Zak stepped forward. He had a firm grip. There was a hint of callus on his warm palm and, for some bizarre reason, that caused a zing of electricity to ground out between my legs.

For the first time in years, I remembered that I owned a clitoris and briefly considered looking for it. I wanted to blame the vibrator, but it was him. Or me—and my utter lack of experience with being single. Whatever it was, I was regressing into prom-night Meg, smiling dopily because he wore his flannel sleeves rolled back, showing off his muscled forearms. His jeans hugged his thick thighs, and his sturdy work boots were oddly reassuring, like he knew how to take command of a situation.

I dragged my attention back to his crooked smile and straight dark brows. The combination made him seem both approachable and stern.

Too young, I cautioned myself. He didn't look like he'd accumulated my level of disenchantment with life. People in their thirties tended to fall into two categories—those like me, creeping up on forty and punch-drunk with family responsibilities, or those like him, who still had the bandwidth for clumsy soccer on a soggy day.

His eyes were really blue. They brimmed with amusement, and I wanted to fall right into them.

I was staring. Damn. I'd caught a case of insta-lust, and he knew it.

"So, um." *I'm due to step into traffic.* "Georgia said her landlord had a daughter. Zara? Is that your wife?" Did I really just ask if he was married? Yes, I did. I wanted to bite my tongue off.

"My sister."

Right. Duh. He had just told me his father was Dale. Could I be more uncool?

He scratched his beard, possibly trying to hide the fact that he was struggling not to laugh.

"We own the building with Dad," he said. "Fun fact—when he signed this lease, he told us the new tenant was a toy store. It wasn't until Zara stopped by after it opened that we learned what kind of toys."

"Oh." I widened my eyes. "Is that a problem?" Was he here to break the lease? Nooo.

"The neighbours aren't thrilled. But we're only hanging on to the building for Dad, so..." He shrugged one well-built shoulder.

"So don't get comfortable?" My heart was sinking on Georgia's behalf.

"I honestly couldn't tell you." He shoved his hands into his back pockets, palms out, and braced his weight in a wide stance. "At first, we thought it was funny that Dad had missed such an important detail. Then Georgia told Zara that Dad was coming in here and getting confused. Zara got him to the doctor, but she has kids and works full-time. She can't run defence on him, too. I moved back after Christmas to live with Dad and..." He shrugged again. "I don't know how long this will work."

Oh. I bit back saying how nice it was that he had come home to help. No one—least of all my husband—had praised me when I helped my mother-in-law after she broke her hip. I'd put school on hold and left our kids with my own mother so I could take care of Mrs. Boyd, because Joel hadn't wanted to cancel any of his lucrative root canals and crowns. It hadn't occurred to any of us—least of all me—that he would. Or that he would look after his own mother. His parents had since moved to the Okanagan, or Joel would still expect me to check on them.

"You're here to ask about rent?" I guessed. "Georgia said Zara let her skip January while she figured things out, but she texted the other day, asking what her plans are."

"I actually forgot Zara was doing that. Yeah, people have been asking what's going on over here." Zak glanced over his shoulder. Brim Stokers Coffeehouse was across the street next to the new microbrewery, Tap That. "There's been some revitalization lately. By that, I mean gentrification. They don't like staring at a dark window."

"Understandable."

"One of them offered to buy the building, but we want to keep it for now. Dad's used to getting up for work every morning. His doctor says it's good for him to stick to a routine. He likes dinking around with his knick-knacks, so..." Another shrug.

I bit back a laugh, adoring how affectionate he sounded.

"Where do you usually live?" I asked.

"Vancouver. You?"

"Toronto. But I grew up here."

"Me, too. I'm a programmer. I had a good job, but I was burning out again. This is a nice break. Mostly I dink around, too. Strip wood. Post photos."

Don't say it.

"That sounds like I post dick pics." His grin flashed. God, he was gorgeous. "Actually, they're chests." He waited a beat. "Of drawers." His mouth twitched with irony.

"I was trying not to ask." I was trying not to ogle his chest, but I could feel a smile teasing my lips.

"How is Georgia?" he asked with concern. "Zara said Dad was making things awkward with her staff and customers. There's been a lot of turnover in this shop the last few years, actually. We should have clued in to what was causing it. Can you let her know I'm here, though? That shouldn't happen as much now." He glanced right as he spoke.

I realized he had done that a few times. He had stationed himself so he could see his own door through this one.

"She'll be off sick for a while longer. She's staying with her sister in Sidney." It was about thirty minutes from the shop, but close to the ferry, which was good since she was seeing a specialist in Vancouver. "She should be back on her feet soon." I was staying positive.

"That's good news." His gaze flickered down, taking in my mint green rain jacket over peg-leg jeans stuffed into ankle boots with faux-fur cuffs.

When his eyes came back to my face, I was prickly and humid inside my damp clothes.

"That you're planning to reopen, I mean." He cleared his throat. "And yeah, rent would be great. My wages over there are less than what the drayman was making back when he was delivering furniture fresh off the lathe."

"I'll see what I can do. Today I just dropped by to get the lay of the land." My voice faltered at the double entendre. "I wanted to see what I'll be working with." I fought the urge to glance at the vibrators but couldn't look at him either, certain he'd be laughing at me again.

"Sure," he said easily. "I won't bother you, but one thing has been driving me crazy since I spotted it through the window. That's why I came roaring over here the second I heard you come in. What the hell is that?" He pointed at the cash desk. "I can't find anything like it online."

I blinked at what looked like a tripod made of clear plastic dildos, all of different lengths and widths. They connected at a point that formed what I assumed was a handle.

"Um…" I was equally mystified and walked over to gingerly pick it up.

"Are they flexible?"

I tested one branch. "No." It was solid and weighted at the base so it wouldn't tip over.

"Who uses something like that? I'm not being judgmental." His expression became boyish, one eyebrow quirking upward while his hand flailed in bafflement. "It's a real question. What goes where? How? There's not enough room for three people to use it at once. I honestly don't think it would be comfortable for one. Maybe that's the point?"

I was just as perplexed. If someone wanted to rotate through poking me with three differently sized dildos so vigorously that they needed a common handle, I would have a lot of questions first.

"I can't figure it out," he continued. "And believe me, I've put in the hours."

"I'm picturing you over there with a corkboard and red yarn."

"Mostly doodling on the back of provenance certificates, but it keeps me from worrying about Dad."

I tucked my smile into the zipper of my jacket. "Perhaps it would be kinder to keep you in the dark, then."

"Please don't. I've reached my limit for edging my curiosity."

Oh heck. I was really starting to enjoy this.

I lifted my chin, trying to project some level of competence while I admitted, "Full disclosure, I'm new to all of this. Fortunately, I can phone a friend." I snapped a photo and texted it to Georgia with a question mark.

"So you don't… do this?" He drew a circle with his finger to indicate the store.

"Sell adult toys for a living? No, I'm an accountant. Helping small businesses pay their taxes is my day job. I'm friendly and punctual, and Georgia says it's no more awkward than selling cans of soup, so I agreed to pinch-hit." I was starting to think she'd misled me on that front. I was feeling extremely awkward as I set down the X-rated version of Poseidon's trident, trying not to imagine which one went up my bum or how much it would sting.

How hard could it be? had been my naive assumption about working here. And there I went with the dirty puns again.

"Pro tip? You can sell anything with a story. This trunk was supposed to be on the Titanic." He waved at an imaginary trunk at his feet. "It was accidentally left behind and went to the passenger's cousin, who found a pearl-handled knife inside—one that was later found to have been used in a murder."

"You make stuff up?"

"No." He frowned, insulted. "I'm saying you need to pique curiosity. I guarantee you could sell that thing if you told your next customer that your vanilla landlord has been obsessing about it for weeks. They won't care what it's actually for. They'll buy it for the story."

"Maybe I'll keep it as a conversation piece, then."

"No," he warned sternly. "Never get sentimental. If you can sell it, *sell it.* You can tell I haven't had anyone new to talk to in a while, can't you?" His mouth twisted with self-deprecation. "I should get back, make sure Dad's okay." He canted his head. "But if you find anything else that stumps you, run it by me. I'm genuinely interested."

"I will, thanks. And I'll let you know what I learn." I nodded at the trident of dildos.

"Great. See you tomorrow." He left with a jangle of the sleigh bell.

I opened my jacket to air out the trapped heat. Talk about trial by fire! I had gotten through it, though. Maybe I could handle this job after all.

My phone buzzed. I tilted the screen to read Georgia's reply:

It's a condom tree, so people can see the textures and patterns. Change it up for the holidays, but don't use flavoured ones. People will lick it.

CHAPTER TWO

ZAK

The phone was ringing as I walked back into Twice Is Nice.

I looked for Dad, but the place had always been a rabbit warren of tallboys, standing mirrors, and folding screens. As a kid, playing hide-and-seek in here with Zara had been a riot. Playing hide-and-seek with Dad? Not so much.

"Dad?" The phone was still ringing, which didn't necessarily mean he wasn't in the office. I'd caught him in there two days ago, watching it ring, but yesterday he'd answered it like he always used to.

From the back of the shop, I heard a cry of pain and the thump of something hitting the floor. I veered toward the workroom, where I'd been stripping a table.

Dad was standing next to it, clutching his own hand, looking at it with a mix of confusion and agony. The heat gun was on the floor.

Fuck me.

"Let's get that under cold water." I yanked the plug from the wall on my way to bringing him into the bathroom, then guided his hand so cold water washed over the pink crescent in his palm.

How had we missed that he was getting this bad?

It wasn't actually a mystery. I hadn't been here because I was a workaholic who'd been saving for a wedding and a house. Zara had a husband, a job, and three kids. I suspected her marriage was also on the rocks, but maybe it was just this situation with Dad putting stress fractures into their relationship. I didn't have the nerve to ask.

"I thought it was your mother's hair dryer," Dad said, giving me a baffled look.

"It's the heat gun for stripping paint. I was using it on the table." He'd been using it himself last summer when I'd visited. "It's my fault. I shouldn't have left it out."

I had to start thinking of him like Ollie, Zara's youngest, but it was a mental shift I didn't want to make. Dad had taught me how to refinish furniture, for Christ's sake. As well as how to drive, how to get a car loan, and how to change the oil. Sure, this was the YouTube generation. Every life skill you needed was one skip of a five-second ad away, but *he* was my Google.

Nothing in me wanted to accept that he couldn't remember the difference between a heat gun and a hair dryer. Or that Mom was dead.

"Does that feel better?" The mark had faded and didn't look like it would blister. "Let's get some gauze on it, then you can hold a cold bottle of root beer. Sound good?" I needed to stop pushing sugar on him. We didn't need him diabetic on top of the Alzheimer's, but part of me wanted to believe his absent-mindedness was just low blood sugar.

"That does sound good," he said, and I thought, *What the hell. If it makes him happy.*

I got Dad settled in the office with his root beer, then went back to the workroom and put away the heat gun, the scrapers, the turpentine—anything I thought could be a danger to him. There was only a wooden turning latch to keep the cupboard doors closed. It felt like a dick move to put a padlock on it, but I guessed I'd have to.

I added it to my to-do list, a living document in my phone that still had *Pick up ring* on it. Then I returned to the office to listen to the message from the call we'd missed. The recording from the credit bureau warned me that my credit card was blah, blah, blah.

I deleted it without listening to the rest, but now I had to wonder how easily Dad could be tricked into entering his credit card number. I would talk to Zara before removing his cards from his wallet. We were in the middle of getting power of attorney for his finances anyway, but this felt like a next-level piss-all-over-his-self-esteem move. Maybe we could just lower his available credit to an amount we were willing to lose.

I heard a muted tinkle and got out to the front of the shop just in time to see the door to Afternoon Delight go dark again.

At least I had a cute neighbour now. One who knew even less about sex toys than I did.

I'd never really fucked with them. Literally. Erica had had a vibrator, but she'd never wanted me to use it on her. I'd wandered through stores now and again and seen shit online, but my hand did the job—and it was always there.

My curiosity had grown since I'd seen that candelabra-looking thing through the window, though. I'd spent way too much time trying to find it online. Turns out, looking at toys was almost as effective as looking at porn. It made me really horny.

Now I would be picturing Meg in her snug jeans, dark-blond hair, and flustered blushes as she fondled those things. Yes, please.

"Zak? Did that couple ever call back for this coffee table?" And just like that, he was back—shrewdly running the least profitable business in Canada.

"I think she wanted it, but he wasn't as keen."

"I think you're right." He took the Reserved sign off it and set a bowl filled with wooden fruit in its place. He gave the arrangement a little adjustment, always so loving with the clutter in here.

I had a lot of feelings about this place. Some were nostalgic, some were overwhelmed and annoyed. These days, I had to wonder if this smorgasbord of disarray was a peek inside Dad's mind. It was filled to the brim, but everything was jammed together and unusable. The thing you might actually want was buried behind an umbrella stand, covered in dust so you couldn't see it. That didn't mean it wasn't here.

"I was thinking of pork chops for dinner," he said.

"Sounds great. Should we knock off early and pick them up on our way home?"

"Let's do that. It's good to have you home, Zak. I like the company." He gave my shoulder a pat, smiling in a way that made me feel goofy, like a kid earning Dad's praise for catching a ball.

It's okay, I thought. He's okay. Everything was going to be okay.

But then he noticed the bandage on his hand and began to pick at it with puzzlement, trying to figure out why it was there.

My heart sank. He was not okay.

CHAPTER THREE

MEG

I pulled into the driveway and parked beside my mother's Toyota Camry. Her first car had been a Camry that my father bought her. Every four years since then, she had traded it in for the latest model. Dad's first car had been a used Pontiac Firebird—"Like Rockford used to drive." He had always planned to restore it to its original glory, and it was still on one side of the garage, waiting for him. The other side was packed with a metric crap-ton of homeowner detritus, so Mom and I parked outside, even on a blustery day like today.

Our house had been the fanciest on the cul-de-sac when I was growing up. Oak Bay was full of well-kept heritage homes and modern mansions with ocean views. Dad had been a family doctor, so we weren't poor, but we weren't "mansion with ocean view" money either. That was Joel's family.

No, we were "tear down a post-war bungalow for a custom-built eighties-colonial" middle-class money. Mom had insisted on an Oak Bay address. She had wanted a bay window in the living room—our view was the street—an island in the kitchen, and a patio out back. Dad had wanted to be close to his office and a good school for me. He had also wanted a small lawn so he could golf and fish rather than do yardwork.

It was a very nice location only a short walk from the beach, but the neighbourhood had grown up over time. New, twenty-first-century behemoths made our house look like what it was: dated and in desperate need of TLC.

Like me.

Mom's gardens were still in the barren stage, choked with moss and full of last year's rotting stems. The concrete steps to the porch were cracked, the stucco stained, and the front door key needed an extra wiggle to make it open.

I kept threatening to call in a handyman to change it out for a button lock, but every small job was part of a bigger one. The door actually needed levelling, or even replacing, if we took the warped panel into account. If we changed one door, we'd have to change all of them. If the doors were coming out, we should probably look at the windows. The seals were shot on at least three of them.

The bigger the job got, the less prepared we were to tackle it. And so it went.

"I'm home," I called as I entered what had always been a claustrophobic foyer. It was a postage stamp of tiles with a tiny closet next to the stairs that doubled back over the door to the basement. On the left were double doors into the living and dining room. Straight ahead was the door into the kitchen and family room. Hang a right and you'd find the powder room and Mom's bedroom.

As I toed off my boots and hung my jacket in the closet, my pits grew clammy. I was such a child.

"You bought more wine." Vickie Crutcher came to the door of the family room, drying her hands on a tea towel. Her white-blond hair was in the chin-length bob she'd worn all her life, framing a face that had accumulated a few lines over the years, but she mostly looked exactly as she always had—short, slim, and stylish. "Is Georgia not improving?"

Mom seemed to think my alcohol consumption was due to concern over Georgia and had nothing to do with the fact that she was stonewalling on selling this house.

I had a flash of Zak moving home to look after his father and reminded myself that I was lucky to have a parent whose only affliction was an obstinate belief that she was always right—along with a distressing ability to prove it.

"She's worried about her shop." I was laying the groundwork for my announcement. "Let me change, then I'll help with dinner." I handed her the wine before I started up the stairs.

"I bought a frozen lasagna," she called after me. "It's in the oven."

I stifled a sigh. I understood Mom's loss of interest in cooking, but I liked making food from scratch. My roasted chicken breasts and riced cauliflower pilaf always earned compliments. Would she let me touch so much as a carrot peeler in her kitchen? Hell, no.

The house was a three-bedroom, but after Mom had a string of miscarriages, she'd settled on raising an only child whom she had resolutely refused to spoil. The spare bedroom became her craft room, and nowadays, you couldn't get near the sewing machine without running an obstacle course of an open ironing board, two standing fans, and several tubs of craft supplies.

Down in the basement—what we had always called the rumpus room—Dad's fly-fishing gear was littered amongst the furniture he'd brought home from his office when he retired. The hide-a-bed sofa was covered with his clothes, but that was as far as Mom was prepared to take them.

I already had a full-time job cleaning out this house, yet I had agreed to work for Georgia. *What had I done?*

I tapped my laptop to wake up the screen while I peeled off my damp jeans and pulled on a pair of yoga pants. I glanced at my email as I took off my bra without removing my top.

Peterson, Londale, and Funk had a policy that you weren't expected to check email while on vacation—but it absolutely was expected. I had nine from Cameron, most of them shoving work onto me that was now in his purview, like scheduling and reports.

I'd gone in to work Monday, on my first day of vacation, to be told "Maybe next time," about the promotion I'd applied for. I was still trying to see the silver lining in not having the extra responsibility of managing a team when I had so much to do for Mom, but there was no silver lining to sexism. That's what my being passed over was, and I'd said so. HR hadn't been able to do anything about it.

"Cameron is seen as a team player, Meg. He's *seen*. You've worked remotely a lot in the last three years."

Only because my father had been dying and I'd been going through a divorce, but I had never missed a meeting or a tax filing. For the last eight months, I'd performed the death march known as commuting into downtown so I could be in my cubicle full-time, trying to earn that stupid promotion—but what*ever*.

In other ways, Monday had been the happiest day of my life. I had handed Joel the certified paperwork on our divorce. It had been my last act as his unpaid personal assistant. Then I'd hopped on a plane, planning to spend two weeks getting this house emptied and ready to list. Instead, I was taking on managing an adult toy store.

I stared at stupid Cameron's stupid emails. It was the story of my life that I put other people's needs before my own. I was the daughter of a doctor. A teen mom. I married too young. After Joel cheated the first time, I stayed for the kids.

I couldn't change the way Peterson, Londale, and Funk were treating me, but I could change myself and how I reacted to their decision.

That's what Georgia was really giving me a chance to do. Georgia had always lived on her own terms. I wanted to live my life the way she did—even if it was only for a few weeks. That yearning had been crackling as a low fire of defiance in my gut since she'd made her outrageous suggestion.

Did I feel bad about pulling the rug out from under Cameron? Sure. He seemed like a nice enough dude. He had a wife and kids and probably a dog, and a boat he couldn't afford. It wasn't my fault he'd been promoted above his level of competency, though.

As for the partners who had promoted him over me? They would soon have to decide what I was worth to them—as tax season loomed.

Mom was right. Georgia did ignite my rebellious streak.

But I wasn't *quite* ready to pull that pin. I went down to the kitchen.

"I'm letting it rest," Mom said of the steaming lasagna on the stovetop. She set out the wine glasses, then went back to emptying a bag of salad into a bowl. She was quick to judge me for having a drink every evening but also quick to join me.

"How was the thrift store?" I asked as I twisted off the bottle's cap.

"I found a cute top that would suit you. It's in the wash."

"Thanks." Much as I bristled at Mom treating me like a teenager who needed a curfew, she had great taste, and second-hand didn't bother me—especially from the thrift store she worked in. It was full of upscale cast-offs.

"Mom, I have something I have to tell you." It was the same way I had opened my announcements that I was pregnant and that I was getting a divorce. I tore that bandage right off. "I'm quitting my job. I told Georgia I would run her store while she's off for her surgery."

Mom froze with her glass halfway to her mouth. Her hand tightened on the edge of the counter. She stood straighter and looked down her nose at me, even though I was actually an inch taller.

"You're not serious, Margaret."

Oof. I was pretty sure that was exactly what she'd said those other times, too.

"It's a *good job*," she pressed.

"I can freelance." I sat down at the table. "It's a thing women do these days." So I'd heard. "They quit their corporate jobs and work on contract for twice the compensation and more favourable terms."

"In this economy? Good luck." Mom raked out her chair and sat down. "I don't know how they let you work from home as much as you have. Is this because of that man who was promoted over you?"

"Yes, among other things. They don't appreciate me."

"Mm-hmm." Mom put on her buttoned-lip look and cast her gaze out the window, where dusk had thrown the backyard into heavy gloom.

"Tell me again that I didn't appreciate Joel. That I expected too much from him," I dared her. "Should I have stayed in Toronto the whole time Dad was sick, instead of being here with you?"

"You're looking for a fight, aren't you?"

Yes. I was feeling very defensive. Everything Mom was thinking behind that sour expression, I had already said to myself in her voice. I would be throwing away a secure, flexible, lucrative job on what amounted to a midlife crisis, but I was tired of making safe choices.

I had married Joel because I was scared to do anything else. And yes, sometimes I blamed my mother for pushing me into marrying Joel when I got pregnant—as if being a young, single mother would have been easier. As if I could imagine a life where the kids I loved with my whole heart hadn't been born at all.

I was exactly where I had allowed myself to wind up, but that's why I was determined to make new choices now. Divorce had sucked, but it was done. I was glad. Leaving my job and starting something new was also going to be hard, but I didn't want to hate myself in ten years for staying with a company that also took me for granted.

"It's only for a few weeks," I said, trying to reassure both of us. "It depends on when Georgia can get her surgery and how quickly she recovers. But this is a time in my life when I can do something off-brand. It's not like I have young kids and the Parent Advisory Committee watching my every move."

"Only your mother and her friends," she said under her breath. "Will Georgia pay you?"

"Minimum wage, but she needs help, Mom. She might lose all the money she put into that business. If I can bring it back to turning a profit, at least she'd have a shot at selling it, if she can't actually go back to work."

"Why wouldn't she be able to work?" Her eyes widened in alarm.

I explained about the tumors on Georgia's spine. Initially, she had thought the pain in her back was from an old injury—falling off a stage—coupled with the stress of setting up her new business. Eventually, she'd been in too much pain to move.

"Cancer?" Mom's expression reflected the same combo of PTSD and mental leaps I had made when Georgia had told me. Cancer *sucked*. But watching Dad's battle had taught us how to navigate that journey. It was a marathon. Pace yourself.

"They're still doing tests, but they're pretty sure it's benign. They're hoping she'll be able to walk after the surgery, but it's spinal surgery."

Mom nodded, brow furrowed. "I'm very sorry to hear that. Does she have a date?"

I snorted. I would defend socialized health care with my dying breath, but the wait times these days were awful.

"She has a really good specialist. He's optimistic, and so is she. We are, too," I decided for both of us. "She's in a lot of pain, though. She was filling online orders using stock from the store, but her sister can't run into town every other day to pick things up. Gail has her kids and work, and now Georgia needs more help."

"Georgia can't hire someone else?"

"She had someone quit right before Christmas." Right when Georgia might've made enough to sustain herself a little longer. "I guess it was getting awkward with the landlord. He owns the whole building and works at the antique shop next door."

I didn't mention Zak. He wasn't the reason I was doing this, and I didn't want Mom jumping to conclusions. I'd been married for over twenty years to the man who took my V-card, but as far as she was concerned, I was incapable of keeping it in my pants.

"I guess he has dementia. He walks in, then gets upset that it's not the fabric store that was there ten years ago."

"Oh, that's sad. Does he have family to help?"

"His kids, yeah. They gave Georgia a break on rent for January, but they've been texting, asking what she plans to do. When she moved back here to open that shop, she thought it would support her for the next twenty years. Then she could sell it when she retired."

"That's optimistic."

"Not really. Sex doesn't go out of style. Some of us grow out of it, but it's always popular with the kids."

"And it produces the next generation of customers," Mom mused. "It's actually the perfect business model."

I chuckled, relieved. If Mom was making jokes, she was coming around.

"Is there nothing we can do for her on the financial side instead?" she asked. "How much does she need?"

I groaned inwardly, wishing I could parlay helping Georgia into selling this house.

"I offered her money and said I could talk to the bank for her." Helping small businesses rejig their finances was something I did all day, every day. I firmly believed the biggest reason I'd been passed over for the promotion was because I was too valuable at the client-facing grunt work. Clients loved me for my reassuring voice and my bossy ability to impose order onto chaos.

"You know what she's like, though. She doesn't want to need help. She wants to fix it herself—and can't."

It had been really hard to see Georgia chewing on so much frustration and despair, never having expected her body to let her down. When she said she didn't want to be forty and starting from scratch, I'd almost said, *I'm turning forty and starting from scratch.*

Not total scratch, obviously, but when I looked back on the last twenty years, I had to wonder what I'd done with my life. I love my kids. I'd die for them. But I could see how I had repeatedly settled back into my safe little rut—my comfortable job where I was overlooked and taken for granted.

"I wish I'd had an ounce of Georgia in me when they told me that Cameron—the guy I *trained*—was going to be my new manager. I should've told them to go fuck themselves."

"Meg," Mom murmured in protest at my curse. "What if Georgia can't walk again?" Her brows came together in worry.

"I'm confident she'll walk through the door of the shop within a few months and pick up where she left off. But she can't let it languish. She has to pay her bills."

Mom sighed and rose, moving to the plate cupboard.

I held my breath, wanting her approval even though I knew I wouldn't get it.

"We're really doing this?"

"*We*?" Record scratch. "You want to work in an adult toy shop, Mom?"

"No. But I can't let you risk Georgia's future along with your own." She set two plates on the counter.

"I've worked retail. I can handle it." I got up to get the cutlery.

"No, you're running her business. That's not as easy as it sounds. I know from running your father's office." She handed me the bowl of salad.

"I did the books for Joel's dental clinic!" I had hired and fired most of his staff. I had designed his website and maintained it right up until I emailed Wanda four days ago with the login credentials. "I'm an accountant, Mom. I work with small businesses every day. I know how they run. I know what they need."

"Do you know what her clients need?" she asked condescendingly.

"I like to think I'm intelligent enough to learn. Why? Are you offering to help? Tell me about your vast experience taking Dad's dictation."

She paused mid-jab, her serrated knife buried in the lasagna. "Don't be crass."

"I'm just saying, don't rush to help. Think about it first. Long and hard."

"Stop it." She aggressively cut rows into squares.

I smirked and set out the cutlery, then brought the salad to the table while she brought our filled plates to the placemats.

"I'm open-minded, if not particularly adventurous," I said once we were seated. "Thanks to you, I'm also pathologically responsible. Georgia asked for my help, so I will help her." Honestly, Georgia was doing me the favour—shoving me off the ledge. We both knew this would be good for me.

Mom huffed out a sigh. "What will you tell your children?"

"That I'm working for a friend."

Mom's brows went up in challenge.

"I'll tell them as much as they need to know." I might've watered down various details through the years—especially around the divorce and Dad's illness—but I didn't keep secrets from them. "I'm as entitled to a private life as they are." *Hint, hint.*

Mom used the side of her fork to cut away a bite of lasagna. "What about the house? I thought you wanted me to sell it?"

"I do." But throwing out expired cottage cheese got her back up. I didn't expect her to change her attitude any time soon.

"You said you were going back to Toronto in two weeks. What about Roddie?"

"I'll ask Roddie to come for spring break. Maybe he'll want some of Dad's things." I highly doubted it, but Mom perked up at the suggestion.

"He'll need the sofa bed. I'll take your father's clothes to the thrift store the next time I go." She had been saying that every day since I'd arrived. I had a feeling she dreaded seeing them on the racks—or worse, on someone in town—but she was too loyal to the Ladies' Hospital Auxiliary to take them anywhere else.

"Let me know when you're ready. I'll help carry everything to the car," I said, exactly as I had every other time. "Do you want more wine?"

"That would be nice, thank you." She pushed her empty glass across the table.

CHAPTER FOUR

MEG

At five minutes to midnight Thursday night, I quit tinkering with my resignation letter and hit send.

My email to Cameron—oh yes, I sent it to him because I was that much of a passive-aggressive bitch—referenced "an unrelated opportunity that necessitates my leaving by the end of February." That was almost three weeks of notice, two of which were the vacation time I was currently taking. I said I would continue to work remotely until then and expressed my gratitude for the experience I had gained at PLF. I provided a status report on my current workload, promised to tie up loose ends before I left, and offered suggestions for client reassignment. I even mentioned I'd be open to training my replacement, if that would assist the transition.

It was the most politely worded shove-it in the history of take-this-job-and.

Starting at six a.m.—nine Eastern time—texts and emails began flooding in, but I had set my phone to Do Not Disturb. I rose at ten to eight and climbed into the shower after only a glance at the number of unread messages.

I felt like such a badass ignoring them. Pathetic, I know, but I hummed a smug tune as I dried off and massaged body butter into my thighs, shins, and heels.

"Mr. Peterson wants you to call," Mom called up the stairs when I came out of the bathroom in a towel.

I looked down to see she was wearing her chenille housecoat and had helped herself to the coffee I started brewing on my way to the shower.

"He called you?"

"On the landline. Are you in trouble?" Mom looked worried.

The strangest sensation came over me, one I had felt a few times during the divorce. At one point, Joel had insisted on keeping my grandfather's pocket watch, even though he never wore it. Sentiment and a sense of stewardship had told me to dig deep for a second wind of battle fury, but something else in me had dried up and blown away. I had ceased to care that Joel was in the wrong. I had simply wanted out, no matter what it cost.

I'd been told women lost all their fucks at forty. I'd honestly believed that was a reference to sex, but in this moment, I understood it was broader than that. It was about priorities and who deserved my attention. As I contemplated what Mr. Peterson might be thinking of me or what he might say, I reached for my jar of fucks and found it empty. In fact, there was no jar.

It was disconcerting but incredibly freeing. I stood there in bare feet, hair dripping onto my shoulders, and was struck by how unafraid I felt. How light.

"I'll call him back after I get dressed."

But I didn't.

I pulled on jeans and the top Mom had bought me—a light knit in pale blue that hugged my boobs and waist. White cords crisscrossed the V-neck, and the flared sleeves fell past my knuckles. It was casual, kind of hippy-dippy, but flattering. The colour picked up the ash tones in my streaked, dirty-blonde hair.

I never wore my hair down unless I was going out for the evening, but after drying it, I left it loose, giving it a light spritz of hairspray to keep it off my face. I used minimal makeup, only doing my eyes and applying a nude balm to my lips. I looked great.

When I was ready for "work," I skimmed through the emails and texts, replied to one from a client that seemed pressing—I was still a professional—then told HR what my hourly rate would be if they wanted to hire me on contract. It was an exorbitant amount, and I felt no guilt or shame.

I ate my half of the grapefruit Mom left out, poured my coffee into a travel mug, and walked outside to embark on my new life.

It was fucking snowing.

CHAPTER FIVE

MEG

It's not like it never snowed in Toronto. Winters there were biting.

But it was the story of my entire childhood that I would lose a good hair day to a drippy, mashed-potato day like today. There were always enough mild, sunny days in February to have you believing spring was around the corner, then a day like today would kick you in the face.

Not that my looks mattered. My dishy neighbour wasn't at work yet. There was a sign in the Twice Is Nice window that hadn't been there yesterday: "If we're here, we're open. If we're not, we're closed."

I refused to be disappointed. I was on a journey to love myself. I had no interest in starting up with any man, especially a younger one. Even a cute, funny one.

Unfortunately, I came from a bloodline of co-dependents. We found our value in serving others. That's why I had brought our snow shovel to work and quickly pushed the layer of slush off the portion of the sidewalk that the awnings hadn't covered.

I was both sweating and shivering by the time I got into Afternoon Delight. I turned on the heat and lights and set my phone to stream music through the Bluetooth speakers behind the cash desk.

Then I unrolled some pastel condoms onto the tree and stuck it in the window display with a rabbit-style vibrator and a couple of insertable egg-shaped toys. Sacrilegious? Probably. Definitely not a stellar first effort.

I snapped a photo and sent it to Georgia, asking her to call me with some tips.

An hour later, all the shelves and inventory were dust-free, and I had just put away the vacuum when my phone started buzzing in my pocket. It was Georgia.

"Hi!" I greeted her. "How—um." The lights came on next door. *Focus*. "How are you?"

"I'm in the twilight period where my pill is starting to work, but I'm still lucid. Are you okay? You sound weird."

"Fine. Did you see my photo? I feel like the window display needs zhuzhing."

"It does. Also, it's Valentine's Day next week. Do that before Easter."

"Right. Damn." And didn't my obliviousness to that special day say everything about how I came to be divorced?

"Maybe get a couple of stuffies from the dollar store. Or some flowers. No chocolate. They melt in the sun and send the wrong message."

"Voice of experience?"

"Yup. Any customers?"

I double-checked that I had flipped the sign to Open.

"Not yet, but there are three online orders I'll fill today. Hey, I've been thinking about how to get the word out that the shop is open again. What do you think of a relaunch event? I could advertise with a little discount to get some traffic in the door. Do you think you'd be up for doing an interview?"

"With who?"

"I don't know. I was listening to the local radio station on my way in, and they had a spot with the owner of a shoe store. That made me think of it."

She made a noise of reluctance. "Maybe if it aired during the drive home? Commuters won't pick up a vibrator on their way *to* work. But I don't know how persuasive I am these days. I sound like a crypt keeper." Her voice reflected her medication-dulled mood and weeks of angst.

"Someone will find that sexy," I teased. "You know that."

"Mmm, my brand is all about personal empowerment and independence and self-care. I don't want to explain why I'm relying on you to run my store."

"Hey, self-care is recognizing when you need help. Plus, you're giving me a chance to explore my own independence and learn something new—so thank you. How about I start with a post to social media? I'll write it up and you can tweak it so it sounds like you. Do you have a newsletter?"

"Yes, but it only has nine subscribers."

"Better than none. Give me your credentials. I'll send out a notice that you're open again. Maybe I'll survey them? Ask them what they liked about your store? Oh, I could get some testimonials for some ads."

"Good God, you sound like Vickie. I mean that as a compliment," she hurried to add. "Remember that time she took measurements for the entire volleyball team and made us new uniforms? *After* her fundraiser was so successful that we could have just bought fresh tank tops? Granted, we looked fly as hell, but why does she have to go the extra mile?"

"Type-A needs an A," I said with a grimace of guilt. "Do you know what she said when I told her I was doing this? She offered to work here with me so I don't ruin your future along with my own."

"Did you tell her that ship has sailed?"

"I—" My heart soared as the sleigh bell jangled and Zak held the door open.

He stepped one foot inside and stared at the condom tree in the window. One dark eyebrow angled up in a bent wing as he shot a questioning look my way.

"That's it," I told him. "It's a display thingy to show how pretty the condoms are."

"That's *it*?" He looked both outraged and crestfallen.

"I was bummed, too."

He sighed and gave a little chin chuck in acknowledgement that I was on the phone. "Talk to you later." He disappeared as abruptly as he'd arrived.

"Customer?" Georgia asked hopefully.

"No. Try not to hate me, but your landlord has a son. He's very hot." I was still grinning at his reaction.

"Zak?"

"You've met him?" I asked. "He thought I was you."

"Zara mentioned him. They're twins." Georgia yawned and swore. "That's it. I'm fogging out."

"Okay. I'll text if I have questions."

I hung up and began composing posts, considering whether to add photos. I snapped out of my concentration when a young woman with blue hair hesitantly entered.

"Hi. Are you, um, open?"

"I am. Hi," I said with my friendliest smile. "Come in."

"I work at Brim Stokers." She pointed across the street. "I'm on my break. I was just curious. This place has been closed since I started."

"I'm Meg. Have a look around. Let me know if you have questions." I was proud of how confident I sounded.

I realized Georgia had a blog page on her website and started writing something for it, giving my customer some privacy.

She was like a cat in a new house—moving cautiously and glancing into all the corners, relaxing marginally as she realized we were the only two in here.

"I've never used anything like these before," she said, giving a little wave of her hand toward the vibrators and dildos.

I thought about Georgia's innate honesty and Zak telling me to tell a story. Selling was about establishing a connection—and this store was all about intimacy, right?

I set aside the tablet and gave her the truth.

"I haven't really, either. My ex-husband bought a few toys over the years, trying to spice things up. I never really got off on them… Maybe that's why he's my ex!" My wry joke earned a glimmer of a smile.

"I guess the first question is whether you're interested in finding something for yourself or if it's something you and a partner would use together?"

"Probably just me. For now," she tacked on faintly.

"Sure, um…" I scanned the array of vibrators. Shit, there were a lot of choices. "Maybe ask yourself if you want something, um, internal?" When she didn't say anything, I continued. "Do you have any allergies? To latex, for instance? I think most of these are silicone." I picked up the box to read the back. Cans of soup these were not.

"How loud is that one? I have a roommate. And does it come in blue?"

"I would have to check." I was still trying to figure out what it was made of.

"Is it really two hundred dollars?" Her voice squeezed into a whisper.

"Because of the Bluetooth, yeah. But we have others that aren't so expensive." I knew I had seen something like it. I scanned for it.

"I don't think I can choose right now." Her face was a mirror of the confused overwhelm accosting me.

"No problem. I'm glad you came in to look around." Letting her leave without buying anything tasted of failure, but: "I'd hate to sell you something you don't like and can't return. I hope you'll come back when you have more time."

She nodded and took a few steps toward the door.

"I'm Ali, by the way."

"Hi, Ali. I'll come by for coffee one day soon."

"Sounds good." She smiled and reached for the door. "Bye, Meg."

It didn't feel so much like a failure now that we were friends.

"Oh," Ali said as she almost bumped into someone coming in. She held the door open.

Zak? My heart gave a little skip.

Nope. *Mom.*

CHAPTER SIX

MEG

"You need to wash the window," were the first words out of Mom's mouth.

I would have been more annoyed if she'd been wrong.

"I was waiting for it to warm up outside."

"So... June?"

I fetched the spray and a paper towel since I had meant to do the inside of the glass while I was dusting. I gingerly stepped into the window display. Up close, the winter grit on the outside of the glass was even worse than I'd realized. I'd also need a step stool to reach the top of the window from the sidewalk.

"What on earth made Georgia want to open a store like this?" Mom asked with a note of disdain as she wandered, purse hugged tightly under her arm.

"I think she wanted to provide a place where people don't feel judged." I looked over my shoulder.

Mom held my stare. The silence thickened before she returned to browsing.

"What are rabbits and cages?" She turned the small, tented sign on the table I had just uncovered.

"The cages are male chastity devices. The rabbits are those vibrators with the two prongs like ears. They stimulate the G-spot and the clitoris at the same time."

"Do they work?"

I froze with a spritz running down the glass, bunched paper towel poised. "I don't know, Mom. Do you want to try one and report back?"

"That sounds as though you're judging whether I should or would," she pointed out.

Ugh. I scrubbed the glass, polishing out the final streaks before stepping down to the floor.

"Let's call a truce. We both want this to work for Georgia, right? If you want to help, then I have something I know you'd be good at."

Her spine stiffened.

"I'm not being facetious. Come here and tell me what you think would help this window display. I realize it should be Valentine's Day, but what's your first thought?"

Her mouth pursed as she came over to inspect it. "It needs more colour and texture—something inviting and playful. This isn't a hospital."

I always, always took remarks like that as criticism against myself, but she was on the right track, and I suddenly saw an opportunity.

"I don't want to spend a bunch of Georgia's money. Do you have anything in your craft supplies that you could loan her?" Maybe forever?

She tapped her chin. "I have a table runner with red roses and a white fringe that I made when I was trying to get back into quilting. It doesn't bear up under close inspection, but it would work here. Let me see what else I can find." She took a step toward the door, paused, and reached into her purse, withdrawing a paper bag. "I brought you a sandwich and a banana."

"No juice box?" I was being facetious, but she took me seriously.

"We don't have any. I'll pick some up when I get the rotisserie chicken for dinner."

I opened my mouth to say I could roast one myself, but instead said, "I'll pick one up on my way home, so it'll still be warm. Do you want potato salad or coleslaw?"

"You decide," she said absently, still studying the window display. "Once things are spruced up, you should host a grand reopening to let customers know you're here."

"Good idea, Mom."

Georgia was right. This apple had fallen directly under the tree.

CHAPTER SEVEN

MEG

"I made my first sale!" I bragged to Georgia when she called that evening. "A clit stimulator."

Ali had come back after her shift. By then, she'd done some research, and I had too. We compared notes and, after a little more browsing, she settled on a model that attached to her finger. It cost less than thirty dollars. I was proud as punch, and she looked like a kid who'd gotten exactly what she wanted for Christmas.

"Doesn't it feel great to make the world a better place, one orgasm at a time?" Georgia teased.

"Can I paint that on the wall? Live, Love, Orgasm? Oh, hey—Mom came by and has some great ideas for the window. I'll send you a photo tomorrow, and you can let us know if we're on the right track with your vision."

I heard a small hitch in her breath.

"George? Am I overstepping?" Shit. "You're right about the two of us being way too keen when we've got a project. I won't do anything you don't like."

"It's not that. I appreciate the enthusiasm, I do, but I'm having a shitty day. They're delaying my surgery because they want another specialist to weigh in."

"Nooo. For how long?"

"I don't know, but I had wrapped my head around it happening soon, and now I have to wait and…" She sniffed. "What if they find something else? What if they say I have to live like this? What if they cancel everything and tell me to put my affairs in order?"

I gripped the phone harder. "Have they said any of that?"

"No," she admitted sullenly. "They're hoping they can use a different procedure that'll be less invasive. They say I'll recover faster, but my paranoid brain is convinced I shouldn't buy any green bananas."

My chin crinkled under a pained smile. I loved that she always kept her sense of humour, but my heart had sunk into my churning stomach. I resisted the urge to tell her not to worry. Everything about what she was going through was terrifying.

"You're trying to brace for all possibilities. I get that," I said gently.

"Yeah. And I don't have the bandwidth to care about what happens at the store, which makes me so sad. I read the posts you sent me. They're fine. I won't rewrite anything." She took another shaky breath. "Make it clear that you're running things—and run it. Is that okay?"

"Of course. But…" I wished I could do more for her. "Do you want me to keep sending photos and updates? Or is that too much for you right now?"

"You can send stuff. I'll answer when I can, but don't expect too much. I need to let go of the store for now."

"Okay." The weight of my role settled crushingly on my shoulders, even as I promised, "Don't worry at all. Focus on yourself. The shop will be here when you're ready."

"Thanks, Meg." I heard her swallow.

"Thank *you*. I'm having fun with it." I sipped the wine I'd brought to my room after dinner. It left a burning ache behind my heart.

"Which one was it?" she asked, her voice a little steadier.

"Which what?"

"The clit stimulator."

"Oh." I told her the brand.

"That's a popular one. It's good, too. Reliable."

"Is it creepy that I asked her to report back on whether it works for her?" I hadn't, but I'd wanted to.

"Yes," Georgia sputtered. "Respect a customer's privacy, Meg! But also tell me what she says."

We both laughed.

CHAPTER EIGHT

MEG

Like any true artist, Mom didn't let censorship impede her vision.

The next morning, she handled all the products like they were designer purses and haute couture. She focused on their colour and shape, not where they'd end up. I was proud of her—patronizing, I know—but I'd always thought of her as a prude, even though Mom had gotten pregnant with me while Dad was married to someone else.

Yeah. Mom had her own history of not keeping it in her pants. I was the unplanned result of her affair with her boss.

That had made me philosophical fourteen years ago, when I realized Joel was screwing his dental hygienist. I understood how that happened. I'd had a rough pregnancy with Roddie so in some respects, the woman had done me a favour. I wasn't in the mood for sex, and she assured me it was consensual. I had to ask, since I was Joel's HR manager. We'd just moved to Toronto, where Joel opened his practice. We were deep in debt. Shelby was at a new school. I didn't want to lose my home, job, and husband while nursing a newborn, so we went to counselling. I forgave him and wrote a nice reference letter that Joel signed.

He didn't do it again. Until two years ago. That I know of.

Last May, however, he admitted he'd been screwing the woman from the car dealership while I was helping Mom hospice Dad. Best part? He told me when Wanda was in labour with his son, Freddie.

Once again, I was more inconvenienced than outraged. Wanda had fucked a married man, sure, but a married man had fucked her. I knew who the real culprit was when it came to the infidelity.

Besides, Wanda had also done me a favour. I was genuinely glad to be out of my marriage. I'd felt trapped since the first time Joel cheated. Since we married, if I was super honest about it. For twenty years, I'd been a hamster on a wheel—running myself to death but stuck in place.

No. I'd been the wheel. Joel had been the hamster. He got a lot of use out of me; I was there for him, never the other way around.

Being the wronged party gave me a high seat on the horse, but it wasn't like that for Mom. If anyone suggested she'd broken up Dad's marriage, she'd correct them and say that Dad had always been married to his practice. *That's* why his first marriage failed. She was third or fourth fiddle after his patients, me, and probably fishing.

They loved each other, though. I saw it. Maybe she made sure I saw it. She always made clear Dad wasn't a cheater who'd taken up with a tart—something I was happy to call Wanda if my kids weren't around.

Mom worked especially hard to prove their mutual love to Dad's family, even though his mother and sister were relentlessly awful to her. Gram-gram was gone, and Aunt Linda, who'd always been tight with Dad's first wife, barely spoke to Mom at his funeral. Some people are jerks—even when they give you Gram-gram's earrings and money for your kids' college funds.

I accepted both and wrote Aunt Linda a thank-you card.

That was Mom's influence. She always took the high road. When everyone came to town for Dad's funeral, Mom insisted on having Aunt Linda and her family over for dinner, even though I offered to take them to a restaurant. She wanted them in our home—to prove it *was* a home.

The relentless judgment of Mom as a homewrecker was the reason she had always been relentless about keeping me in line. She was hell-bent on making sure I wouldn't be criticized—or become a source of criticism on her mothering skills.

To forestall that possibility, she criticized me mercilessly, which is why I was equally critical of her. It was the circle of life.

That's also why I'd always seen her as uptight and sexless. After her oopsy pregsy with her married boss, Mom's only path to redemption had been to never do anything remotely immoral or fun again. Being the mother of a pregnant, unmarried teenager had been inconceivable, so she talked me into marrying Joel and here I was.

But the truth is, Mom had seen things. She worked in a doctor's office. She knew how bodies worked. She knew sex was human.

She also had a sense of humour—when she let it out to play.

Along with the table runner, she'd brought a pair of pillows with heart-print cases, a heart-shaped chocolate box, and a teddy bear with XO stitched on its belly. She arranged them around every heart-themed sex toy she could find in the store—the butt plug with a heart-shaped jewel at its base, the mask with heart-shaped eye covers, the glass dildo with suspended hearts, the flavoured lube with the hearts on the packaging, and the panties with a heart-shaped crotch cutout.

She even brought a miniature chalkboard and easel, on which she'd written: "Get your heart on this Valentine's Day."

"Mom." I pretended to be shocked, but I was genuinely impressed.

"Oh, please. It was low-hanging fruit."

"Perfect slogan for the testicle toys." I pointed at her.

"Tsk." She brushed chalk dust from her hands and glanced around. "Shall I do something with that table?"

"Sure. But I also need a theme for the relaunch. Do you have any streamers at home?"

"You want something classier than paper streamers, Meg. I'll see if I can find my fairy lights. I had a box of electric tealights at some point, too." She tapped her chin and scanned the shop. "When is Mardi Gras? Maybe we could use the beads and masks?"

"That would be fun in the swag bags. All I've got so far is a condom and a coupon."

"When are you planning the relaunch?"

"The sooner the better, but I want to check next door to make sure they're okay with it."

"Why wouldn't they want you to bring foot traffic to their door?"

I thought of Dale. "They're my landlords. It's polite to ask."

I'd briefly seen Zak again yesterday when I bundled up and went out to wash the window. He poked his head out of the antique store and said, "I'll do it with the squeegee."

Ten minutes later, I got a far-too-brief demo of his economical movements. We hadn't spoken since.

Mom grabbed her purse from behind the cash desk and was heading to the door when it opened.

"Oh, excuse me." She politely stepped aside.

I looked up, heart skipping. But it wasn't Zak.

A lean Black man walked in. He had wide shoulders and a muscular build beneath a red tracksuit with stripes down the sleeves and legs.

"Good morn—afternoon," I corrected myself. "Browsing, or looking for something in particular?"

"I was hoping Georgia had returned." His voice was deep and smooth. Soothing.

"She's still off sick. I'm her friend, Meg. I'm covering the store until she's back." I stepped forward and offered my hand.

He shook it. "Negasi."

"This is my mom, Vickie. She's compensating for my lack of artistic flair."

"You're not her sister?" He shook Mom's hand, too.

"Oh." Mom fell for the compliment and flushed with pleasure. "I wasn't *that* young when I had her. And I'm sorry to run off, but I've been put in charge of swag bags for the relaunch. I hope you'll come. Meg will fill you in."

"You had me at swag bags. Nice to meet you, Vickie."

Mom left, and he turned back to me. He was really good-looking, with that bored, half-lidded gaze that oozed sexy indifference. I wondered how well he knew Georgia.

"When is the relaunch?" he asked.

"This is why I've asked Mom to help. She's shameless," I said wryly. "I'm still planning. Maybe a week or so? I guess we'll have snacks and raffle off a gift basket or something. I could take your email and send the details once it's finalized?"

"Do that. I'll tell everyone at work."

"Thanks." I picked up the tablet. "Where do you work?"

"Right now? Dinner theatre in the old church on Clover. It's usually plays and musicals, but they brought in our drag production for the spring run. It's called Pretty Please." He framed his jaw with flat hands, tilted his head flirtatiously, and fluttered his lashes.

"Fun. Where are you from?"

"L.A. That's how I know Georgia. We've worked together at different times. She told us they were looking for something. That's how we got the gig."

"It sounds fun. Mom's birthday is coming up. Is the food good?"

"It is." He nodded.

"Decision made. Email?"

"Negasi Jackson…" He spelled out the whole address.

"Got it. I'll text Georgia you stopped by. Did you want to leave a message?"

"No. She was going to help me with something once she felt better. I saw the shop was open and figured she was back."

"Soon, I hope."

"Me too. See you at the show." He winked and left.

I texted Georgia to say he'd dropped by. Then, since the store was quiet, I stuck a note on the door explaining I was visiting Twice Is Nice and slipped across.

An older man with white hair and an argyle vest greeted me with a beaming smile. His blue eyes and offset grin were exactly like Zak's—still handsome, but weathered and crinkly around the edges.

"You came back for the medicine chest! I knew you would. I saved it for you. The one with the glass door, right? Or was it the mirrored one?"

"Um, no." Oh, shit. Georgia had told me how to handle Dale if he came into her store acting confused, but not the other way around.

"The wardrobe?" he asked with a small frown. "It's here. Let me show you."

"Actually, I was looking for…"

I trailed off, scanning the store for Zak as I followed Dale into a cluttered impression of a Victorian drawing room. Narrow paths wound between aged wooden furniture. Splashes of colour came from needlepoint cushions, bold lampshades, and saucy red vinyl stools. It smelled like cedar and mothballs and my grandmother's attic, where I'd played with my cousins as a child. I felt snug and safe, and I wanted to poke around for hours just to see what I could find.

"A magician bought one of these for his disappearing lady trick." He opened one dark wooden door of a six-foot-tall wardrobe. "Do you know how he did it?"

"How?" I was instantly rapt, excited to learn a magician's secret.

"Layaway."

A guffaw escaped me, mostly because he had led me right into that joke. I was sure he had told it a thousand times.

"Which is something we could arrange for you." Zak's voice startled me into turning. He wore his jeans and boots with a pale blue Henley, sleeves pushed up to his elbows. He was wiping his hands on a cloth as he smoothly continued the pitch. "We could also convert it into something more suitable for today's lifestyle. A television cabinet, perhaps? Or a baking pantry?"

"Very slick. I'll take two."

"Be careful. We have two. This is Meg from next door, Dad. You haven't met her yet. She's running the new shop next door. This is my dad, Dale Halligan."

"Hi, Dale." We shook hands.

"Meg. Right. The new shop. I remember." Dale nodded, but confusion clouded his eyes.

I felt a tug in my chest. He didn't remember but thought he should. That distressed him. I could tell.

"My hands are covered in turpentine." Zak showed me his wide hands, dry white lines traced into every whorl and crease. "I'll be right back."

"Sure." I averted my eyes from his departing jeans, asking Dale, "Have you had this shop long?"

"Oh, yes. Almost twenty years. My wife, Tammy, inherited her grandparents' farm when we married. She began refinishing their furniture as a hobby and sold it through here. When the bachelors who owned this store wanted to retire, she used the money from the farm to buy the building. We have three tenants—two upstairs, and that's Debra next door in the quilting shop."

I didn't correct him, but I did look for Zak, who was still washing his hands.

"The twins come by to help after school," Dale continued. "They'll be off to college soon and Tammy thought she'd be alone here, but I got my buyout package from the railway so she railroaded me into working with her." He touched his nose, inviting me to enjoy his pun.

I gave him the chuckle he was looking for, but it was tempered by the realization that his spiel had come out via muscle memory. My heart panged with compassion.

"Oh, I see you take books." I looked to the table where leather-bound books were spilling out of boxes. "My mother has my father's medical textbooks. Would they be worth anything?"

"Let me show you what to look for." He opened a book and gave me some tips on determining whether it was a first edition. "Like anything, it's a matter of doing your research, then finding a buyer. Books are more personal than furniture, so they're harder to sell—but everything is wanted by someone. The trick is making the match."

"There should be an app, like dating. Swipe right if you're interested in *Diseases of the Ear, Nose, and Throat.*" It was a solid joke, but the wrong audience.

Dale nodded politely, setting down the book he was holding.

"Did you need something?" Zak came back in time to hear me bomb. "Or is this a social call?"

"A little of both." I turned to face him. "I was curious about your shop, but I want to do a splashy reopening next door. I thought it might affect you, so I wanted to ask first."

"When?"

"Thursday next week? I'll put it on social media, obviously, but I'm hoping to get some spots on the radio and entice people to drop in on their way home from work."

"The microbrew will love that. We'll stay open late, too. Keep the street bright."

"Really? That'd be great. Thanks."

"A street party? We should talk to Debra about that." Dale started toward the door.

"No, Dad—" Zak caught him back.

I winced an apology and pointed to my untended store.

Zak nodded, and I left him patiently repeating to Dale that Debra wasn't there anymore. I really did need to appreciate my mom more. I couldn't imagine how helpless Zak felt.

At least he'd been okay about the relaunch. With the date decided, I could turn my attention to getting the word out and hoping customers showed up.

CHAPTER NINE

ZAK

My sister walked in the back door while I was making a salad to go with the shepherd's pie I'd already put in the oven. I wasn't exactly Wolfgang Puck, but I'd lived alone a lot, and Erica was a nurse—she only cooked when her twelve-hour shifts hadn't left her comatose. I'd also gone through a period in my early twenties when I survived on junk food and barely left my apartment. One way I'd pulled myself out of that pit was by signing up for budget cooking classes.

"Hi," I greeted.

"Hi." Zara left her boots on the mat and draped her damp jacket over the back of a chair.

"Hey, Dad," she called, poking her head into the living room just long enough to see he was engrossed in his game shows. "Doing okay? Need anything?"

"A better noggin," Dad said, same as he'd been saying since his diagnosis. Then he blurted, "Clavell," at the TV, and I once again wondered why we were even worried about him.

"You want a beer or something?" I offered as she came back into the kitchen.

"No. Jade's at dance. I only have a few minutes before I have to get her." She picked up the can I was nursing, though, and took a few healthy swallows.

"Everything okay?" I asked.

"Just a busy day."

The way she did these little drive-bys made me painfully aware of how much I'd left on her shoulders for the last decade. Sure, she'd filled her life to overflowing by having three kids, but even when she'd only had Lance, and Dad had still been fully on his game, she'd dropped by a few times a week to check on him. When she had gone back to work at the insurance office, she hadn't been able to help Dad as much with the shop and the building. She hired someone to shift his bookkeeping online and build him a website, but look where the man worked. He didn't know much about computers and didn't want to. Everything she'd done added up to her doing more work, not less. I hadn't done a damned thing to help.

"How's the shop?" she asked.

"Fine." Boring as hell, but she knew that.

I had a sudden flash of Meg chuckling at Dad's very, very tired joke about the magician. *Don't encourage him*, I might have said in the past. Instead, I'd been grateful that she indulged him, helping him look and feel like himself for a few minutes.

"Oh," I remembered. "Meg from the toy store? She's doing a relaunch on Thursday. I said I'd keep our shop open late, too."

"And take Dad?"

We both looked toward the living room, aware we were supposed to keep him in a routine. Zara was way more strict about it—she was a working mom and ran a tight ship.

I shrugged, still figuring things out.

"Have you heard from Erica?" she asked, picking a carrot disk off the salad.

"Not since she asked me what I want to do with the condo."

"What did you tell her?"

"That I haven't decided. Calm down." I held up a hand as her eyes widened. "Not because I want to move back there."

I liked keeping that option open, though. It was only a ninety-minute ferry ride between Vancouver and Victoria, but that fucking ferry. It was the reason I hadn't visited as often as I should have.

I wasn't prepared to be an island guy again—not that I had much choice. Erica had always been very ambivalent about moving here. All her family was in Abbotsford and Chilliwack—drivable from Vancouver in an hour or two and you didn't have to book a hundred-dollar ferry reservation first.

"Erica isn't in a position to buy me out, and the condo is a good investment," I explained. "I don't pay anything here, so I might as well keep paying my half of that mortgage. Why? Did she ask you about it?" I had the impression they were still texting.

"No. She sent me an invitation to a Galentine's thing. I think she was just being nice—kind of letting me know she wanted to stay friends or whatever—but it made me wonder if she was taking the temperature here. Maybe she regrets not coming with you."

"Maybe she does. And I say this with love, Zara, but don't you have enough to worry about?"

"Yes, but I feel like this is on me," she mumbled around the strip of red pepper she stole off the cutting board.

"You feel responsible for our breakup? Why? Did you make that happen?" I thumbed toward Dad in the living room.

"I told you to come home."

"For Christmas. She was working anyway."

"You know what I mean."

I did. Zara had had a small nervous breakdown on Christmas Eve, crying so hard Kyle had to take Dad and the kids for a drive to look at Christmas lights without us.

I'd felt like a giant asshole, finally seeing how much stress she'd been under. I said I'd come back until we figured out what was next for Dad. In that moment, I only wanted to comfort my sister and pick up my share of the burden. Maybe I'd thought there was some kind of protocol for how to deal with something like this and that I'd only be here a few weeks while we put a plan in place.

Erica had straightened me out when I got back to Vancouver. She knew what I was in for better than I did. Sure, there was a protocol and a process—one that would go on for years. We'd have to make thousands of decisions, and they were all going to suck.

Before Christmas, she'd agreed to marry me and we'd talked about trying to start a family once we were married. But she wasn't prepared to quit her very good job, move to the Island, and help me care for a parent whose needs were only going to grow more complex.

Fresh off seeing Zara's exhaustion from trying to juggle that with a family of her own, I couldn't blame Erica for dumping me—but I couldn't ignore what was happening here either.

We agreed to split, but here was my sister trying to hand me a ticket for a guilt trip because I hadn't fought harder for my relationship with Erica.

"You want me to go back to Vancouver and patch things up with her?" I asked.

"No," she said glumly. "But you seem really bummed lately."

I snorted and waved toward the living room. What did she expect?

"I know, but…"

"It is what it is. Let it go."

Breakups sucked, and my feelings were hurt, but I didn't regret being here.

There should be an app—like dating. Swipe right if you're into diseases of the ear, nose, and throat.

"I have to get Jade," Zara said, snapping me back to reality.

She went in to drape a hug across Dad's shoulders, then came back to shoot her arms into her jacket while kicking into her boots.

"Next Thursday is book club. I'll see if the group wants to swing by the sex shop on our way to dinner. Could be fun."

I nodded, grateful. If she came by, she could sit with Dad for a few minutes and give me a chance to chat with Meg again.

CHAPTER TEN

MEG

Roddie had texted me that he had a quiz to study for and a basketball game Friday night, but promised to call me over the weekend.

When he decided to live with Joel, it had been about staying closer to his friends and his high school, which he liked for its music program.

I told Roddie I understood, but I still wavered between guilt and bitterness.

I'm that hypocrite who complains about becoming a mother too young but I'm not ready to lose any of the crushing weight of that responsibility. Who am I if I'm not a mom? I envy my daughter for being single and thriving in the carefree college life I never had, but I haven't figured out how to enjoy being single myself.

I could have fought Joel for the house in Rosedale, and Roddie probably would have stayed with me there. But Joel had a baby on the way. I was happy to downsize into a North York condo near the university, in case Roddie decided to study there. Also, Joel had screwed Wanda *in our bed* while I was helping Mom with probate. That soured any lingering sentiment I felt toward our home, so I let him buy me out.

The only thing I regretted about my current decision was leaving Roddie again. I'd already missed too much of his life. Big things. Roddie was fourteen, and I hadn't guessed he was gay until he told me and Joel right before school started in September.

I was still furious with myself for not realizing it sooner, but between Dad, the divorce, and returning to the office full-time, I'd been phoning in my parenting for at least three years.

I'm not proud of that.

But I was doing everything I could to be present now—as evidenced by the fact that I was waiting for him to call me because I wasn't *there*.

Ugh. Mother of the Year again.

I texted that I was free all day tomorrow if he wanted to talk, then started going through the books on my bedroom shelves, hoping to find a first edition Harry Potter.

Are you home now?

Yes, I replied.

A FaceTime notification popped up.

I dropped the book I was holding and accepted the call, moving to the bed and piling pillows against the headboard. "Hi."

"Hey." He was on his laptop with gaming headphones on, not looking at me as he emptied his school backpack onto the desk.

"It's Saturday night. I thought you'd be out." I glanced at the clock. It was nine there—he still had an hour before curfew.

"Like with Tyson? He's with *Bethany* now." His lip curled, and his eyebrows pulled into that winged shape Joel's always made when he was annoyed. I found it patronizing in his father, but when Roddie did it, I loved it.

"Really?" I was genuinely shocked. Agog. Things had been very new between them, but—"Bethany?" I couldn't believe it. She'd been his best friend since kindergarten.

"Right? He acted like he liked me, but I guess he actually liked her? And she likes him? That's fucked up, right?"

"It is." Now wasn't the time to scold him for swearing. I didn't actually care if my kids swore. I almost never said anything about it.

Roddie's brows had thickened with adolescence, forming strong, masculine lines over his golden-brown eyes. In so many ways, he looked like the young Joel my young self had fallen for—especially with that kicked-dog look on his face. It reminded me I had genuinely loved his father. It helped me forgive myself for staying with Joel that first time. I had done what I thought was best for our kids. I didn't regret it, but I knew now it hadn't been the best thing for *me*.

Hindsight, man. Always twenty-twenty.

"I'm really sorry to hear that, bud. I can see you're angry." And hurt. Oh, my little man.

"I am. School sucks. I switched to remote learning, but I have to go in for music and science lab. They're on my fucking *bus*."

"Oh, buddy. That sucks."

"Yeah." There was a crack in his voice.

I wanted to hug him so hard right then. "Do you want to talk about it?"

"I just did."

Right. I didn't laugh because there was a sharp ache sitting in my chest. He might be starting to look and sound more man than child, but I felt as though I'd abandoned my baby.

"Did you see my text about coming here for spring break?" I asked tentatively.

"Yeah. You're staying longer? How come?"

"Grandma's having trouble parting with stuff." That was true, but I'd noticed that my own room was a time capsule, so I was trying not to be too hard on her about it. "I've also started working for a friend who's sick. It's a long story, but there's a chance I'll need to stay through the summer to get everything done. I can fly you out here anytime, though. I have tons of points. Grandma would love to see you."

Visiting Grandma in Victoria had been a lot more fun at four than it was at fourteen, so I was genuinely surprised when he said, "Can I come next weekend? We've got a PA day Friday, and Thursday's online. I could leave Wednesday after my lab in the morning, then do school from there on Thursday."

I was taken aback. What fourteen-year-old wanted to hang out with his mom unless he really, really missed her? A lump formed in my throat.

"Done," I said. "I'll book it as soon as we're off the phone."

"Thanks, Mom."

"No problem." I forced some lightness into my voice. "Anything else going on? Have you talked to Shelby?"

She and I texted constantly—mostly memes and rants about the patriarchy—but despite the seven-year age gap, she and Roddie were still remarkably close.

"She's seeing someone called Weston. I said it sounds like she's dating a refrigerator."

"And she said little brothers are awesome and she misses you?"

"Pretty much. I'll tell her I'm coming to see you. Maybe she can come see us."

"That'd be nice. I'll look at flights for her, too." God, I wanted my arms around my kids right now.

"Okay. I'll go tell Dad."

"I'll go tell Grandma that we have to clean up the rumpus room."

"That bed," he groaned.

My kids had been sleeping on that pull-out since they were little. There was an infamous bar that dug into their backs, which had grown worse as they grew bigger and heavier and the mattress grew older and saggier.

"I'll buy a foam topper tomorrow. I'm really glad you're coming. I'll text you the details in a little while."

"Thanks, Mom. I love you."

"I love you, too, Rod." I was smiling as I ended the call.

It faded as I realized I'd have to fess up about my career change sooner than I'd expected.

CHAPTER ELEVEN

MEG

The days leading up to Valentine's Day were busy with a steady stream of walk-ins and several online orders. I stayed late to fulfill them, glad to see a small bump in sales for Georgia.

After reviewing her sales from the few weeks she had been in business, I set some targets for myself. My low-bar goal was to match her average weekly sales, even with the "five dollars or five percent off" coupons I was handing out. If I could do that, I'd cover the rent, my modest wages, and the amount I'd budgeted for the relaunch.

I wouldn't have been able to make the party nearly as splashy without the full force of Vickie Crutcher behind it. Along with her keen eye for stylish arrangements, she brought a few vintage pieces from the Ladies Auxiliary that set a tone of elegance. One was a cocktail dress with a green velvet bodice and black polka-dot netting over a green satin skirt. She also brought colourful bow ties, a burgundy fedora, a gorgeous red cape, and a black mini dress that laced down the back like a corset. These were all strategically hung around the shop to define spaces and add flair.

Between the social media posts and the newspaper ad, people were coming in steadily—a blessing and a curse. While Mom pinned a *Phantom of the Opera* poster to the wall, I did my best to help a customer.

"Is it waterproof?" the young man asked.

"Um, yes." I pointed to the blue teardrop I'd added to the price tag on every item I'd identified as waterproof.

"Good. She said she wanted the waterproof one. And this one's okay for, like, front and back? 'Cause it says 'anal' here."

"That's how it's marketed but—" I cleared my throat and pointed. "See, it says it can also be used vaginally. Just be sure to clean it well between uses. Obviously."

"Right. Is this the only one you have?"

"This one's a different brand. It's not purple." I picked up the box. "It's also more expensive."

"That's the one she wanted." He practically snatched it out of my hand. "Yeah, with ten speed combos. This is the one." He sounded really excited—not so much sexually, more like a prospector who'd struck gold. *Eureka*. He was grinning from ear to ear. It was cute.

I grabbed the tablet and ran his credit card, then wrapped the box in tissue paper and slipped it into one of the bags discreetly embossed with the store's initials.

"Let me give you one of these coupons." I showed him before adding it to the bag. "We'll be handing out more at the relaunch in a few days. The details are on the back. I've got more stock coming in for that, so I hope you'll drop by with your partner."

"This basket needs something." Mom frowned at the gift basket I was planning to raffle for the low price of joining the newsletter. "I'll see what I can find and come back after lunch."

"Thanks, Mom."

She left, and I helped two more customers before Zak strode in.

"Hi." A zip of electricity jolted through my limbs—but how could it not? He was all sexy in his faded jeans and open flannel over a shirt that read, "Favourite Uncle, Only Uncle."

"Hi." He stopped short and took in the masquerade theme. "This looks great."

"Credit to Mom. She's worried I'm not doing enough to get the word out, *and* that it won't be good enough if people do show up."

"Tell her I've invited everyone from Dad's church."

"Great." I scratched my upper lip. "Did you really?"

"Dad hasn't been to church since Mom died. Me neither. Zara's coming with her book club, though."

"That's great! Hey, Mom thinks this gift basket needs something." I gestured at the square basket filled with a bottle of white wine, two glasses, flavoured lube, furry black handcuffs, and a bright pink dildo. "Is this worth giving your email for?"

"You already have it."

"For the newsletter? Wait—you're not Tinfoil, are you?" A notification for a new subscriber had popped up the day after the store reopened. The timing had struck me as odd, but I hadn't thought much more about it.

"Yeah. Twice Is Nice…TIN. Get it? It was my first alias account. I still use it for subscriptions and stuff I don't check very often. Let me give you my number so you have it if you need anything."

My brain half-exploded, but this was only as significant as I let it be. We weren't exchanging numbers. He was being professional. He was the landlord.

Even so, I was flustered as I tried to call up my contact book on my phone.

"You can just tell me your number, and I'll call it," he pointed out.

"Right." Clearly, I had never given a man my number before.

I told him, and my phone rang once.

He ended the call and nodded at the basket. "I have an idea. I'll be right back."

While he was gone, I fiddled with my phone, adding him to my contacts.

"I want you to treat this with the reverence it deserves," Zak said when he returned. He set a *Penthouse* magazine from the mid-seventies on the desk. A young woman on the cover was removing her black bra, revealing uptilted nipples on small, pert breasts.

"The articles *are* worth reading," I noted as I scanned the callouts. One was about Castro and another about Paul Newman. "Did you know this?" I pointed with mock alarm. "Streaking leads to making love in public?"

"It's a gateway kink." He nodded somberly.

"Who knew?"

"*Penthouse*." He nodded again. "Take a photo and post it. You will get offers and they will be generous."

"Really?" I wrinkled my nose in skepticism, then I narrowed my eyes. "Where did you get this? Do you have a secret room in the back?"

"Where I polish wood? Yes. And I'm not embarrassed to admit it."

My pulse tripped, and I bit my lips together to hide my smile.

"Nor should you be." I fought to keep a straight face. "I'm working with a different product, so it's mostly about keeping the dust off, but, you know. Same diff."

A twinkle entered his blue eyes. He crossed his arms and rocked on his heels.

"Here I thought you'd be so busy receiving packages, you wouldn't have time to dust."

"You're about to ask me where I receive those packages, aren't you?" I was fighting back a bubble of mirth. "Front of the store. That's why I'm doing all that maintenance. Keeping things in good working order."

"Quality assurance."

"Exactly. No shame in that." My bravado was thinning along with my voice. My face was on fire. It took everything in me to hold his laughing blue gaze.

"Why would you be ashamed? It's more of an obligation to those who… Hmm." He winced. "I was going to say 'come through the door,' but…" He winced in dissatisfaction.

"I appreciate how hard you wordsmith your comebacks."

"Now you're just talking dirty for the sake of it."

We were both struggling not to break, but the air was crackling in a way I hadn't felt since I didn't know when. It was like being tipsy and stoned and horny all at once.

He glanced away, biting the corner of his crooked grin.

"So where did you really get it?" I asked. "The magazine."

"Hmm? Oh. An estate sale. There was a stack in one of the nightstands. I haven't read the articles in that one yet."

"Then how are you staying abreast of current events?" I dropped my jaw in mock discovery. "Do you think that's where the expression comes from?"

"Abreast? Gotta be."

We were both openly grinning now. Damn it, I really liked him.

"This does class up the basket, doesn't it?" I busied myself tucking the magazine behind the wine glasses. "Do you want anything for it?"

"Just the right to come talk to you when I'm bored."

"Is that why you're here now?"

"Yeah. Dad fell asleep and I found myself researching what mermaids eat."

"Are you thinking of getting one? Goldfish are quieter."

"Sirens are the noisy ones. I always thought they were the same as mermaids, but they're different—half bird. Did you know that?"

"Oh, dear. Boredom that acute could result in serious injury or death. Look, there's no price of admission here. C—" Don't say it. "Come anytime. I won't make you buy anything."

"No? Why not? I'm curious." His gaze wandered to the shelf I'd labelled Penis Pleasure. "I've never really played with toys. My ex had a vibrator, but that was for her 'me time.' Where do you even start?"

Mom had tried to set up his and hers sections, but I switched it to labels that were less binary. The clit stims and vaginal vibrators were under Joie de Vulva. There was an All Things Anal shelf and one called Knick Knacks for Nipples.

"In this store, you start by allowing a novice like me to ask you a bunch of intimate questions. When you're really lucky, my mom is *right there.*" I pointed to the floor next to my foot. "I was helping a customer choose a strap-on harness and Mom was humming 'Innocence.'" When his brows came together I added, "Harlequin."

"I'll have that song stuck in my head all day now. Thanks. Did the customer notice?"

"No. Mom's off-key as hell. But I'm always trying to make a connection with them. Kind of like what you suggested. I tell them about my own experience—of which I have none—so that's a pretty short conversation. I'm dying to ask if they'll report back, but that's gross, right? 'Enjoy your butt plug. Call me with a postgame.'"

"I'll do it. I'm serious," he insisted when I sputtered a laugh. "Sell me something. I'll let you know if it does anything for me."

"I'm not going to make you buy a toy just so I can get better at selling them."

"Why not? I'm not Mr. Gates, but I've worked for his competitors. I can afford a couple of toys, especially if it'll benefit humanity."

He picked up a cock ring with an anal bulb attached. He tested its stretchiness, then closed his fist over the bulb. "Be real. Is this to check your blood pressure after sex?"

"You really are bored, aren't you?"

"So bored." He winced, seeming to want to bite back his words. He set the toy down. "That sounds like I don't want to be here." He shifted so he could see the door to his own shop and folded his arms. "In the big scheme of things, I don't. I wish this wasn't happening. But it feels good to get back to woodworking. And now that it's sinking in that Dad really is losing his memories, I want this time with him."

"How is he doing? Because the day I met him, he seemed… okay-ish?"

"That's about where he's at. Half the time I wonder why I'm even here. He gets dressed and helps me make breakfast, and we agree that it's too soon to start mowing the lawn. Then he forgets something basic, like how to turn the key to unlock the door. Or that Mom is dead."

"He said something yesterday that made me wonder. When did you lose her?"

"I was twenty, so…" He rubbed his beard. "Twelve years ago?"

I nodded in empathy. "It's been almost two since we lost Dad. It sucks."

"It does."

"Is he still hanging on to some of your mom's things?" That was a dumb question, considering the store had been hers. "I ask because Mom is having trouble letting go. I don't know how hard to push. I'm only here because she agreed to sell the house and move closer to me in Toronto. But things like this—" I pointed at the red and gold Mardi Gras beads spilling from champagne glasses "—are about all she's willing to part with."

Even at that, I expected her to ask for them back next week.

"I wondered about that," he admitted. "Why you moved in with your mom when she seems healthy and fully on top of things."

"Oh, her mind is a steel trap. It's me who failed to remember that she drives me nuts." I scrunched up my face. "That was in bad taste. Sorry."

"It's fine. If you can't joke, how do you get through it?"

"Do you want a serious laugh? My son, who's fourteen, is arriving tomorrow night. He doesn't know I'm doing this." I waved at the store. "What do I tell him?"

"I don't know, but can I be there when you do?"

"I had a feeling you'd enjoy that."

"I would. What time—oh." He quickly stepped over to open the door for my mom. "Hi, Vickie. I was just telling Meg how great it looks in here."

"Hello, Zak. It's nice to see you again."

Mom strode in with a pair of white tapered candles, a bag of white feathers, and a roll of white satin ribbon speckled with hearts.

"Zak brought something for the basket." I pointed at the *Penthouse*. "He says these vintage magazines are worth a lot to collectors." I still wasn't convinced.

"Is that true?" Mom brightened. "I have hundreds that belonged to my husband. Could you sell them for me?"

CHAPTER TWELVE

MEG

The Victoria airport was delightfully jarring in its simplicity, especially coming from Pearson in Toronto. Sometimes you even got lucky and found a direct flight, but most of the time you had to wait in Vancouver for a connection. That's what Roddie had to do.

Roddie had made this trek with me at least once a year since he was two months old, but this was his first time travelling alone. He'd texted that he was on his connecting flight, though, so I wasn't worried. Not about that, anyway.

I was still trying to come to terms with my father, the GP, collecting boxes—plural—of pornography. And the fact that my mother had hung on to them!

"I didn't know where to take them," she had said with a flustered shrug.

Zak had politely offered to come by the house to pick them up one day soon. Then he'd left and was probably still busting a gut over the flabbergasted expression that must've been on my face.

Who was I to judge? I still hadn't figured out how to tell my son about my new, equally titillating occupation.

*Pre*occupation? I'd fondled every toy in the shop, wondering how each one worked. *If* it worked. Honestly, the only thing stopping me from trying them was not knowing how I'd ever say to a customer, *Oh yeah, I really like that one. It got me off three times last night.*

Meanwhile, I had gotten off three times after dinner, thinking about Zak getting off. Which wasn't my fault. He'd started it, with all his banter about polishing wood and test-driving toys. I kept telling myself he wasn't serious, but what if he was? What if he actually bought a toy and—

Oh. People began trickling through the sliding glass arrivals door. I spotted a chestnut forelock poking out from under a raised grey hoodie, layered beneath a heavy blue winter coat. My heart swelled, and a wide smile spread across my face.

"Hi, bud."

"Hi, Mom." He dropped his backpack by his feet and hugged me. Hard.

"Did you grow again?" It hadn't even been two weeks since I'd hugged him goodbye, but it felt as though he towered over me.

"Did you shrink? Where's Grandma?" He looked around.

"Home. She was tired." From organizing my relaunch event. "Was your flight okay? Is that all you have?" Just his school backpack? He was only staying a few days, but still—I'd expected a carry-on.

"I checked a bag." His gaze moved to the carousels.

"Oh. Big spender." We walked over as people began to gather. "Did you bring your ski gear?" Shit. We'd done that as a family sometimes when visiting here over Christmas. Mount Washington was three hours up island, though. "I didn't even think of that. Sorry, bud. I don't think I can take you. Maybe I can get you one of those day trips, though?" Skiing alone wasn't as fun.

"No. It's not—" He clenched his eyes shut, mouth flat and brows drawn together. "Can I stay?" He opened his eyes, still tense, as if bracing for rejection. "With you? Until you go back? Please?"

My heart lurched so hard it nearly burst out of my chest.

"Yes," I said, instantly. Instinctively. Dumbfounded, but there was only one answer to such a request. "Always." I pulled him into a hug. Through his thick layers, I thought he might be trembling. "I love you. You always have a place with me." My heart was pounding. *What happened?*

The conveyor belt started. He let go and swiped the heel of his hand across his eye.

"Do you want to tell me why?" I asked gently. My mind raced to bullying at school and all the terrible things that could happen to a kid.

"Dad and Wanda fight all the time. Even today, about who would take me to the train."

Joel hadn't driven him to the airport? Sure, airports are a pain, but Roddie had a full-sized bag. I was livid, but I did what I always did: I made excuses for that fuckwit.

"New babies are hard on everyone. No one gets any sleep. Tempers are short." It was all true.

"Freddie isn't that bad. He cries a lot, especially at night, but he's cute. I feel really bad about leaving him, but Dad is never there, and Wanda is always mad about it. When I told Dad about Tyson and Bethany, Dad said, 'Don't miss your bus.' That's *all*. He didn't even offer to drive me to school that morning. Wanda hates that I'm doing school from home even though I'm in my room all day. I hate being there."

He didn't feel welcome in his own father's home. In the home that had been ours, when we'd been a family. My heart wrenched itself into jagged shards.

"What about science? I thought you had to go in for that. And music?"

"I can retake science or make it up over the summer. I was hoping I could move in with you when you go back. Starting a new school can't be worse than—" He stepped forward and yanked a black suitcase off the carousel. He plonked it in front of me and snapped the handle up. He hung his head, peering from the depths of his raised hoodie. "Are you mad?"

"No." Not at him. "What about your dad? Did you talk to him about this before you left?"

For a second, he looked five years old again, begging me for a puppy. "Can you tell him?"

"Sure." Joel would be defensive, and I'd have to soothe his ego, but that was nothing new. Also, I was getting something I wanted, so I was more than happy to make that phone call. "Grandma will be excited that you're staying."

I was pretty sure. We had shifted things around in the rumpus room, but Mom had not been persuaded to take Dad's clothes to the thrift store. My mind began assembling a long list of to-dos if Roddie was staying longer.

As I pulled the SUV fob from my pocket, the key to Afternoon Delight flashed silver.

Right. There was also that.

CHAPTER THIRTEEN

MEG

W*e could all use a break.* That's what Joel said when I told him Roddie wanted to stay with me until further notice.

I actively tried not to hate Joel. He was the father of my children; they wouldn't exist without him. As much as I wanted to blame him entirely for our divorce, I couldn't. Yes, he cheated. More than once. But I wasn't perfect either. I could be uptight as hell. I ran our chequing account like I was collecting for the mob. In the last years of our marriage, I was always working, carting the kids around, or in Victoria. I knew we were drifting apart, and I did nothing to stop it. Looking back, I think I *wanted* to be apart, I just didn't have the balls to end it until he gave me the excuse.

So no, I didn't hate him—I hated his selfish streak.

I swear, when I told him that Roddie wanted to stay here with me at Mom's, Joel nearly asked if he could come stay here too.

I got it. Newborns are brutal. I respected Wanda for calling Joel out on leaving all the baby care to her. I hadn't done that. I was the child of a doctor, raised to believe it was my job to defer to Dr. Joel's higher needs—as a freaking dentist—even when I was so sleep-deprived by a colicky baby—and then another—that I was afraid to walk anywhere with them for fear I'd drop them.

I'd trained Joel to expect me to run triage with the kids and only loop him in once the crisis had passed—when he had time to absorb and process it.

But could he not go through the motions of fighting for his son? For Roddie's sake? Did he have to be such a numb-brained prick all the time?

As I came back to the kitchen, where Mom was microwaving leftovers, Roddie lifted his attention from his phone and frowned with concern.

"Is he mad?"

"He understands." I let go of my anger. This was what I wanted. From the moment I packed my bags, I told Roddie he could live with me. It might not be ideal to have him here while I ran Afternoon Delight, but I'd make it work.

"Thanks, Grandma," he said as Mom set a plate in front of him, piled with store-bought chicken fettuccine from earlier.

"Want milk? Or one of those green things your mother takes to work?"

"Water's fine, thanks." He scooped up some noodles. "I asked Grandma what you're doing for your friend. She said to ask you."

"Did she?"

Mom shot me a buttoned-lip look as she filled a glass from the tap.

"Right. So." I sat across from Roddie and grabbed the edge of that metaphorical bandage. "I've got something to tell you."

"Oh, shit." He dropped his fork with a clatter.

"What?" I flashed back to telling him about the divorce. "No, it's fine. I just quit my accounting job."

"Why? Does Shelby know? Is that why you came here? Are you staying?"

"*No*. And no. I'll tell her in a few days." When I worked up the nerve. "It's not a secret." I glanced at Mom as she set down Roddie's glass of water. "I'm helping Georgia at her shop. She needs surgery."

"Oh." He looked at both of us, waiting for the other shoe. "So…?"

"She needs someone to run it until she's back. It's temporary, and it gives me space to figure out what's next."

"Okay." He was still frowning, but losing interest now that he knew it didn't directly affect him. He tapped a notification on his phone and asked absently, "What kind of store is it?"

"Adult toys," I mumbled and quickly added, "We're relaunching tomorrow. I'll be out all day and probably working late. It won't always be like that. Mom, do you think we need a banner in the window?"

"Wait." Roddie had, for once, forgotten he was holding his phone. "Like vibrators and stuff?"

"Yes," I said with breezy casualness, as if it was totally normal. Because it was. "Afternoon Delight is a sexual health store that serves the needs of a diverse customer base. Grandma's been helping me there."

Yes, that was the Downtown Express I pushed my mother under. With both hands.

"I'm assisting with merchandising," Mom said stiffly, yanking open the top door of the refrigerator to pull out the ice cream. "Providing themed decorations. That's *all*."

"Themed." Roddie was still slack-jawed, but the corners of his mouth were twitching.

"It's like selling anything else," I insisted. "Nothing to get excited about."

"I think the point is to get excited, but what do I know?" He shovelled more noodles into his smirking mouth. "I'm just a kid."

"I know this is unexpected." Understatement of the year. "But could you keep it to yourself for a few days and not tell your sister? Or your father?" Or anyone?

"I don't know. When your mom comes out as a dungeon master, you kind of want to tell your friends. But since I don't *have* any…" He glowered at his plate.

"I appreciate your discretion. Finish up and get to bed. I have a big day tomorrow, and you have class."

CHAPTER FOURTEEN

MEG

You quit your job to sell sex toys? Shelby texted as I was opening the store the next morning.

"Really, Roddie?" I muttered under my breath.

Yes, I texted Shelby. *I'm busy doing that right now. Long day today. I'll call tomorrow.*

Then I texted Roddie before I finished my opening routine.

Tattletale.

It didn't really bother me that he'd ratted me out. I was glad my kids were close enough to share secrets with each other. I had always wanted a sibling and always worried I'd waited too long between my own children. Shelby was in kindergarten before we began trying for another baby. It hadn't happened right away, which added even more space between them.

Still, both of my kids now knew I had quit my job. I would've preferred to have a broader plan in place so I didn't come across as unhinged by my recent divorce, but so be it.

The door jangled. Zak poked his head in. "I'm going for coffee. Want anything?"

"Sure. Thanks. Whatever their drip of the day is, with a splash of cream." I would be vibrating, but I had a lot to do today.

"You don't want something fancy? Pumpkin spice latte or whatever?"

"I do not want that, and if you ever buy me one of those, I will marry you purely so I can divorce you and take all your money as punishment for not knowing how disgusting that is."

"Yes to pumpkin spice. Got it." The door clattered again as he left.

I watched him stride across the road without using the crosswalk, shoulders hunched in his blue puffer jacket, hair tousled by the wind.

Nutbar.

A customer came in, one I privately classified as 'covert.' His jacket was zipped to his chin, and he wore a baseball cap pulled low over his eyes. He moved with stiff purpose, grabbing a butt plug and some lube, bringing them straight to the cash desk and setting them down with the quiet defiance used by every woman when buying tampons—until she stopped giving a flying fuck that the cashier knew her uterus was shedding.

"Good morning. I can give you five percent off with today's coupon." I flashed it at him. "It's our relaunch today."

"Oh. Great." His wall of reserve crumbled. He broke into a wide smile. "Thanks. You don't have to bag it. I'm in a hurry."

"Sure." I rang it through. He shoved the items into his jacket pockets as he left.

I tried not to wonder what sort of butt-plug emergency he was racing to, but I was quickly distracted when Zak returned with my coffee.

"Thanks." I came to the door to accept it so he could stay positioned to keep an eye on his own shop's entrance. "What's the occasion?"

"Dad always helps with breakfast, but whatever went into my mouth this morning wasn't coffee." He made a face, but he wasn't joking. Beneath the grimace was brooding concern.

"I'm sorry." I wanted to squeeze his arm.

"Yeah. I can't tell Zara. She gets upset. I bought you a coffee so I could stand here and bitch to you about it." He took a tentative first sip.

"You already gave me a *Penthouse* for that." I nodded toward the basket. "I've had offers, by the way. I told them to come by your shop, knock three times, and ask for Zak."

"Tinfoil," he reminded me with exasperation. "You think I want my dad knowing I'm cutting side deals in vintage porn? I should check on him." He reached for the door. "But hey, good luck today."

"Thanks. And seriously, anytime."

"Thanks." He nodded and slipped into his own shop.

I thought about him between the small rushes of customers I had through the morning, wishing there was something I could do to help Zak.

Like what? I chided myself. Buy him a toy to cheer him up? He had said he was curious.

I'd spent a lot of time examining the vagina-focused toys and had finally brought home a small vibrator marketed as 'stealth' for its near-silent vibration. It delivered solid orgasms. I had no complaints, but it wasn't changing my life or anything.

Since the store was quiet, I took a closer look at the penis-focused toys. I'd filled a lot of online orders for super high-end products with Bluetooth controls that could be used via an app for long-distance lovemaking. Most of what I had on the shelf was mid-range in price and focused on masturbation sleeves and prostate stimulators.

A rimming plug? How did that work?

The door jangled.

"Mom?" Roddie walked in.

For Christ's sake. I dropped the plug.

"What are you doing here?" My heart was fully outside my chest, running away.

"I texted you." His gaze swung like a scythe from wall to wall.

I checked my phone and there it was. *The wifi isn't working. I'm going to the library.*

"How did you get here? Did Grandma drop you?" I looked toward the street.

"No. She had to help someone named Barbara at the thrift store." He came further into the shop and peered around the shelf to see what it held. "I checked the bus schedule, then hopped off down the street."

"Did you text Grandma?" I started to text her.

"Uh-huh. I said I going to the library, but I saw online that the coffee shop across the street has free wifi. I brought my school stuff." He adjusted his backpack on his shoulder while tilting his head back to see how the sex swing was affixed to the rafter beam.

"I've been thinking of upgrading it. The wifi," I clarified as Roddie's gaze crashed down to meet mine. Was I starting to blush? Ugh. "I'll talk to Grandma tonight."

"I went by a high school on the bus. If you're really going to stay until summer, you could drop me there on your way to work and I could walk here after."

"You want to go to school here?" In Milestone? When I was growing up, my mother hadn't let me date anyone from this neighbourhood. Zak had probably gone to that high school, though. Why did knowing he was from the wrong side of the tracks make me warm to him even more?

"For music and science, so I don't fall behind. It's only a semester," Roddie said absently, still taking in the toys that his grandmother had arranged so painstakingly.

"If you want to walk up to the school and ask whether they'll let you do that, go ahead, but I can't go with you today. I have—" I pointed at the customer coming in. "And they like privacy, so you have to leave."

"'Kay. Can I have some money for the coffee shop?"

I rolled my eyes but found some cash in my purse. "Bring me a scone or something, would you?"

CHAPTER FIFTEEN

MEG

Things got busier as the day wore on.

I had Roddie bring me a rice bowl from Nooners, the café up the street, before Mom came by to take him home. She asked if I needed help, but she caught me in a quiet moment, so I said I was fine. The minute she left, people began streaming in again.

Fortunately, one of them was Gail, Georgia's sister. She worked for a concierge service at the Oak Bay Marina, which she mostly loved. The hours were flexible, which meant she didn't need a lot of childcare and every day was different. Over the years, she had encountered what she called "seriously posh knobs."

She also looked amazing at all times—full makeup, eyelash extensions, tasteful nail art, and trendy yet professional clothing. Today's wig was a sophisticated, chin-length bob that made you instinctively believe she was in control of whatever might be freaking you out in the moment.

Like me, right now.

"It's busy," Gail said, with a wondrous look around.

"I know. Any chance I can recruit you?"

"I can stand at the desk and do the cash sales."

"That would be amazing. Thank you."

"I want it to go well. Georgia's so stressed."

"I know," I said, concerned. The good news was that Georgia was a candidate for the less invasive surgery. The date was set for next week. It was weighing on me, so I could only imagine how frightening it was for Georgia and Gail.

Having Gail at the desk freed me up to wander with my trusty tablet, looking up items for more information or running transactions if people paid by credit card.

A couple of women in the corner were laughing in bursts, clearly enjoying themselves as they pointed at different items.

"Any questions?" I asked as one of them noticed me.

"Are you Meg? I'm Zara." She reached across the prostate stims to offer her hand.

"Hi! Good to meet you finally."

Zara's resemblance to her father was more subtle than her brother's. Her hair was streaked with ash-blonde, and her figure was voluptuously curvy. She wasn't as tall as Zak, but she had his blue eyes, a firm handshake, and that winning Halligan smile.

"Zak told me you were coming with your book club. Welcome." I smiled at her friend.

"Wine club," Zara said out of the side of her mouth. "And only Imani could make it tonight."

"Oh. I was going to pitch you a book from our erotica collection, but wine club sounds fun, too," I said.

"*Erotica* sounds fun," Imani said. "We met through a friend who made us read the most depressing books."

"The first meeting after she moved, we got drunk and talked about how much we hated all the books she'd chosen." Zara tucked her chin as she confessed that.

"It was actually our most lively discussion ever." Imani said. "We wouldn't have met if she hadn't started the club and, to be fair, the goal was to read more diverse books, which we did, so we try not to slag her too much."

I smiled at this; I'm such a sucker for British slang.

"But also, fuck her and her fetish for suffering," Zara said.

"We specialize in fetishes with happy endings here." I did a game-show wave at the table of products they'd been giggling over. "Can I show you how some of these vibrators work?"

"Sure. Oh, hey, Zak." Zara looked past me and bit back her smile.

CHAPTER SIXTEEN

ZAK

Meg turned with a kill-me-now expression. "Hi."

God, she was pretty when she was flustered.

One of the things I liked most about her was that expressiveness in her face. All of her thoughts and emotions were right there to be read with ease. It made talking to her really fun.

"Hi." I suppressed a chuckle, gave a nod to include my sister and Imani in my greeting, and looked back at Meg.

Her hair was still in a ponytail and she hadn't changed, which meant she'd been here all day without a break. I'd been glad to have another excuse to see her today, but perhaps showering, trimming my beard, and putting on my best jeans was over the top.

"Are you going on a date?" Zara asked, puzzled.

"Did Meg not tell you?" I ignored how transparent I felt and deflected with, "She's going to demonstrate the vibrators on me. Where should I undress?" I asked Meg.

She threw her head back in a big laugh, which I enjoyed way too much. Imani chuckled too, while Zara frowned at me.

"Is Dad next door? Alone?"

"No." Why couldn't she trust me? "Carl came over to watch the game with him." I usually tried to work on my programming contracts when Carl visited, but tonight I'd come back to open the shop, like I promised I would.

"I've been over there listening to this party for an hour," I said to Meg with mock annoyance. "Can you keep it down? I can hardly hear the clocks tick."

"You here with an eviction notice?" she guessed.

"Not until I've browsed the erotica." Zara held up a halting finger and started toward the book rack, pausing to ask Meg, "If we pick a title, would you order one for each of us? And join the group read?"

"An alcohol-fuelled discussion about sex?" Meg brightened. "Sign me up. Be sure to enter the raffle while you're here."

"Oh, right. Kyle told me to do that." Zara glanced toward the counter, then shuffled toward the book rack with Imani.

"I thought you said you were getting offers for the skin mag." I noticed her jar of entry slips only held about a dozen pieces of paper.

"I'm shamelessly misrepresenting the odds. My post online has a QR code. I've had at least a hundred entries."

"*And* you got people in the door."

"I know." She glanced around with a little smile of pride, then wrinkled her nose at me. "But I should probably pay attention to the real customers."

"I am a real customer." One who had put conditioner in his beard. I clearly needed to get laid. "Sell me something."

She lifted her brows, skeptical, then said in a smoothly professional tone, "Did you have any thoughts on what interests you? Do you have a budget in mind?"

"You've been practicing. That sounded great."

"Thanks," she said dryly.

"Money's no object." I was helping Dad with some bills, mostly so I knew they were actually getting paid. There was no mortgage on the house or this building. I was only working on a casual basis at a considerably lower pay scale, but my programming take-home was still very comfortable. "I'm curious about the prostate stuff, but I'm not ready for that." I let my eyes skim past that section toward the masturbation sleeves.

How was she not in a perpetual state of horniness all day? I was aroused 24/7 just thinking of her over here. Thinking of her, to be honest. She was on my mind a *lot*.

"Do you know what I find is the oddest thing about this job?" She leaned closer to speak more quietly as we walked to the Penis Pleasures shelf. "People share very openly, like I'm a doctor. I don't mind, but it's disconcerting."

"Is it weird that I mentioned ass play?" I also leaned in, mostly because I wanted to. "It felt weird as I said it."

"It's weird that I have such intimate conversations with complete strangers." Her eyes widened in amused perplexity. "It puts a lot of responsibility on me. I wasn't prepared for that when I signed up for this."

"You think of me as a stranger?" I put a hand on my chest where there was a genuine pinch as I wondered if I was reading her all wrong. "You're getting such a pumpkin spice latte tomorrow."

Her mouth twitched. "My safe word is Frappuccino. Macchiato means keep going."

"I better write that down." I mimed reaching for a pencil behind my ear and scribbled on my palm. "I know I'm going to mix those up."

We shared a long look that was mostly laughter with a hint of speculation. Okay, it wasn't my imagination. We were definitely into each other.

That cheered me up enormously.

Meg dropped her lashes and righted a toppled box. "You don't really want to buy something, do you?"

"You're a terrible saleswoman. Yes, I do." I wanted to keep talking to her without worrying about having to get back to Dad. "What's this Darth Vader thing?" I picked up a black cuff shaped like a swirling cape. Inside were ridges and a silicone pad with tiny pins.

"That's for the frenulum."

"Just the tip? Like a toe in the water? Way to meet me where I'm at, Meg."

Her teeth flashed in a grin and I wanted to kiss her. I wanted it to be just the two of us in this store and all the time in the world to see where things might go.

"What's this, a lamp?" I made myself reach for another item—a clear silicone casing. It looked decorative on its stand, but the embedded balls bulged when I squeezed it.

"It stretches around the penis." She took it and tugged to show its flexibility. "The firmer shapes add stimulation. That's the only one out of its box, but you can get it with ridges or—I thought I had another one." She searched the shelf.

Another customer came to peruse the shelf so I pulled out my wallet.

"I'll try the ridges. And the 'Luke, I am your father' one." I handed Meg my card.

"You need lube," she said. "Water soluble, or it'll break down the silicone."

"Might as well sell me a five-gallon bucket. My nights are quiet."

"I'll give you this tiny free sample." She stole it from a jar on the counter, smiling at a drag artist chatting with the woman behind the counter. "If you come back for more, I'll know the toys were a hit."

"That'll be in seven minutes," I assured her, fishing for another laugh. Another minute of her sparkling eyes on me. "I've got an empty store and heightened curiosity."

"Buddy, the longer I work here, the less that kind of talk fazes me. You do you." She was smiling as she rang me up, though, filling my chest with a warm glow

"Do you hit all those double entendres on purpose," I had to ask. "Or is it a gift?"

"It's the *store*. If I started a drinking game for all the puns, I would be hammered all day every day." She handed me the bag. "Enjoy your evening."

"Pretty sure that's a given."

Truth was, I already had.

CHAPTER SEVENTEEN

MEG

I was dragging my ass the next morning, feeling hungover even though I'd only had one glass of wine when I got home. A big one, granted. I'd chugged it before falling straight into bed.

After my shower, I glanced at my laptop and saw it was blowing up with messages from Peterson, Londale, and Funk. I might not be irreplaceable, but they'd realized my departure was going to be a pain in the ass. Some clients were very pissed to be losing me, and HR was pressuring me to finalize terms for contract work.

Suddenly, the firm had very deep pockets. *Assholes*.

I was thinking about that while I poured my coffee into a travel mug. At the same time, Roddie was peppering me with instructions on how to enroll him in part-time classes at the high school. It involved phone calls and filling out forms online.

"I'll get started if I have time at work, okay? I've got to get in there to tidy up and fill the online orders before I open for the day." I stole a slice of his toast.

"Hey." He frowned.

"What. You don't even have school today. Look through Grandpa's stuff downstairs. Let Grandma know what you might want to keep for yourself. You kids be good."

I was halfway to the shop when I reached for my coffee and realized I'd left it on the counter. That's the kind of day it was going to be.

I was early, so Zak and Dale weren't at their shop yet. I texted Zak.

I forgot my coffee. What's your poison?

Large double-shot Americano. One sugar, no milk. Dad says no thanks.

Brim Stokers was busy, but I had a brief chat with Ali while I waited for my order.

"I had to work my other job last night," she said over the hiss of foaming milk. "I couldn't come to your thing. How'd it go?"

"Really good. I'm giving away the last of my coupons today. Come grab one on your break."

"I will, thanks."

Yes, I knew damned well that a half-dozen people overheard me. I made sure of it. They could find one in the local paper if they looked, but scarcity had a way of motivating people to act. Sure enough, a couple of people followed me across the street when I returned to the shop.

I had texted Georgia the receipts last night. This morning, before I began straightening the displays, I sent her a couple of photos of the wreckage along with, *Nice problem to have*. I had to consolidate here and there and brought out what stock I had in the back to fill the gaps.

Surprisingly, a lot of clothes had sold. I would put Mom on the hunt for more.

"Good morning." Zak strode in with a jangle of the bell and descended on the waiting coffee cup I pointed toward. "You're a lifesaver. Things went sideways last night with my niece. She's fine, but she gets nosebleeds that don't stop. Zara and Kyle were at the hospital until midnight, so Dad and I kept the boys overnight. I love them. Genuinely. But Ollie—the two-year-old—goes until he stops. He wouldn't settle, so I brought him into my bed. I've been taking kicks to the kidney all night. Then I had to get Lance to school this morning, drop Ollie off with Zara. Needless to say, I did *not* get a chance to play with my new toys."

"No review for my newsletter? You're so fired. Give me back that coffee."

"Tomorrow. I promise." He took a sip, realized it was almost cold, and started gulping.

"No pressure, but when do you think you could pick up those boxes of magazines from my mom's? And is there a chance you'd want one of those old wooden stereo cabinets? Roddie's staying here, so he needs a dresser. The stereo's in the way."

"He didn't file for emancipation when he heard about this?" Zak pointed a finger from the hand holding his cup and drew a wide circle to indicate the store.

"When it provides endless reasons to mock me? Heck, no."

His grin kicked sideways. "Sounds like my kind of kid. Does it work?"

"I spend a lot of time re-examining my life choices, so yes, I guess it does."

"I see what you did there." He nodded in approval. "Does the *stereo* work?"

"I'll check. Where does it go if it doesn't?"

"Take out the guts and use it as a dresser. But if it works, bring it in here." He nodded at the wall where there was space beneath the crops and paddles hanging on the wall. "I assume you have vinyl records? If not, we have some."

"We have tons. Dad liked psychedelic rock and—" I gasped with excitement. "Mom loves ballads. 'I Feel the Earth Move.' 'Let's Get It On.' 'Kiss You All Over.' 'Good Vibrations.'"

"'How Deep Is Your Love?'" Zak lifted his brows.

"Oof. But yes. You're a genius."

"This isn't just a hat rack, you know." He pointed at his head. "Since it sounds like I need the van for all your dad's porn, I can pick up the stereo at the same time."

I looked at the wall again, already seeing the stereo there. "When?"

"Let me check our schedule. We're booking into—Just kidding. When do you want me there?"

"Sunday?" It was my only day off, and I had work to finish for

Peterson, Londale, and Funk, but screw those guys. "I haven't asked Mom yet if she'll part with it."

"Okay. Let me know. I should get back to Dad. Thanks again." He saluted me with his cup and left.

CHAPTER EIGHTEEN

MEG

Mom agreed to the stereo cabinet being rehomed. When I told Georgia, she remembered it and was as excited as I was.

While I waited for Zak to show up, Georgia and I had a good chat about how well the event had gone and how steady the store traffic had been on Friday and Saturday.

"It'll slow down. People get their toys and stay home to play with them. They forget about the shop for a while," Georgia said. She'd worked at an adult toy store when she lived in California. That's how she'd learned the products and started the online business.

"It's like they're only in it for one thing," I complained.

"Right? Hey, what are you up to with Zara's brother? Gail said you two were flirting."

"I sold him a couple of toys. It was completely professional. But he'll be here soon to pick up my stereo."

"Is that a euphemism for sex? Like hauling your ashes? I should let you go, then."

"It should be, shouldn't it? No, I have time if you want to keep talking." I didn't want to prod her with *How are you feeling?* but I really wanted to know.

"I'm done talking. I'm freaking the fuck out over the surgery, but I also don't care anymore. I can't stay like this."

"Yeah," I murmured. "I told Gail I'd come hang out with her while you're in surgery. She said you'd rather I stay here and keep the store open."

"I would. There's nothing you can do during the surgery anyway. I'll tell her to text you with updates."

"Okay, but call anytime if—"

There was a knock on my door.

"Mom?"

"Yeah, bud?"

Roddie poked his head in. "That guy is here."

"That guy is here," I repeated to Georgia. "I'll send you a photo once the stereo is in the store."

"Thanks. Oh! Negasi might come talk to you. He wanted to pick my brain about starting his own business, but then this happened. I told him he should talk to you. Is that okay?"

"Of course." I said goodbye and followed Roddie downstairs to the living room, where Mom was standing with Dale and Zak.

"Oh yes, I know them well," Mom was saying. "You must have been acquainted with the McIntyres, too?"

"We bought our station wagon from them," Dale said with a nostalgic smile.

"Hi Dale. Hi Zak," I greeted.

Dale gave me a startled look, as though I'd appeared out of thin air.

"This is Meg, Dad. Vickie's daughter. You met her once. She took over Debra's shop. We're here to pick up some furniture from her."

"Right, right, of course. It's good to see you again." He was such a sweet man, shaking my hand like we were old friends. "And this is your son?"

"Roddie, yes."

"You're a strapping lad. We can always use some muscle at the shop."

Dale gave Roddie's biceps a squeeze as he shook his hand. "Come by if you're looking for an after-school job."

"Thanks." Roddie glanced at me with a mix of amusement and a request for guidance.

I had a feeling it was Dale's way of getting people in the door so he could sell them something, but I said, "Let's get school figured out before we worry about what you're doing after the bell rings."

"Would you like to sit down?" Mom asked. "What can I get you? Coffee? Iced tea?"

I saw Zak open his mouth to refuse, but Dale said, "A cool drink sounds nice. Thank you."

"Of course. Zak?"

"No, thanks. We don't want to be in your way long." His concerned gaze flicked toward Dale, who was settling onto the sofa.

It's fine, I wanted to assure him. Mom was a grandmaster of small talk, and caregivers needed breaks. Mom and I both knew that.

"Let me show you the stereo. It's down here."

Roddie came with us as I led the way to the basement rumpus room. Thankfully, there was an exterior door to the backyard. Carrying the thing around the outside of the house wasn't ideal, but it beat dragging it up the stairs, through the narrow foyer, and out the dogleg of the enclosed porch.

Roddie had been instructed to tidy up but hadn't gotten far. He'd folded his bed into the sofa and stuffed my father's clothes into some canvas yard-waste bins. Mom had drawn the line at garbage bags. The bins were shoved into a corner with Dad's fishing gear, leaving plenty of space around the stereo cabinet.

"Nice," Zak said, stroking the top edge before opening the lid to check out the record player and stereo knobs. "This here's your top-of-the-line 1971 Zenith Allegro Stereophonic Hi-Fi. I can polish up this walnut once it's at the shop. Does the eight-track work?"

"Mm-hm." Roddie nodded. "I'm kind of bummed Mom's taking it.

My sister and I used to listen to all of these." He opened the front door to reveal neatly sorted tapes from Animals to Yardbirds.

"You have a daughter?" Zak asked me.

"Shelby. She's in Calgary. Second year."

"Your daughter's old enough to be in university?" Zak's brows shot up.

"Child bride. What can I say?"

"Huh." He seemed to reconfigure his impression of me as that sank in.

I caught Roddie looking between us and redirected his attention by waving at the tapes.

"I should throw those into a box."

"Yeah, this thing is going to be heavy as fuck. Sorry." Zak grimaced in Roddie's direction.

Roddie turned to me with an expression of mock innocence. "Mom, what does *fuck* mean?"

"I'll tell you when you're old enough to understand. Let me see if there's a box in the garage." I started for the stairs.

"If you don't have any, my brother-in-law can pick some up on his way," Zak said. "I figured this was a job for three men and a boy, so I told him to meet us here. You're not the boy," he told Roddie. "Lance is. Dad's not as steady as he used to be."

I left them chatting while I emptied some cardboard boxes in the garage. When I returned, Zak was deep in conversation with Roddie.

"Oh, it's nerdy as fuck, but I guess I have a touch of obsessive-compulsive because I kind of like it," Zak said.

"What's that?" I asked.

"Researching old furniture. Roddie asked how I knew this was worth about $165. Truth is, it would fetch more like $150, but I add $15 so the buyer can talk me down. I wouldn't give you more than $75, though, so I can double my money. Bottom line: the worth of nearly anything is whatever someone's willing to pay for it."

"Zak said I could do my homework in his shop and earn a commission if I sold something. That's what he and his sister did growing up," Roddie said.

"You're a hustler from way back. That tracks." I began shifting the tapes into the box.

"My sister was the hustler. I'd be about to close a sale, then she'd elbow in and say, 'You can't sell that! I have someone coming back for it!'" He used a high, panicked voice and mimed a dramatic *Home Alone* expression. "The people would hurry to pay, and she'd insist she earned half my commission."

"Ruthless," Roddie snorted.

"Kyle's on his way," Zak said, checking his phone. "While we wait, I'll put the skin mags in the truck."

"Skin mags?" Roddie repeated with a choke of laughter. "Do you mean, like… porn?"

"Yes. Before there was internet we had to sneak them from our dad's toolbox in the garage," Zak said.

"They were Grandpa's." I held up a hand. "I didn't know about them either, so don't hassle me over it."

Roddie quirked a bemused brow. "Can I see—"

"*No*," Zak and I said together.

CHAPTER NINETEEN

MEG

Georgia was right. Monday was really quiet, and after last week, it felt too quiet.

At least I had time to enter reorders and call Roddie's school in Toronto.

I was perched on the stool at the cash desk, working on my laptop, when Zak burst in with his usual bull-in-a-china-shop energy.

"I brought this for the cabinet." He held up a rag and a capped bottle. "Sometimes a little rub with oil is all it needs, rather than a full strip and finish."

For a long moment, the innuendo hung in the air.

He nodded. "You're right. It's the store."

I smirked, closed the laptop, and folded my arms on the desk.

"Need me to stop the music?" Air Supply was "All Out of Love."

"Nah, I'll do a small spot for now, see what it needs." He crouched at the back corner of the cabinet. "Want my report?"

"On? Oh." Right, the toys. I left the stool and came closer to open the cabinet so I could lower the volume.

A lemony scent rose from where he worked.

"I'm ready. Hit me."

"So first, the squishy thing? Interesting. Not ground-breaking, but it mixes things up. Easy to clean, but you have to get up and do that before you can go to sleep. I'd rather grab a few tissues from the bedside, roll over, and saw logs."

"Good feedback. I didn't think about cleanup."

His gaze flicked up to mine. Apparently, this was a reciprocal conversation.

"I don't have that problem very often." I glanced at my non-existent manicure. I wasn't really a squirter, but didn't feel like I was missing out on much. My orgasms were reliable and satisfying. Who needed wet sheets to prove it?

"The frenulum thing has ten speeds. It was too much at first, until I figured that out. Then it was like, fuck. Really great. Blew my load up to here." He cut his hand across his collarbone. "Was that TMI?"

"Not at all." I was stifling a laugh. "I'll be sure to tell future customers. I'll need you here so I can demonstrate the distance travelled, though." I moved my hand through the air to where his neck might be if he stood beside me.

"Velocity is really what you're wanting to convey. Speed, power, and velocity."

"An effective method when you're in a hurry?"

"Sure. And discreet. I'm wearing it now."

The toy was the size of a groin guard, but I played along. "Comfortable enough to wear all day. Noted."

He stood, mouth quirked with amusement, but only nodded at the cabinet. "What do you think?"

I refused to look at his fly and shifted closer to him so I could see the richer contrast in the bottom corner. "That looks way better."

"Yeah, I can't do it all today. Maybe if Dad's neighbour can hang out with him for a few hours, I'll come by one evening."

"Let me know. Do I owe you anything?"

"Nah, it's something to do." He stuffed the rag into the back pocket of his jeans and closed the bottle. He tilted his head and slid his gaze to mine. "Are you gonna tell me what you've tried?"

"A vibrator. It was fine." I folded my arms, defensive for some reason. "I kind of think you have to be into toys to enjoy them. It was time-efficient, but a little like what you said. Too much too fast. Like, where's the foreplay? How about a *kiss*?" I moved to the vulva shelf. "I was thinking about trying this clitoris thing, though. It's supposed to be like oral. People online seem to like it."

"Hmm." He picked up the box to read it.

"This is the penis version for simulated BJs." I pointed.

"All right. Let's see what it does." He picked up the suction sleeve.

"You don't have to buy it!"

"Oh, is this a library? Can I borrow it for a week and pay fifteen cents a day if I'm overdue returning it?"

"I mean, you don't have to buy something just because I pointed to it."

"We're not going to have this conversation again, Meg. I have money. Shit tons. Wedding money that—"

"You're married?" I gasped.

"No." He snort-scowled. "No. My ex-girlfriend and I were talking about getting married and had started saving for a wedding, but after I came home for Christmas, I decided to take a leave from work and move home to help Dad. Erica wanted to stay in Vancouver, so..." He shrugged and looked away, but I caught the flash of injury behind his eyes.

I remembered him mentioning his ex. I hadn't been sure how recent that had been or how many exes ago.

"I'm sorry." He was so funny and flirty, I had no idea he was fresh off a breakup. That made me kind of wistful. Whatever I had thought was going on between us suddenly seemed much less significant. Not that I had expected it to go anywhere anyway. It was just a good reminder that I shouldn't read into this casual friendship we'd formed. "You must have been together a while if you were thinking about marriage."

"Three years. We moved in together early in our relationship because we both had such insane schedules. Erica's a nurse. I work in tech. I thought we'd see more of each other if she moved here with me, but she likes the job she has. I don't know." He grimaced. "I kind of think we started talking about marriage because we thought it would make us feel more connected, but… I was hurt that she didn't want to come with me, and I feel like I keep failing at basic partnership. But I'm not heartbroken, so maybe we weren't likely to go the distance anyway."

I could see how uncomfortable he was admitting that—how much he felt the breakup was a failure in himself.

"I don't think breakups and divorce are failures per se. Relationships are complicated. They're made up of smaller successes and failures, so how can you judge the whole thing as one or the other? Anyone who knew Joel and me would have called our marriage successful, but on the inside, I always put myself second to him, his career, and the kids. Our marriage was really only successful for him. For me, it was a disappointment. I'd characterize our divorce as successful, though. We're civil. I told him Roddie wanted to stay here with me, and Joel's annoyed that he'll have to pay more support, but he isn't taking me to court over it."

Zak was listening attentively. "What happened to make you decide to call it quits?"

"He cheated. Again. So do we call it a successful relationship because we got through his infidelity when Roddie was a baby? Or was it a failure on my part that I didn't leave when I had the excuse? I think we all do our best in the moment and figure out later whether it was a success or a learning point."

He snorted. "Yeah, I'm living on learning points these days. They are so pointy. It's like a bed of nails." His voice was self-deprecating, but I heard the despair beneath it.

I wanted to hug him.

"I need distraction, Meg." He deliberately injected a lighter note into his voice. "Ring me up a simulated blowjob, would you?" He pulled his wallet from his back pocket. "And get yourself something nice, sweetheart. Throw in that clit thing." He gave a magnanimous nod toward it.

"On the understanding that I have to tell you if I like it?"

"Not if you don't want to." He looked pretty heartbroken at the idea that I wouldn't, though.

"For Georgia, I will let you buy me this toy." I took his credit card and rang it through.

"Awesome. I've always wanted to make two women happy at once." He took back his card. "Check *that* off the bucket list."

"Joel always had that fantasy, too. Except he wanted twins. I never saw the appeal, but…" I tilted my head and let my gaze wander across Zak's shoulders and chest.

"I know where you're going, and I'm going to stop you right there." He gave me a very stern look as he pushed his wallet back into his pocket.

"But you must have had offers." I blinked, feigning innocence. "Zara is very—"

"Nope. Shut up. I'm leaving." He plucked his toy from my weak grasp. "I hope you're happy because you have ruined sex for me *forever*."

The door clattered loudly, and he was gone.

I burst out laughing.

CHAPTER TWENTY

MEG

I was still snickering over Zak's reaction as I unwrapped the toy and gave it a wash on my way to bed. Mom was already asleep. Roddie was in the basement, gaming online with a friend, noise-cancelling headphones on. He occasionally shouted out a curse but was very much in his own world.

I locked my door and climbed into bed, thinking only of Zak. His sister *was* striking, sure, but sibling sex was a taboo too far. Besides, I'd never truly been into women. I could admire curves and great hair, but any flicker of desire was always dimmed by envy. Four months from turning forty, I was still grappling with my love-hate relationship with this body I'd been given. It was time I learned to celebrate it.

Would Zak celebrate it? Men his age tended to be drawn to bouncy twenty-five-year-olds, not breasts that flattened when I was on my back or a stomach that possessed the tension of a deflated balloon.

I should get a wax, I mused while applying lube to my inner labia. I'd let the bush grow through the divorce, more out of laziness than defiance. I shouldn't cave to impossible beauty standards—but if Zak ever went down on me, I'd want a clean slate.

I clicked the toy on low. It nestled neatly in my palm, the small ring pulsing gently. I traced it around my nipples, imagining it was Zak's fingers teasing them erect. His mouth sucking them, sending heat curling into my belly.

My other hand moved between my legs, spreading lube, feeling how much warmer and wetter I was getting as I played with my clit.

Would he push my legs apart and lick me here? I guided the toy into place. There was a sharp, pleasurable jolt as I fitted the ring over my clit. Ripples of need surged through my pelvis. My pussy clenched on nothing, feeling achingly empty. I wished I'd kept a dildo within reach.

Oh, fuck. I was about to come.

I rolled onto my side and pinned the toy between my thighs, muffling my groan in the pillow as a hard orgasm rocked my pelvis.

Holy hell. I had to pull the toy away—it was too much. I let it buzz along my inner thigh, then over my outer lips. It kept me turned on. I imagined Zak eating me from behind as I lay like this, rubbing the toy in the tight space between my thighs, amping up the friction between my lips.

Fresh arousal twisted through my abdomen. I bit my lip and brought the toy back to my clit. I reached back to play with my wet hole as I imagined his tongue there. His fingers.

Oh, fuuuck. I came again, eyes clenched, hips thrusting into the toy that I held pinned to my clit.

I could hardly catch my breath, but I still wanted more. I rolled onto my stomach, one knee raised. I humped that toy with my sopping pussy, reawakening the nerve endings until I was ready for the bite and tickle on my clit again.

I imagined Zak doing filthy things to me. Joel and I had tried anal a couple of times. I hadn't liked it, but I fantasized that Zak was playing with my asshole. Fingering it. Licking it. That's why my pussy was so neglected. He was holding my shoulder and shoving his cock up my ass. Fucking me hard.

Oh, fuck. I nearly screamed—I came so hard.

As I lay there panting in the aftermath, trying to find the energy to turn off the toy, I wondered how I would face Zak after what he had just done to me.

CHAPTER TWENTY-ONE

MEG

Mom had unearthed a few choice pieces from the thrift shop, so she was busy arranging them while I was unpacking shipments in the storage room—receiving packages, as Zak would put it.

I was still tender from last night's friction burns and kind of dying to tell him. When I heard the door at the front of the shop, I half-expected it was him, but it was a woman's voice.

"Oh." The voice had a tense, stridently cheerful tone. "Hello, Vickie."

"Barbara." Mom sounded equally nonplussed. "How did you know I was here?"

"I didn't."

I came out from the back to see one of Mom's friends from the thrift store. They'd all come by the house at different times when Dad had been ill, and I'd seen them all again later, at his service.

"Hi, Barbara," I greeted.

"Oh, Meg. Hello. It's nice to see you again." Barbara gave off a matronly vibe—plump with glasses, her hair a short gray perm. Her faux-fur jacket was buttoned to her chin. Usually, she was very maternal and effusive. Today, she wore a look I recognized—like she expected to be arrested for entering such an indecent establishment.

I took pity on her and offered an exit ramp. "Did you think this was still Debra's shop? The quilting store? She's been gone a while. My friend Georgia owns this shop now. I'm helping out."

"Oh. Um, no. Um…" Barbara turned bright pink but drew a piece of paper from her pocket. "My husband cut this out of the paper. He asked me to pick up these?" She used her thumbnail to indicate the furred handcuffs on the tantalizing list I'd printed on the coupon.

"Of course. Let me bag that up for you. Cash or credit?"

"Cash." She handed me a couple of bills and turned to speak to Mom. I couldn't help overhearing.

"Do you work here?" Barbara sounded astonished.

"I'm helping Meg. I told you about that," Mom insisted stiffly.

"I didn't realize it was *this* shop."

"It's temporary." Mom's voice had shifted to her most obstructive pitch. This conversation was clearly unwelcome.

I hurried to make Barbara's change.

"I threw a couple of samples in there for you," I told her as I handed over the bag.

"Thank you, Meg. Are you back in Victoria for good, then?"

"Just visiting, but I might be here through the summer. It really depends on what Georgia needs."

"I see. Well, I know your mother enjoys having you around. See you at the thrift store, Vickie."

"See you Tuesday," Mom called pleasantly. The second the door shut behind Barbara, she rounded on me.

"She bought *handcuffs*?"

"Mom. I can't betray her privacy."

"You were right there, Meg." She pointed to the spot where they were displayed. "There's an empty spot on the shelf. Why on *earth* would she let Bill put her in handcuffs?"

"Who says she's the one who wears them?"

Mom looked like she'd swallowed her own tongue. With a pissy expression, she went back to clipping a pleated schoolgirl skirt onto a hanger.

I took a moment to kick off my desire to mock or judge her.

"Are you more bothered by what she bought or by the fact that she saw you in here?" I asked gently.

"I'm helping my daughter. There's nothing shameful in that," she said snippily. Then she clacked the hanger onto the rack and turned back to me. "But she practically had me arrested for making an illegal left turn once. No cars were coming. We were late for the garden tour. It was perfectly fine, but you'd think I robbed a bank. She told everyone the second we were inside."

I bit back my amusement. Mom was so sensitive to gossip or being the butt of a joke.

"Now every time I look at her, I'll picture her and Bill playing Dungeons & Dragons." She waved a hand, then dropped it. "Is that what that is? I've never understood that reference."

"Close enough." I started back to the stockroom but paused. "You know you can't tell anyone she was in here."

"I won't. I don't suppose she'll mention she saw me here either."

"Are you really that embarrassed that you were seen here?" It made me sad for her. "Helping people with their sexual health is legitimate work."

"Oh, please."

"There's such a thing as vaginal atrophy, you know."

"And the prescription is handcuffs?"

That pithy tone was everything that annoyed me about her. It was the tone that had assured me you can get pregnant your first time. The tone that said, *I know better, Meg.* The tone that always made me want to prove her wrong, even if it meant overturning my life in the process.

"Maybe it's not for you," I acknowledged. "Maybe you're not feeling sexy, what with losing Dad and everything. That's completely okay. But isn't it nice to know that someone your age can still get horny? And that if you ever feel differently, Georgia has this store you can come to?"

"I do think you're doing a good turn by Georgia." She shook out a pair of Daisy Duke shorts. "I can see she worked very hard to create something that serves a purpose. I'm glad she won't lose everything while she's getting her surgery."

"Thank you." I started again toward the stockroom, then paused again. "I'm just going to say this so it's been said: If you ever do think about dating, don't worry about how I might react. I'm fine with it."

"I'm not thinking about dating. I wouldn't even know where to start! Ask your son to set me up on one of those dating apps?" She knotted the bottom of a white tank top, her gaze sliding over to me with more interest than she probably meant to reveal. "Are you on any of those things?"

"I've thought about it." Zak was ever-present in my mind. "But I don't see the point in dating here if I live in Toronto. I could make profiles for us if you want to try it, though."

"That's silly talk."

I shrugged. "The alternative is to buy a toy and fly solo. Barbara would never know."

"*You* would. So thank you, but no."

"Your birthday is coming up. I could surprise you."

"For God's sake, Margaret. Drop it."

I did. For now.

CHAPTER TWENTY-TWO

ZAK

I heard the bell over the door chime and stopped sanding to listen.

Dad had launched into his magician routine with someone, so I gave my hands a quick wash and went out to find Roddie looking confused by the punchline.

"Layaway is how people used to buy things in olden times," I explained. "Like a loan, but you had to pay it off before you took your purchase home."

"Oh. I get it now. That's pretty funny," he told Dale.

"Dad, this is Roddie." I reminded him that they'd met before and told him where, then mentioned Meg next door.

"Not Debra. The toy store," Dad said, chuckling and scratching the back of his head. He turned to Roddie. "How embarrassing—I thought she was selling toys for kids."

"You think *you're* embarrassed," Roddie muttered out of the side of his mouth.

"Are you?" I asked.

"Nah. I think it's funny."

Better, I supposed. "Did your mom send you over for something?"

"No, I had a spare. I'm on my way to the coffee shop to do my homework." He hitched his backpack higher on his shoulder.

"Do you need a school desk? We have two in the office. The twins used them, but they're at college now. We could let one go," Dad offered.

"Oh. I just came in to look around. I was curious," Roddie said. "Do you mind?"

"No, no. Stay as long as you like." Dad gave a grand wave. "If you don't see anything today, come back tomorrow. Tammy's always bringing in something new. Did you say you're looking for something for your mother? Let me show you the vase she found last week. Now, where did I put it…" He wandered off.

"I need to put my stuff away in the workroom," I told Roddie. I'd learned my lesson on that. "I'll be back in a sec."

"Sure."

By the time I'd locked everything in the cupboard and closed the door behind me, Dad was talking to Roddie again, saying, "People can't buy it if they can't see it."

"The china cabinet?" I guessed, since that's where he was pointing.

"Yes. Since we have Kyle here, we should bring it to the front of the store," Dad said.

"Okay. You start emptying the cups and plates. I'll get some boxes for them. How was school?" I asked as I led Roddie to the gumball machine and turned the crank.

"Meh." He shrugged, then took the orange ball I handed him. "Thanks."

"It was a dumb question, wasn't it?" I felt like one of my aunts who used to pinch my cheek and ask about my plans for my future.

Roddie peered down into the glass case full of odds and ends—wire-rimmed spectacles, old camera equipment, a signed baseball in a protective plastic cube.

"Are you a sports guy? Computers? What's your area of interest?" I asked.

"So you can sell me something?" He gave me the side-eye.

"You need a cookie jar?" I pointed to the fat blob vaguely shaped like a man's head that looked like it had melted in the kiln.

"That's horrifying," he said with a giggle, lifting the lid and replacing it. "No, I'm into music. I joined band, but I have to rent a saxophone while I wait for Dad to send mine."

I nodded, then quit pretending I wasn't dying of curiosity.

"You mind if I ask why you wanted to come here? That high school you're going to is fine, but it's not great. At least, it wasn't when I went there. Either way, changing schools usually sucks."

"I know, but… I don't know if my mom told you—my dad has a girlfriend. They have a baby. Wanda wanted to get married. Dad kept saying the divorce had to be final."

"It's not?" That was none of my business, but I was definitely interested.

"It is now, but they were still fighting. If Mom was there, I could've just moved in with her. But I wanted to change schools because…" More side-eye as he took my measure. "The guy I was seeing started dating my best friend, Bethany."

"Shit." Getting thrown over was a kick in the stomach. And for your best friend? "You want a root beer?"

"Sure."

I led him into the office. The school desks were long gone. There was only the big oak desk with the leather blotter, a sofa, a filing cabinet, and a mini fridge where we kept pop and meal replacement shakes that Zara liked Dad to have once a day, to be sure he was getting his vitamins.

I pulled out two root beers. Bottles, because I was fancy. I opened one and handed it to him, glad to have fresh company.

"Thanks." Roddie sat down and left his backpack on the floor at his feet.

"I was recently dumped, too." I opened my bottle and flicked the cap into the waste bin, where it landed with a ping and a clatter. Then I sat on the edge of the desk where I could see Dad through the open door. "I hereby call the meeting of the Dented Hearts Club to order. First item of business: no social media stalking. Can I get a motion?"

"Ew. Yeah. Guilty." Roddie curled his lip, then promised, "I'll stop."

We clinked the necks of our bottles and drank.

CHAPTER TWENTY-THREE

MEG

I had hoped Zak would show up with coffee and some afternoon banter, but instead, I got a text from Roddie that said, *I'm next door.*

I was disappointed that neither my son nor my convenient flirt came to see me before closing, but I had enough work and customers to keep me from dwelling on being left out.

Also, I managed to pump Roddie for an inside view of Zak's life while we drove home—not that I did it on purpose.

"What'd you do over there for two hours?"

"Nothing much. Zak's office window looks out at the dog grooming place around the corner. There was a lady who couldn't get her dog into her car. Me and Zak were pissing ourselves watching her." He giggled as he said it, making me smile.

"You should see if they have a dresser you like." I could pick something up at a garage sale, but I felt like Twice Is Nice could use the business.

"I looked at one he needs to refinish. Everything he shows me, Zak is like, 'Hey, did you ever see one of these? It's from a million years ago, when blacksmiths were dentists. It's made of lead so it rots your brain. It's worth ninety dollars.'"

"Was Dale okay with you being there?" I trusted Zak would've kicked

Roddie out if it had been an issue, but I suspected he actually enjoyed the company. It had to be hard, staying on guard around Dale all the time.

"He kept calling me Kyle. That's the guy who helped us move the stereo."

"Zara's husband. I remember."

"Zak said Dale probably won't remember I'm not into girls and that I shouldn't take it personally. I told him about Tyson and Bethany."

"Did he say anything?"

"Gave me a root beer. Said he was dumped, too."

"He told me about that." I was glad he'd shown an ounce of sympathy, rather than being a dickhead like Joel.

"Are you two…?" Roddie didn't finish.

"No." Maybe in another life. "He's got a lot going on and needs someone to talk to. I'm convenient. Why?" I put on my best high school Queen Bee intensity. "Did he say something about me? What was it? Do you think he likes me? Like, does he like me? Or *like* me like me?"

He looked out his side window, elbow resting on the ledge as he rubbed his knuckle against the grin he was trying to hide. "You know, if you liked him, I wouldn't hate you for it."

It was almost exactly what I'd said to my own mom, and I didn't know how to take it.

"Thanks," I said, wondering if Mom had felt as conflicted as I suddenly did.

CHAPTER TWENTY-FOUR

MEG

Zak didn't come to work on Wednesday.

I got myself pretty agitated over it, convinced something had happened to Dale. I knew I was making a mountain out of a molehill. My anxiety was really more about Georgia. She was travelling to Vancouver today and checking into the hospital later this afternoon. They planned to run some final blood tests as prep for her surgery tomorrow. I sent a quick text to Zak at lunch anyway.

Everything okay?

Estate sale, was his prompt response.

Now I felt like an insecure girlfriend.

Later that afternoon, I heard the truck beeping as it backed into the receiving bay. Next time, I'd remember to check for it before letting my imagination run wild.

Roddie showed up in time to help Zak unload and flashed me a smug twenty in the car on our way home. I was glad he'd made some quick cash, but I was bummed not to have seen Zak. This time, I was the one who needed a distraction, especially after I got the text confirming Georgia was checked in and everything was set.

I didn't sleep well and was feeling keyed up the next morning at work.

When a statuesque drag artist walked in wearing a sparkly red cocktail dress that hugged their knockout figure, it took me a second to recognize… "Negasi! I saw you talking to Gail the night of the launch and didn't realize it was you."

"Nina Rhinestone when I'm in drag, please, hon. She/her." She gave a slow blink of long-lashed eyelids shimmering in gold and blue shadow. Her lips, slick with glossy red, offered up a cool smile.

"Ms. Rhinestone," I corrected myself. "I didn't expect to meet you unless I came to your show." This was a good reminder that I'd been meaning to look into tickets. "You look incredible, but do they do a breakfast seating?"

"I'm auditioning for *Kinky Boots*."

"Get out. There's going to be a run of that *here*?" I pointed at the floor. "That's great!"

"Vancouver." She offered a negligent shrug. "But they have an open call at a theatre downtown, and the dinner theatre run wraps in a couple of months so I'm looking to what's next."

"Oh? Georgia told me you might be thinking of opening your own business. I told her to give you my number if you want to chat."

"She did." She nodded. "But I don't want to impose."

"Impose," I insisted. "I'm an accountant on hiatus. I'm happy to look at your business plan or answer any questions. You can have my two cents for two cents. What kind of business are you thinking?"

She sighed and her long red nails grazed the hair falling against her cheek, then brushed the tresses to fall behind her shoulder. "It's still more of an idea, but every time I talk with my niece, I think of opening a boutique that caters to trans folk."

"Here?" Victoria was pretty diverse, but I had no idea how big the trans community was. "My first thought is that it might be too niche to be profitable in a smaller city. My second concern is taxes. Are you Canadian?"

"Dual. Born in Winnipeg, baby."

"Oh, the real Canada. I didn't know how good I had it here in the winter until I moved to Ontario. Do you still have family there?"

"Mm." She nodded. "My parents were both musicians and moved us to California as soon as they got work there. Daddy hated shovelling snow."

"Who doesn't?"

"Right? I visit, but I don't want to live there again. I haven't decided where a shop might work. Vancouver, likely. I just want a space where people feel comfortable trying things on and figuring out what works for them. It's intimidating to go into a shop when you're a baby trans."

"Can I ask…" I hesitated. "Are you trans?"

"No, hon. I'm a gay man who can sing and dance and happens to love high heels, but my niece is always looking for school clothes that are comfortable and let her feel like who she is."

"Said every woman ever." It wasn't really a joke.

"You get me. I helped her find binders and shapers online, but you need community, too, you know?"

"Mm." I nodded agreement.

"I looked at what Georgia's doing here…" She glanced around at the shelves and the stereo where Stevie Wonder was crooning about the sunshine of his life. "She's setting herself up for her next stage and that's smart."

"That's what I keep thinking, that she knew what she wanted and went after it. I wish I had such a clear vision for myself. And how do you let go of what you had? Do you just know in your heart that you're done with performing and ready to do something else?"

"Darlin', I'm a whore for being on stage. I *love* it and will never give it up."

I couldn't help laughing at that unabashed confession.

"But it's a lot of travel and hustle and grind."

"I can imagine."

"Real talk? I got into this for the costumes." She waved at her dress. "In another life, I would have been a fashion designer and keep thinking maybe I still can. I see a need and was hoping for some tips from Georgia on how to make it viable."

"I can absolutely help you with that. Let me pull some thoughts together and get back to you."

"I appreciate you. But that's not why I came in. Georgia's having her surgery today, isn't she?"

"She is." I sagged a little, grateful to let my cheerful mask slip. "I didn't want to say anything—privacy and all. How did you know? Did she tell you?"

"Gail told me when I saw her here last week. She said she'd keep you posted, so I wanted to check in."

"I haven't heard anything yet, only that she went into hospital last night for prep. It'll be several hours."

She frowned, concerned.

"That's also why I haven't booked our reservation for your show yet," I explained. "It's Mom's birthday tomorrow. I know I could cancel if I have to, but I want to be sure everything goes well for Georgia. I'm sure it will," I added quickly. "I'm thinking all good thoughts." I mentally sent strength and wellness into my favourite visions of Georgia being sassy and happy and full of her I-can-do-anything confidence.

"Me, too," Nina said in her warm, soothing voice. "And, sugar, you're A-list. You'll always get a table."

"Pah!" I had to laugh at being called A-list while wearing comfort clothes—distressed jeans, a mock turtleneck, and a warm but shapeless red-and-black flannel. Then I blurted, "Do you want to hang out for a bit? The quiet of the store doesn't usually bother me, but today it'd be nice to have company." Especially someone who cared about Georgia as much as I did.

"I have my audition." She glanced at her phone.

"Right. Sorry. Break a leg."

"Thanks. I'll come back after, though. I'll bring donuts."

"*Yes, please.* You can't be anything but optimistic when you have a mouthful of sprinkles."

"Baby girl, don't I know it."

CHAPTER TWENTY-FIVE

MEG

It was a long day, but finally, just after I spotted Roddie walking by the window toward the antique store, Gail texted again. *Georgia is in recovery. The surgeon is happy with how it went. Sedation should wear off by morning. They'll know more over the next few days.*

I deflated with relief, only then realizing how much tension I'd been holding all day.

I locked up a few minutes early and walked into Twice Is Nice to get Roddie.

Zak looked up from tightening some hardware on a cabinet. He gave me a compassionate look that made my toes curl.

"Any news?" he asked. He'd dropped in a few times today, but I'd had a surprisingly busy day as several of Georgia's friends had come by the shop to ask about her.

"She's in recovery. Now it's healing and physio. Hopefully that goes well, too. Hey, buddy?" I looked toward Roddie, who was helping Dale place a doily and a tray of glasses onto a coffee table. "I'm done for the day. Can you go get your stuff?"

He nodded and headed toward the back of the shop.

"You okay?" Zak asked.

I felt as though I was suspended in gelatin. "I spent the day pretending

I wasn't bracing for bad news. Now my adrenaline has drained away, and I want to be home on the couch with a glass of wine and garbage television."

"Perfect evening. Looked like you had a busy day, though. Still getting traffic from the relaunch?" He tilted his head toward our common wall.

"Those were mostly friends of Georgia's dropping in to check on her. It was nice to have the distraction and they were all really great. I'm envious of her." I faltered slightly, realizing how revealing that sounded. "Not just because she surrounds herself with awesome people. I'm part of her circle, so obviously I'm awesome myself." I splayed a hand on my chest.

"Obviously," he echoed with amusement.

"But she's built the kind of life I want."

"News flash, I think you're living her life."

I smiled weakly. Wistfully. Pretty soon, Georgia would return to her great life. I wanted her to. I was glad I was helping her hang on to her dream, but it was her dream, not mine.

"I mean that her life is intentional. I know this didn't just happen for her. It took her time to figure out what she wanted and pull it all together." I thought of Negasi noodling options for his future. It was never easy to make a big change. "But that's what I envy. I want a clear vision and then to be where she is, without all the bullshit of working for it." I wouldn't even start assembling my new life until I got back to Toronto.

"You want an effortless happy ending?" he teased. "Didn't I bankroll something to help with that?"

I scolded him with a look and glanced for Roddie. He was politely allowing Dale to run his magician-wardrobe routine on him.

"Is there a reason you're not letting me wallow in melancholy?" I asked Zak.

"I don't want you to get any on me."

I refused to laugh, but our gazes locked. I let him see my exasperation, but intertwined with it was that tingling sexual awareness that liked to dance and sparkle between us. His expression softened.

"Here's what I think. If I'm full of shit, say so. It's just my impression, but I think you like to feel needed. You came home to help your mom, and you listen to my BS, and you wanted to help your friend by running her store. Now that you know she's going to get better, you're starting to think she won't need you, and that bums you out."

"I had my first kid at eighteen. Of course I need to feel needed to feel valued." I curled my lip with self-disgust. "When Roddie went to live with Joel, I plummeted into an identity crisis." And ran straight home to mother. Dutiful daughter was the only other role I knew. "Sure, he's with me now, but this isn't our home. I have to go back to Toronto and pick up the pieces. What will my life look like when I get there? What do I *want* it to look like? That's what I'm saying. How do I get there without all the growing pains?"

"Yeah, I can't help you with that," he said, shoving his hands into his back pockets and turning his attention to his father. "I thought I knew what I wanted, but that was programming."

"Clever."

"I thought so. Hey, Dad? Meg wants to take Roddie home."

"The draper's rod? I sold it."

Zak gathered his patience with a long inhale. "Sounds like I get to play a round of Who's on First. Have a good night. Enjoy your wine."

"Thanks." I wanted to hug him for no reason. For all the reasons. Because he made me feel lighter and faced his own life crisis with philosophical humour.

"'Night, Zak," Roddie said as he came up to us.

"'Night," Zak replied.

"I'll see you tomorrow." I gave him a little wave.

"You sure will," he assured me, and that made me feel brighter, too.

CHAPTER TWENTY-SIX

MEG

Fortunately, I had my phone with me the next day when I decided to sit down in the swing.

It was the quiet of late morning before the lunch rush, which wasn't exactly a rush, but I usually saw a customer or two. I was forwarding Gail's message to all the people who had dropped in yesterday: Georgia was awake. She had squeezed Gail's hand and could feel Gail's warm grip on her toes. *Good news,* I added.

I hadn't really given the swing much attention before because the customers hadn't either. The seat was a couple of padded straps that looked like they belonged on a red backpack. Black cuffs, grips, and stirrups hung from the suspension ropes.

I decided it was time to learn more and flipped through the illustrated booklet attached to one of the cuffs. One image showed a man spanking a woman's butt. Another showed a woman's legs splayed wide while a man went down on her. One had her heels in the top cuffs while he stood between her upraised legs. Then she was flipped onto her stomach, boobs falling through the seat straps, while he railed her from behind.

Why were they all white hetero couples? And why was it always the woman strapped into the swing?

I pulled out my phone and searched for more positions. I came across a lesbian sixty-nine, a serious bondage scene between a couple of guys, and some playful poses featuring people of colour—even one with a gray-haired partner.

If I was being honest, I was getting kind of turned on by all the suggestive images, but how comfortable could it really be to have your legs akimbo like that?

This was when Vickie Crutcher's voice should have resounded in my head, warning me to have some decorum.

But my brain was in research mode. A compulsion to investigate had me adjusting my position so I could stick my foot in one of the stirrups. Was I smart enough to brace the heel of my boot against the loop? No. I brought the loop up behind my bent knee. Because I was curious. *Research*.

Then I realized the handles and stirrups were adjustable. I tugged the appropriate grip, and my knee went up.

That, right there, should have been enough. I should have stopped there.

However.

My phone was in my lap, and it started to slide to the floor. Reflex had me trying to catch it while still holding the upper adjustment strap. My weight tipped, yanking my right leg higher. The sudden shift opened the two straps cradling my ass. My other leg lifted off the floor.

It was like being stuck in a toilet while holding onto a towel rack.

I hung there swaying, too shocked by my predicament to move. I could almost reach my phone. My fingertips grazed the slippery screen as I gently drifted back and forth above it. My other hand was still clinging for dear life to the adjustment strap.

It was so ridiculous, I started to laugh, which only made me weak and even more helpless. What the hell was I going to do?

Gingerly, I took hold of one of the suspension ropes and released the adjustment strap. It didn't lower my leg. It had some kind of locking mechanism that kept my knee up around my ear. The best I could do was grasp a different strap and try to lean far enough to catch my phone as the swing continued to sway.

What if a customer came in and found me like this? What if my mother or Roddie did?

With supreme effort, I stretched a tiny bit more and managed to pick up my phone. Zak was going to laugh himself wet, but I thumbed for his name and hit "call."

"This is Elvis," he answered.

"Zak." I was still gasping with laughter at the utter ridiculousness of my situation. "I need help."

"What's wrong?" His alarm made it funnier.

"I'm okay. I just need you to—"

"Meg?" The bell clanged. Loud.

He appeared from around the shelf and halted when he saw me. His tension fell away as he put superhuman effort into holding a straight face. His expression was still priceless. He ended our call and tucked his phone into his back pocket.

"Kitten's up the drapes again," he called over his shoulder to no one.

"Have your laugh, then help me."

"This is what you get when you fuck Spiderman."

"My mother warned me, but I didn't listen."

"I hope you have a reserve chute."

"One more and no photos."

"I'm definitely taking a photo." He *did*. The bastard.

Then he came over and scooped an arm beneath mine. He splayed his hand on my lower back, his hard thighs braced between mine. His pelvis was exactly where the illustrations had anticipated it would be. He squashed my boobs against his firm chest as he pulled me upright, then studied the mechanism. He flicked something that released my leg.

In a very swoony move, he finished pulling me free of the swing and stood me on my feet.

I was every breathless romcom heroine who had ever stumbled and landed in the hero's arms, weak and bemused.

"Thank you."

"You're welcome."

We both dropped our hands but stayed where we were, standing too close.

"Good luck with Cirque du Soleil," Zak said. "I'm going to miss you, but I support you following your passion."

"I only called you because I knew you needed a laugh. This stays between us." I tapped his chest—mostly because I wanted another excuse to touch that wall of muscle.

"And Rod. I would text him the photo, but I want to see his face when I show him."

I knew he was joking, but I gave him my most menacing glower.

His mouth was a thing of beauty, digging in at the corners, completely unimpressed by my ferocity. In fact, there was heat and affection and speculation.

I really, really wanted to kiss that mouth.

A flicker from the window made him jolt and look out. He leaned to see who it was, but it was only someone hurrying past on the sidewalk.

Zak gave the back of his neck a squeeze as he turned back to me. His gaze caught mine before he took a step back. His attention slipped away from me and back toward his own shop. His mouth pushed to the side, rueful.

I folded my arms and bit my lips.

"He's a good kid, by the way," he said. "Funny. Scathingly funny. I love it."

"Thanks." We were pretending the almost-kiss hadn't happened, then? "Shelby is, too." A swell of pride warmed me. "I used to think it was just that they grew up knowing how to make me laugh, but no, they're both genuinely hilarious."

"It's cool that you have that." He was splitting his attention between his own shop and our conversation, but there was something else in his expression, a faraway look.

"It is," I said, as a pang of dejection hit me. He wanted his own kids. I could see it.

"When I talk to him…" He closed one eye in a wince, clearly debating whether to continue.

"What?" I prompted.

He gave me a look that was sombre and unguarded. "Sometimes when I talk to certain kids and do the math, I realize they're the age my own kid might have been. It makes me wonder what my life would have looked like if that had happened."

Oh. "Meaning there's a teenager out there with your DNA or…?"

"No." He scratched his beard, his attention swivelling to the door of his shop. "No, my girlfriend had an abortion my second year of college. Mom had just died. I was already struggling with my course load, drinking my face off to deal with the grief. Anyway, she got pregnant and I told her I'd support her if she wanted to have it, but I was shitting myself. She decided the timing wasn't right, and I went with her to the clinic. I was relieved." He lifted a shoulder as he made that admission. "But sometimes I get the what-ifs."

"Of course," I murmured.

"Zara doesn't know about that, so…" He ran an invisible zipper across his lips, locked it, and threw the key over his shoulder.

"This is a safe space. Anything that happens in this room stays in this room." I was sincere, but I sent a pointed look toward the swing.

"This place should be called Little Vegas. Hey, did you ever try that clit stimulator?"

"I kind of can't stay off it." I grimaced with self-reproach.

"Good to hear." His grin was as smug as if he had personally left me in a puddle of my own come. He kind of had.

"Yours?" I prompted.

"More realistic than I expected, especially with lots of warm lube. There are settings to suck the tip or go down the shaft and into the base. It's a total pain in the ass to clean, but I use it in the shower." He gave me a slow blink. "Then I use it again before bed. I may need an intervention."

"Should we hold that here with your dad and sister or…?"

"Invite your mom. Sounds like you need one, too." He reached for the door. "I should get back. I ran out on Dad. But listen, I'll take care of the window washing. You keep two feet on the ground."

"I'm telling you, I did it for *you*. I was fully in control the entire time."

"You looked like one of those illustrations on old maps, where tall ships are being attacked by a giant squid."

"Bye, Zak."

The door jangled behind him.

If I wasn't careful, I was going to be head over heels for that man.

CHAPTER TWENTY-SEVEN

MEG

That night, we went to see the Pretty Please drag show for Mom's birthday. Negasi had told me they didn't allow young children because crying babies and free-range toddlers ruined dinner theatre, but the risqué humour was fine for the average teenager.

Roddie liked music, theatre, and free meals, so there were no complaints from him, not even when I asked him to dress up. He put on clean black jeans, a white button-down shirt, and one of my dad's wide-ass paisley ties in green and pink. He wore one of Dad's blazers from the eighties, too. It was mint green, and after he rolled up the sleeves the oversized fit was great on him. Mom's only comment was a mutter about double-Windsor knots right before she fixed his tie.

The dinner was a riot. The show was loosely based on *Little Women*, where all the campy dialogue served as setup for performers to burst into songs by Lady Gaga, Adele, Rihanna, and Taylor Swift. There were big, colourful wigs and sparkly outfits, lively choreography in platform shoes, and plenty of bawdy jokes.

It was such a delight we wouldn't have cared if the food had been terrible, but it was delicious. When they brought out Mom's dessert, there was a sparkler in it, and the performers gathered around her to sing a couple verses of Rod Stewart's "Forever Young."

"Thank you." I caught Nina Rhinestone's eye as the performers started to disperse.

"No problem. Is this your son?"

"Roddie, yes." I introduced them.

"I thought it was going to be lip-sync, but you're all really good singers," Roddie said.

"We are, aren't we?" Nina flashed a smile.

"Can I ask you something? I took one of these from the bathroom." Roddie showed Nina a card he drew from his pocket. "Do you know if it's legit?"

"It is. Cinnamon Buns runs it. I'll introduce you after the show. I have to get back onstage for our final act. Enjoy your cake." She patted Roddie's shoulder and hurried away.

I leaned toward Roddie and he showed me the card for an LGBTQIA+ club for teens.

I gave it a nod, aiming for mild interest, trying not to go overboard with my support.

When he first came out, I had tried to sign him up for every group I could find. My guilt was in the driver's seat after being absent from his life so often, but I was starting to realize that coming out was a journey and he was still on it. It had been huge for him to admit to me that he liked Tyson, and it ended so painfully I wouldn't have blamed him for keeping his sexuality quiet while he was here. Instead, he had told Zak, and this card was another sign he didn't need me to help him figure out what he needed.

I wanted to hug him but decided to ambush him in the parking lot with one "for no reason." Otherwise, he'd accuse me of being extra. I'd leave that label for Mom. She finished reading the card and took off her glasses and tapped the card with them.

"I know where that is—just a few blocks over from the thrift store. You can come into the store on your way. I can introduce you to everyone."

So extra.

CHAPTER TWENTY-EIGHT

MEG

I turned the page of the book I was reading and followed the randy maid and her regency master up the stairs of his London home and into his bedchamber…

"Close the door and take off your gown." His tone of command made her skin tighten.

She obeyed quickly. He stripped down to his breeches, his suspenders hanging loose. Then he pulled a long, flat box from under the bed and placed it on the bench. Opening it, he revealed several items—many shaped like erect cocks—but also padded rings with chains, which she guessed were for restraint.

"Does any of this intrigue you?"

All of it. "I'm not sure," she said hesitantly.

"Nelly." He placed his hand on her shoulder and turned her to face him. His other hand settled at her throat, where her pulse pounded beneath his palm. "I'm allowing second chances because you don't know me—but those are running out. This is a device for the ass."

Keeping one hand at her neck, he held up a small stone object with an olive-shaped tip and a tapered shaft, its base flared wide with a cord attached like a drawer pull.

"I've told you not to lie to me. If you do it again, I'll put this in you and spank you until my arm tires. It will hurt like nothing you've ever known. Do you want that?"

"No," she said reflexively. Then, to be as honest as she could, added, "Not the spanking part."

"You want this in your ass?"

"I—" She nearly said she knew it was bad and she was trying to be good, but stopped herself. "I'm intrigued," she admitted, letting her gaze drift to the object, trying to believe it was okay to be curious.

His thumb on her neck caressed her skin. He drew her close enough to touch his mouth to hers. She stiffened slightly in surprise, then let her lips soften and part to accept the domination of his.

She hadn't been kissed much. It felt strange. Intimate, considering her naked breasts brushed up against the warm, hair-roughened plane of his chest. She quickly decided she liked it. He fitted his lips to hers and applied suction, as though bringing forth all the passionate feelings that emanated from her depths. He played his tongue against hers in a way that made her nipples harden, and she leaned into him, seeking the soothing stimulation of firmer pressure.

He released her, and she staggered slightly to find her balance, murmuring, "I'm sorry."

"I want to put this inside you and undress before we continue. Kneel on the edge of the bed with your elbows in the middle."

The bed was high, which put her ass in his face, but he didn't seem to mind. He played with her pussy for a long minute, rubbing and stroking his fingers into her cleft, arousing her until she—

The door jangled. "Pumpkin spice latte?"

I slammed the book shut and blinked at Zak.

"That's an even guiltier look than yesterday, when I caught you bungee jumping without a licence."

"It's this book." I showed him the cover. "Your sister and her friends are reading it for book club. It's historical erotica. I just read a filthy story where a married woman pegs a duke who was not her husband."

"Did he like it?"

"He loved it. There's some guy-on-guy stuff that's next level, and now this maid's about to get a spanking."

"You ever tried that? Spanking?" He crossed his arms and tilted his head with curiosity.

"Never saw the appeal."

"The appeal is there's an ass in your lap. That seems self-explanatory."

"You presume *you're* the spanker then."

"I guess I went straight there, yeah." His self-deprecating grin turned into a faraway smile, as if he was still there. As if he was considering both sides of that particular play. His gaze came back to me and the book with heavy interest. "So is that getting you horny?"

"So horny," I admitted on a chuckle, not caring that I was blushing because I was already flushed and hot. "I was seriously considering locking the door and going into the bathroom for some self-maintenance."

"Do it." He shrugged.

"Ha." I rolled my eyes.

"I'm serious. Do you know how many times I've jacked in the can next door? I could paint it twice."

"Gross!" I laughed.

"What the hell was I supposed to do, coming in from high school all worked up from looking at bra straps and whale-tales all day?"

"And now? Since you've been back?" I challenged lightly.

"I might have. Once or twice." He scratched his nose.

"I'm starting to think that's all you do, you know."

"You're enabling it, pushing all these toys on me. I'll remind you that I'm doing it for *you*." He pretended to be very affronted and glanced toward his shop.

"I thought it was for humankind."

"It is. I'm a very magnanimous person. So go. Do it. I'll stand here and watch the shop. Because I'm nice that way."

"I suspect you're actually kinky as hell."

"Getting there, but either way, you get an orgasm, so where's the problem?"

The problem was that I'd be rubbing one out while he was standing right there. Which made *me* a little kinky—but the heavy, wicked pressure already sitting in my pelvis told me I didn't care. And something about him knowing exactly what I was doing was titillating. It wasn't as though he didn't know I masturbated. We'd been reporting our orgasms like birders logging yellow-breasted tits.

"Take that in there if you need to," he said, nodding at the book.

"No, I'll leave it here for you to peruse." I set it on the edge of the desk like a dare and sauntered into the bathroom.

I closed the door, glanced once at myself, then turned my back on that lusty-eyed bitch. Leaning my hips on the sink, I lifted my skirt. It was a three-quarter length, button-front in striped cotton—perfect for the moody spring weather. I set my feet wide in my boots and found the placket of my thong damp.

I pushed it aside and plunged my fingers into the slick valley of my pussy lips. I was so wet it barely gave enough friction. But I was so aroused, the rush of stimulation hit instantly. I closed my eyes, bit my lip, and imagined Zak walking through the unlocked door.

He'd unzip, pull out his hard cock, and thrust into my needy, clenching pussy—

I gasped as climax broke over me in swift, pounding waves. I had to fight to keep my moans trapped, my mouth open in a silent scream of bliss.

Panting, I kept circling my clit with lazy fingers. I could've come again. Four more times. What I really wanted was a thick, hard cock. Right now. Desperately.

Georgia might have had the nerve to crack the door and invite Zak to bend her over the sink, but I wasn't there yet. I cleaned up, washed my hands, and walked out with more ease than I expected. I met his heavy-lidded stare without embarrassment.

He was standing at the desk with the book in his hand.

"Thanks," I said.

"My pleasure." He set the book down. "Watch the door to my shop, would you?"

Then he walked into the bathroom like it was nothing and shut the door. I didn't hear a lock—just the zip of his fly.

Oh, fuck. I nearly bit the spine off that hot-ass book.

Before long, a low, throaty groan resounded behind the bathroom door. Seconds later, the toilet flushed, and water ran.

When he came out, his cheekbones were flushed, his eyelids heavy, and he wore a relaxed smile.

"Which one did you read?" I had to ask.

He gave a slow shake of his head and held my stare with magnetic force. "I was thinking about something else. We should do this together more often. Coffee?"

My mouth went so dry, I could only squeak, "Sure."

"I'll be right back." He winked and left.

CHAPTER TWENTY-NINE

ZAK

Meg was right there at the shop door when I leaned in to hand her the coffee I'd bought for her.

"Thank you." She dipped her chin, wearing a pleased little smile that seemed to say she was thanking me for more than just the caffeine.

"Anytime." Oh, I felt smooth. Physically. Like all my sharp edges had been sanded off.

Considering the amount of time I'd been spending with my toys lately, I should feel like this all the time, but messing with them only took my mind off things for the seven minutes between squirting lube into my palm and cleaning up. Then the tension, worries, and stress over Dad would come rushing back.

Not today. I felt properly stoned. That had been really hot, thinking of her pushing her fingers into her—

"Your sister's in there."

"What? Where?" I dragged my gaze up from the fit of Meg's jeans.

"Your shop. I wasn't fast enough to say hi. She was moving like she was on a mission."

Ah, shit. How had I missed seeing her? I always kept an eye on the store from across the street. But I'd been thinking about Meg.

"Okay, thanks."

I walked into Twice Is Nice, and Zara glared at me from the office door, hands raised in a silent, *What the hell?*

"I went for coffee. You want some?" I held up my cup.

"No. But you can't leave him alone." She drew the office door closed as she came out.

"He's asleep." He fell asleep on the sofa most days after lunch. "Meg was watching the door. She would have stopped him from wandering if he tried to leave."

"What if he fell?"

"What if I was sanding in the back room and he fell? I can't be right behind him all day, every day. Maybe familiarize yourself with the labour codes, because I'm entitled to a coffee break—"

Her mouth tightened, and her eyes started to gleam.

I shut the hell up. I knew that look. I'd seen it at Christmas.

"I take that back." I held up a hand. "You and I are not going to fight."

We could, and we had, back when we were still young enough for it to be a fair fight. We loved the crap out of each other, but the older we got, the more different we became. Zara could be bossy. I was sarcastic. She had been an outgoing cheerleader; I was a computer nerd. After Mom died, she dealt with her grief by leaning on friends. I ate my feelings. Now she was a wife and mother. I was a single man living with Dad.

Still.

"We're on the same side," I reminded her. "This situation is going to get on our last nerve sometimes. We can't take it out on each other."

"I know." She blinked fast and took a few long, shaky breaths. "But for a minute, it felt like it was all on me again. I couldn't take it." She ran her thumb under one eye.

"I'm not going anywhere. I'm here for the long haul." The words felt heavy coming out. It was a hard truth I'd been avoiding, but this was what life looked like for the foreseeable future.

"Okay. Thanks," she murmured.

"You want a hug?" I opened my arms.

She came in for a quick one, then darted away to straighten a doily under the lamp, saying tentatively, "Kyle has to work late on Monday. Can I leave the kids with you so I can go to book club?"

"For that erotica book?" I pictured Meg looking all flushed and sexy from reading it. "Sure."

"How do you know what book it is?" She frowned at me.

"Meg told me." I waved my cup in the direction of her store, then took a sip.

"Is there something going on between you two? You were laughing and talking a long time the other night."

"We chat sometimes." About sex. Today, it had escalated into taking turns at self-abuse within earshot of each other, but that was something friends did all the time. Didn't they?

"Like Dad and Debra?"

If I started thinking about Dad doing shit like that with Debra, my brain would snap in half.

"Her son comes by after school so he doesn't have to wait for her at the coffee shop. He's patient with Dad. Funny as hell. I like him."

She swore and looked for her purse. "I think I have one of those. A son. I have to get him from preschool."

"Last time I checked, you had two. Just a friendly reminder."

"That one has soccer, and I think he's going with one of the other parents. I should check that."

She left, but I didn't move for a long time. I was processing what I'd said about being here for the long haul while remembering what Meg had said about getting back to Toronto to start rebuilding her life.

Good thing we were only friends.

CHAPTER THIRTY

MEG

I was dying to tell Georgia that Zak and I had taken turns wanking in her shop's bathroom, but I doubted she'd find it as titillating as I had.

She was in such good spirits, though, she might just laugh herself right out of her wheelchair.

At least she was home with her sister again. It was Sunday. Gail and her family were out, but she'd encouraged me to come sit with Georgia so she wouldn't worry.

It was great to see Georgia smiling, even in pajamas and still a little dopey from pain meds.

"It's a different pain," she told me. "I can tell it's healing pain. I can live with that. What's all this?" She peeked into the bag of samples I'd brought. "I have my trusty-reliable."

"I registered for an online trade show. I wanted the education workshops, but that was the swag bag they sent attendees. I thought you might want to test drive a few, or tell me which ones are worth stocking."

"I'll look through it later." She set it aside. "Tell me what's been going on."

"It's so hard and so fun, pun intended."

I told her about the long hunt for a replacement charger for an older toy and how excited one guy had been when he found out there was a product to replicate his penis for his girlfriend.

"He wanted me to help him take the cast of his erection. Literally. I was like, 'Read the box. You can do it yourself.' He was so sure something would go wrong."

"That poor girl. His dick sounds like the only useful part of him."

"Right? Oh. You're going to die when I tell you what happened the other day." I told her about the swing incident.

She laughed so hard, she kept saying, "Oh, shit," and clutched at her lower back. "Please tell him to send me that photo."

"I will not. He asked me what my plans were for today. 'Robbing the Bellagio?' He thinks he's so funny."

Georgia chuckle-winced again. "But you like him."

"I do," I admitted sheepishly. "Not that I see it going anywhere beyond flirting. Maybe a little torrid sex."

"Just a little."

"A teensy bit of extremely vigorous boning while I'm in town, but eventually I'll go home and…" I shrugged, wistful.

"Will you?" She sobered.

"Yeah," I said reluctantly. "Roddie expects us to. *Joel* does. Even if I stayed here, there's no guarantee Zak would stay here, too. Or that he wants a relationship. He's only here for his Dad and that situation is pretty heavy and unpredictable. Even without those factors, he's too young for me."

"Not that you've given it any thought."

"None," I said facetiously.

"I thought Zara was our age. How is he too young?"

"Thirty-two or three at most. It's more about the fact he doesn't have kids yet. He'll want some. And this factory…" I pointed to my abdomen. "Is boarded up."

"Did he *say* he wants kids?"

"It's implied. He was engaged last year to someone who lived with him. If he wants anything from me, it's rebound sex and I'm here for it. But tell me about Bruno." I leaned forward. "He came by to ask about you the day of your surgery."

Bruno had been really hot in a sexy, gym-bro way, and sincerely worried about Georgia, which had instantly drawn me to Team Bruno.

"Ah, Bruno." She looked to the ceiling. "We hooked up a few times, but it was complicated with his work hours, and he had some family stuff. Then I opened the business and had my own stuff. We couldn't get on the same—" She see-sawed her hand.

"Time zone? He told me he works nights."

"I was going to say wavelength, but that, too. Then we had this Romeo and Juliet moment one day when he threw open his window as I was leaving the store. He yelled, 'Are you looking for me?' and I said, 'Nah, dawg, I work here.' It was pretty funny when we realized that he lived upstairs from my new shop, but I was already having problems with my back and..." She shrugged.

"I think he really likes you."

"He texts me sometimes. I answer sometimes."

I left it at that, and we went on to talk about how Afternoon Delight might offer workshops and which topics to cover first.

CHAPTER THIRTY-ONE

MEG

On Monday, Mom came by the shop to give it a spring makeover. She'd picked up a clear umbrella printed with rainbows, some silk tulips from the thrift store, and a pair of bright yellow rubber boots.

She arranged a few shower toys with a book on natural aphrodisiacs and some colourful tubes of lube. Her sign read: *Have fun! Get wet!*

"You could start a business doing this, you know."

"I doubt it." She reached into the display to adjust the angle of a boot. "People don't even go into stores anymore."

"Because their window displays suck."

"I'm retired. People would think I'm broke and taking the only work I can get."

"Screw what people think. If you like doing it, do it. It's flexible. You could take only the clients you like and only as many as you want."

She waved her hand in dismissal. "I already work at the thrift store."

"For free. Doing *this* for free."

"Because I have friends there." I could see the little hamster in her head running in its wheel, though.

"It would get you out of the house and help you meet people once you move back east with us."

She sighed the way she always did when I brought up moving, big and heavy. "This is where I live, Meg."

"I know." It's where I had grown up, and I couldn't remember why I had hated it so much. My life had seemed very small back then. Restricted. But I'd been a kid.

"Roddie seems to like it here," Mom pointed out.

"Because it's still new." Also, he had made his first sale at the antique store. It was a fluke because the mirror was the size the customer wanted, but he had earned fifteen dollars for five minutes of work. "His dad and baby brother live in Toronto, though."

"His sister is closer."

"I know, but—"

The door jangled. Mom turned.

"Dale," she said with a warm smile. "It's nice to see you again."

"Debra." His wide smile faltered. His expression became confused as he looked around.

Oh, shit.

"Hi, Dale." I made myself approach him without hurry, holding out my hand in hopes that he'd recognize I wanted to introduce myself. "I'm your new neighbour, Meg. We've met a few times. This is my mom, Vickie. You've met her once or twice, too."

"We had a nice chat about some of our favourite haunts, like the diner out by the rail yard," Mom said with a nostalgic smile.

"Right, right." Dale's smile was brave, but his eyes grew damp with upset.

"Should we go back to your shop and talk with Zak?" I asked.

"Yes. I think so." He looked around, and I realized he was completely disoriented and didn't know where the door was.

Oh, Dale.

"I'll walk with you. It's this way." I motioned toward the door.

Through the glass on our door, I saw a middle-aged couple leave the antique shop to duck into the rain. Zak came out right behind them, shoving open my door with a hard push.

He pulled up short as he saw it was only Mom and me in the shop with his father.

"Hey, Dad. Everything okay?"

"Totally fine." I projected all the calm reassurance I could. "We were just about to walk back and see you."

"Debra retired so now Meg is in this shop," Zak explained to Dale. "Did you want to look around? Or come back to our shop?" Zak was trying to pretend he was unbothered, but I could feel the tension that gripped him.

"I thought this was a toy shop," Dale said with a husk of laughter as he peeked into the window display. He blushed. "That's what I told your sister. That a toy shop was moving in."

"Yeah, we were all surprised as hell when we saw what kind of toys," Zak drawled. "That looks nice, Vickie. Brightens up a dreary day."

"Thank you." She had sobered at Dale's obvious distress but found a smile for Zak.

"What would Debra think if she knew?" Dale asked Zak. "That woman wouldn't say 'shit' if she had a mouthful of it. Now they're selling unmentionables in her store?"

"She was pretty straightlaced." Zak was relaxing. "She washed my mouth out with soap once for saying 'fart.' I still taste Irish Spring when I swear in here."

"I wondered why your breath always smells so fresh," I murmured.

Zak's mouth twitched, and I was entirely too proud that I'd given him something to laugh about.

"Debra was a good listener, though," Dale said.

"Let's give her a call, see if she has time to chat. You can talk to her while I empty the china cabinet."

"You sold the china cabinet? It's about time. God, they're a bitch to move."

"We'll put some blankets around it." Zak opened the door, nodding at Mom and me.

"Bye." I waved. Then I sighed. Big and heavy.

"I thought the only thing that could feel as bad as losing your father would be losing you or one of your children. I can't imagine how Dale feels, though, losing himself." Mom was staring at the wall as though looking through it to where the men had entered their own shop.

"I can," I blurted, then immediately regretted it.

Mom shook off her introspection and waited for me to continue.

"That's why I quit my job." I crossed my arms, not wanting to be defensive, but I was. "I feel like I was lost for twenty years. Now I want to figure out who I am when I'm not a wife and mother. I want to find *me*. And I know you feel lost, too. That you're trying to figure out who you are without Dad."

"I know exactly who I am," she dismissed. "And I agree that helping Georgia was the right thing to do. But throwing away your career is throwing away something valuable." Her voice edged toward impatience. "You're not replacing it with anything."

"I'm making room for something else. Something better."

"Now you sound like those hippies who come into the thrift store, always telling me how they rake the sand in their aquarium, or rearrange their crystals to fix their auras."

"Mom," I kept my voice as gentle as I could. "If raking crystals makes them happy, and that's who they are, who cares?"

"They can do whatever floats their boat, but you're not broken, Meg. You're *fine*."

"I don't want to be fine," I snapped, temperature spiking. "I want to be fabulous."

I made myself take a breath.

"Look, I know Aunt Linda made you feel guilty about your affair with Dad, that you've always felt we have to live a certain way to make up for that. But guess what? Dad was the one who cheated. With his secretary. I really hope it was consensual, but quit carrying all the blame for his affair. Tell Aunt Linda to fuck off."

Her expression shifted from shock to consternation to mild irritation.

"I can't, can I? She gives your children money for school." She picked up her smart blue raincoat and slid her arms into it, letting me know this conversation was over.

"She does. And I appreciate it. So maybe just say it in your head." I chewed my lip, wondering if I'd gone too far.

"It was consensual, for the record." She belted her coat, avoiding my gaze. "I was naive about what I was getting into, but your father gave me—*us*—a very good life. I can't say I ever felt lost until he was gone."

Oh, Mom. I wanted to hug her, but she was already digging through her purse, searching for her keys.

"For what it's worth, *I* know who you are, Meg. You've always liked to help people, so this—" She waved at the store. "In many ways, this is exactly who you are. That goes for Zak, too." Her gaze held mine.

How could I be nudging forty and still feel so self-conscious when my mother saw right through me?

"He's not the man-child Joel is, but I can see how you're trying to prop him up."

He's a good person, I wanted to say. *He needs support.*

Did I want him to need *me*, though? I kind of did.

Mom was right. That was a slippery slope if my goal was to make myself the priority.

A gust of wind slapped rain against the window.

"I think we're both fixers, Mom. That's why I'm trying to move you to Toronto, so you won't be so lonely here. We're trying to fix each other's lives so we don't have to figure out our own."

"I have been lonely at times," she admitted with a slow nod. "And I'll admit that as much as this has been outside my comfort zone, helping in here has been good for me."

"Yeah? Does that mean you'll let me buy you a toy? Have fun, Mom. Get wet," I quoted from her sign.

"I was thinking of starting with joining a mixed foursome when golf reopens. Which, for your information, can be a gateway to polyamory." Her gaze clashed into mine, wide with amused forewarning. "I've seen it happen."

"Okay. Well. Make good choices. Use condoms."

"Can you imagine?" she muttered, but we were both chuckling as she left.

CHAPTER THIRTY-TWO

MEG

Joining Zara and her book club gave me an excuse to visit Tap That across the street. I dropped Roddie off at home first and then caught an Uber back so I could have more than one beer. Zara and Imani were already there and had ordered loaded nachos for the table.

"Everyone else will be here shortly. How are you? How's the store? How's Georgia?" Zara asked.

"Good, good, and good." I hung my jacket on the hook between the booths and sat down next to Imani.

"Before I forget, can we talk about making the store wheelchair accessible?" I asked Zara. "Georgia's starting rehab next week, and her prognosis is that she'll walk again, but I'm looking into offering workshops to get more people into the store. One is about accommodating impairments in the bedroom, but with the stoop, the target audience might not be able to get in."

"We've talked about it a few times, but we've never made it a priority. I'll ask Kyle to drop by," Zara promised. "Zak said your son comes into the antique shop after school, the way we used to." Her smile brimmed with reminiscence. "He sounds like a nice kid."

"He is. And I just got a text from my daughter saying she's coming for spring break." I gave a small clap of excitement. "She's driving from

Calgary and stopping in Kelowna to see some friends. She made the drive alone last September, so I'm trying not to be such a mom about it, but…" I wasn't succeeding.

"My oldest leaves for Dalhousie this fall," Imani said glumly. "Part of me has been counting down to that for years. I thought I was ready for the hands-on child-rearing to end, but the more real it becomes, the more I want to throw up. How will she survive if I'm not there to tell her how to live her life?"

"Right? We've spent eighteen years teaching them to eat right and do laundry. We know damn well they weren't listening." I thanked the server who arrived with my cloudy IPA. "Thank you for inviting me." I raised my glass for a toast. "I've been isolated for the last few years. I lost touch with most of my friends while Dad was sick, then I was stuck in the trenches of divorce and bullshit at work. I forgot to hang out with women who swear."

"We've been looking for a name for this group. I think that's it," Imani said.

"Fuck yes." Zara clinked her glass with ours.

CHAPTER THIRTY-THREE

ZAK

Were the kids okay last night?" my brother-in-law asked me when he came by the next morning to help me load the van.

Kyle and I were in the receiving bay behind the shop. It was a covered, concrete pad with a big rolling door into the woodworking area of my shop and a couple of man doors that accessed the sex shop and the apartments upstairs.

"Fine." I had babysat at Zara's house so I could put the kids to bed. "Ollie got a case of the sillies when it was time to brush teeth, but Jade read him the riot act. What do you even need me for? She seems to have Ollie and Lance firmly under control."

"The Zara is strong in that one," Kyle agreed from his end of the oak tabletop. Maybe it was exertion that made his tone sound a shade more sardonic than affectionate.

"Everything okay between you two?"

"No."

Great. "I should have come home sooner to help with Dad," I said once we'd set down the tabletop inside the van. "I'm here now. I just told her the other day that I'm not going back to Vancouver."

"Does Erica know that?" He looked up from tightening one of the straps.

"I texted her. Said we should talk more seriously about whether she's staying in the condo and how that looks on paper." I'd felt a mix of disappointment and relief as I'd done it, along with weariness at the thought of sorting and dealing with my stuff there.

"What'd she say?"

Nothing yet, but I didn't get a chance to tell Kyle that. The door into the back of Meg's shop popped open. She poked her nose out.

I paused in gathering the table legs so I could take in how pretty she looked. Her blue top was thin enough I could see the shadow of her black bra beneath it. Her hair was loose, and her jeans were the ones I liked—they cupped her ass really well.

"You know you're going the wrong way with that?" she said as I handed the legs to Kyle.

"That's what she said?" I tried.

She snorted and used her foot to slide a paint can into place as a doorstop, then came out to survey all the furniture I'd readied for loading.

Today was the first of March and sunny, but it was always cool back here. Meg folded her arms, keeping me from seeing her nipples stand up against her top.

"Wow, are you *loading* the van? Did you actually make a sale, Zak?" She feigned astonishment. "You assured me that never happens."

"I didn't. Dad did. It's easy when you tell a nice couple from Leavenworth that we deliver."

Leavenworth was east of Seattle. It had been tricked out with a Bavarian theme back in the 1960s, purely to draw tourists. It worked, especially for Oktoberfest and Christmas light displays, but I was looking at a ninety-minute ferry ride, a border crossing, and four and a half hours of driving from here. I was not thrilled.

"I called them back and said if they want us to do that without charge, they have to take the sideboard and the china cabinet too."

"You sold the china cabinet?" She was suitably awestruck.

"Hell, no. But they've taken over an old rooming house and are updating it with new furniture before listing it on Airbnb. They agreed to take the sideboard, then offered a room for the night if I threw in the mahogany bedframe and a night table."

"You drive a hard bargain."

"All the way to Leavenworth," Kyle chimed in with a smirk.

They high-fived in appreciation of their puns. It was friendly enough. Kyle wasn't crossing any lines.

I still didn't like it.

He might have read that in my expression. He gave me a silent, *What?*

"I've never been to Leavenworth." Meg perused the furniture like she was considering buying it herself.

"Hopefully your room is conveniently located near the morning Alpenhorn performance," Kyle said.

"Do they still do that?" I tied off a rope that secured a bedframe to the inner wall of the van. "Mom and Dad took us there the year *after* they took us to Disneyland. You can imagine how that went over. We asked Mom if we could go to Euro Disney, and she said Leavenworth was like going to Europe. Spoiler alert: It was not like going to Europe. I'm still mad."

"At her? Or Leavenworth?" Meg was grinning at my disgust, which made me want to stop working and just stand there talking to her, making her smile and laugh.

"Both," I replied.

"*That's* why Zara is so obsessed with Paris," Kyle dropped his hands onto his hips.

"Maybe take her for a weekend in Leavenworth," Meg suggested.

"Update your will first." I shook out a blanket and draped it over a cabinet. "I offered to let her do this trip, and she told me to shove it up my ass. Sideways. Dad's excited to see the nutcracker museum again, though."

"You're taking your dad?" Meg lifted her brows.

"Sure. What could go wrong?" I deadpanned, even as I reminded myself to go in and check on him. He'd been fiddling with some books and I would have heard the chime on the door if he left the store, but still.

A distant jangle from inside Meg's shop had her looking in that direction. "I have to go. Safe travels. Try not to get arrested."

"That depends on whether Thelma behaves herself, doesn't it?"

She closed her door on her way through it.

Kyle gave me a long look.

"What?"

"You and her…?" He cocked his head toward her door.

"We're friends." It was true. But also a white lie, on my side at least.

"But you told Erica you're not coming back," Kyle pressed.

"You want me to put the kettle on? You can tell me what's going on with you and Zara while we're at it?"

"No."

"Then shut up and load the truck."

His mouth curled into a friendly smirk and we finished up.

CHAPTER THIRTY-FOUR

MEG

It was odd how much I noticed Zak's absence. Afternoon Delight had slowed down a lot since the advertising blitz of the relaunch. That gave me plenty of time to work on my instructional slides for the contract work Peterson, Londale, and Funk had offered me. At least now, when I trained titmice like Cameron to take jobs I would never be offered, I would be amply compensated. And you'd better believe I would tell any women I trained exactly how much they should ask to be paid.

The next day was an even longer, slower day. Roddie went to his first LGBTQIA+ meeting after school. It was nice that he had somewhere to go, since Twice Is Nice was closed. He caught the bus to the meeting and texted me the address so I could pick him up on my way home.

If I hadn't been so bored, I might have stayed late at work, but I closed right at five and swung into the grocery store, killing time before I had to get Roddie.

Mom had let me start cooking now that Roddie was here. With Shelby coming for the weekend, my mind turned to a menu that felt a little more celebratory. She was vegetarian, which always presented a challenge, especially because Mom was firmly old-school, meat-and-potatoes.

I was trying to remember what I might need for black-bean patties when I came around the end of the aisle and found Zak standing in front of the dairy cooler. My heart leapt with way too much joy.

"Zak! You're back."

"What?" He turned his head. His expression was just… devastated.

"Oh my God. What happened?" I released the handle of my cart and stepped closer. I grasped his arm. He looked as though he was about to topple off a cliff and needed someone to hold on to him.

He swallowed, fighting to keep his composure. "Dad didn't recognize me. I came out of the shower and he thought I was a robber or something. He yelled at me to get out of the house. He was *scared*."

"Oh, Zak." I slid my arms around his waist, trying to press warmth into his stiff frame. "Is someone with him? Can I call Zara?"

"She's there. Carl went over. Dad thinks she's Mom." His hand came up, but instead of wrapping it around me, he wiped his cheek where a tear had leaked out and started to run. "I had to leave so he would calm down. I thought I should pick up some groceries while I had the chance."

He was trying to carry on. Sounded familiar—that's what I did when my world flipped upside down.

"Let's get a drink," I said. Maybe ten or twelve. I rubbed his back, then plucked my purse from my cart and left everything where it was. "Do you have your car?"

"No, I walked."

I wondered how far. We were about a kilometre from our shops, and he lived within walking distance of the building, but the evening was chilly and he wasn't wearing a coat.

I turned on the heat in my car while I drove us to Tap That. We each ordered a beer and a burger, then I called Mom to ask her to pick up Roddie.

"I'm fine," I told her. "But Zak had a rough day. I'm buying him dinner."

"Oh?" Her voice held both concern and speculation. "I'll see you when you get home, then."

"Thanks." I ended the call and texted Roddie, then turned to Zak. "How was Leavenworth? Was it exactly like Europe?" I was trying to draw him out of his tailspin.

"Yeah," he snorted. "Couldn't tell the difference."

"Was it okay for your dad? Disorienting, maybe?"

"Maybe. I don't know." He sat back and nodded his thanks as our beers arrived. "We got there and the buyers helped me unload the van. They took us out to dinner and put us in a room with two beds. Dad was confused when we got up, but we had a great morning wandering around town."

"You saw the nutcrackers?"

"So many nutcrackers." He shook his head. "He read me every little sign about them like they were clues in *National Treasure.*"

I propped my elbow on the table and leaned my head on my hand, adoring him for indulging his father that way.

"The drive home was fine. The roads were clear and dry. Dad knew where we were. He said stuff about the different towns. 'Your mother bought a dress there once.' Things like that. We got home, and I put on his game shows. I usually shower when he's watching those. He likes them so he doesn't get up and wander outside or start cooking."

My heart stuttered at what that told me about how closely he had to watch Dale, so his father didn't become a danger to himself or others.

"I walked across to my room, got dressed. I guess he heard me because he was in the hall when I came out. He was really scared. Wanted to know what I was doing in Zak's room."

I could see how bewildered Zak was. How hurt.

"The doctor warned us this was likely to happen at some point." He rubbed his face. "They said we shouldn't, you know, correct him or try to make him believe reality, but I couldn't help it. I said, 'I'm Zak.' He said no, Zak was out with his wife. And where was Zara? What had I done with Zara? He was really angry. Really upset. I thought he was going to hit me."

"Oh, Zak." I reached across to squeeze his hand. He gripped mine tight. I could feel him shaking.

"I tried to distract him," he continued in a hollow voice. "I asked what he wanted for dinner. I just wanted him to accept that it was okay I was there, but he was so scared. Of *me*." He released my hand and used his thumbs to wipe both eyes again.

I unravelled a paper napkin from around a bundle of cutlery and offered it to him.

"Thanks." He pressed the napkin into each eye. "I couldn't stand there terrifying him."

"No," I murmured, heart breaking right along with his.

"I went over to the neighbour's, asked him to try calming him down. He's lived next door since Zara and I were little. Dad let him in, and I could hear Dad saying he wanted to call the police, that he'd had a break-in. I called Zara, and once she was there I just started walking."

"That sounds so upsetting." He looked so lost I wanted to slide around the booth, sit beside him, and hug him again, but our food arrived. I'd never been less hungry.

"I should text Zara, see how he's doing." Zak took out his phone.

"Of course." He tapped out his message, and a minute later his phone buzzed. He didn't talk long.

"Dad is calmer. She's going to stay the night with him," Zak relayed after he ended the call. "I'll sleep at her place. Tomorrow we'll get him to the doctor, but…" He shrugged. "There's nothing they can do. We already know that."

This situation was the absolute worst.

"Do you and Zara belong to any support groups?" I asked.

"We've talked about it, but I think we've been in denial about how bad it is. It went so fast. One day she said, 'I think Dad's becoming absent-minded,' then suddenly it was, 'Dad can't live alone.' What the hell do I do now?" He sat up straight and rubbed his face. "I can't live with him if he's afraid of me. What do we do? Put him in a home where nothing is familiar? Where no one cares—"

He stared at the back of the booth, clenching his eyes shut against fresh tears.

I thought again about moving to his side, but he picked up his burger. He looked like it took all his effort to chew and swallow.

"You don't have to eat it," I said gently.

"No, I'm hungry. I just…" He trailed off.

"This is the shittiest of shitty situations, Zak. I'm so sorry."

"It really fucking is."

The helplessness was killing me.

"Hey," I said, remembering something as I shook vinegar onto my fries. "I've been talking to a facilitator who specializes in senior well-being. I'm trying to organize some info sessions at the shop. I'm sure she'll know of some good groups for caregivers. Let me get the details for you, save you calling around."

"Thanks," he said, though his voice lacked enthusiasm.

I really wished there was more I could do.

After a minute, he asked, "Do you mean you want to host dementia caregiver therapy sessions in your shop? Next to the dildos?"

I absolutely did not, but I gave him my best look of wide-eyed innocence.

"Is it bad taste to invite burnt-out, emotionally distressed people into the shop under the guise of helping them so I can push sex toys on them?"

"Works for me. *As you well know.*"

A wave of happy-sad laughter hit me. I was glad to see him rallying toward humour, but I realized how much he used jokes to cover up genuine anguish—deep, rough, rocky emotional waters.

"We actually have enough space in our shop to hold meetings there," he mused. "God knows we have enough furniture." His gaze drifted into the middle distance, but the idea was a glimmer of movement out of his dark spiral, so I encouraged it.

"What I'm hearing is that you want to poach my workshop attendees and sell them your dusty old knick-knacks. Shameless."

"Never claimed to be any different."

We stuck to meaningless banter for the rest of the meal. I offered to drive him to Zara's after I paid.

"Thanks. And hey." He stopped me in the parking lot. "Thank you for this. I felt like I'd been hit by a truck when you found me."

"Now it's only one of those little two-seater cars?"

"Self-driving electric. No one at the wheel to blame, just a short-circuit somewhere. Bad luck."

"No kidding. But seriously, anytime."

"Thanks." His arms came up then faltered.

I moved in to hug his waist.

He folded his arms around me and held me tight and hard. Really hard. His chin rested against my hair. "I mean it, Meg. Thank you."

The sky was spitting on us, but he was warm and strong—and so shaken I had to rub his back, trying to soothe him. He could hold me as long as he needed. I only wished I could give more. Do more.

Oh, God. I really was in free fall, wasn't I?

He took an uneven breath, his chest rising under my ear, but he didn't let me go.

"I knew you would feel like this." His voice sounded different. Still unsteady, but for a different reason.

I ignored the way my blood turned to warm honey.

"How's that?" I lifted my face to look at him in the light from the bulb mounted on the side of the building.

"Good." His grin tugged sideways. "I think about you a lot. How it would feel to kiss you. Do other things." His brow lifted. "I thought maybe you should know that."

"That is very unexpected news, considering ninety percent of our conversations revolve around sex." I was trying hard not to let his words mean more than they did.

"Tell me you think about it too, so I know I'm not a degenerate."

"That ship has sailed, sir."

"Fair." Another sideways grin, this one fuller. More lighthearted.

We were still holding on to each other, pressed close, sharing amused smirks.

"I do think about you in certain ways," I admitted ruefully. "Ways that are not helpful when you're going through so much."

"Don't. That's not what this is."

I wrinkled my nose, pretty sure he was simply clinging to the nearest solid object—me—but I was okay with that, since his arms felt really good around me.

"I'm a grown adult and I'm sober. Mostly." He'd had a second beer. "I happen to be having a bad day. If you think letting me kiss you would be taking advantage of me, then lucky me. Have at it."

"Maybe today isn't the best day for me to do that, is all I'm saying."

"Hmph. But is it definitely possible that at some point you're going to use me like a ten-speed, hands-free, water-resistant vibrator?"

"Until I'm too weak to leave my bed."

"Swing," he corrected. "Let me have that one."

I adored him. "Do you think maybe we should get out of the rain?"

"Do you think maybe we should kiss? Just once? Just to see?"

"Once," I allowed. "For science." I immediately got all nervous and fluttery. My smile wouldn't relax.

He was grinning too. He dipped his head to brush his mouth at the corner of mine. The bristles of his beard grazed my chin. I liked it.

We both laughed, self-conscious, then pressed our lips together with more purpose.

The flood of sensations was incredible. We were both shivering and shuffled closer, warding off the cold. Speckles of rain dampened my face and the heat of our skin practically made the drops sizzle.

A rush of excitement struck as I realized I was finally kissing this man. I'd been waiting and waiting, and it was every bit as lovely as I'd hoped.

We found the right angle, the perfect fit, and settled into it. For those few moments, nothing else existed. My whole body felt like it glowed.

When the hiss of tires on wet pavement neared, we broke the kiss and caught our breath, suddenly aware of where we were.

I pulled all the way out of his arms and zipped my jacket up to my chin, freezing to death now that I wasn't snuggled up to him.

"That felt really good," he said.

"It did," I agreed. Way too good. Like, change-your-life-for-a-man good.

Been there, done that, and sent that worn-out old T-shirt to the rag bag. *Never again, Meg. Never again.*

"Where does your sister live?" I blipped my fob to light up my SUV.

CHAPTER THIRTY-FIVE

MEG

I didn't see Zak the next day, but he texted:

If anyone comes to the store [laughter emoji], tell them we'll be back tomorrow. Specialist with Dad.

I almost tagged his message with a heart but wondered if that was too Valentine-y after our kiss. Instead, I texted back:

If anyone comes to your store, I'll poach them the way I always do.

His response took long enough that I started to wonder if I'd been too flippant—especially considering he was still reeling from what had happened with Dale yesterday.

Then he texted:

I don't want a war, but I can compete if I have to.

He added a photo of something that looked like an old-fashioned egg-beater but with a phallus instead of beaters.

A hand-cranked vibrator? I pictured a man between a woman's thighs, rolling his wrist like he was landing a marlin, trying to get her off with that contraption, and laughed on and off for an hour.

Zak and Dale were back in the store on Saturday, but I didn't see Zak until Zara's husband, Kyle, was in my shop, taking measurements of the doorways and looking at other modifications to make the shop more accessible.

"The alcove entrance is the biggest stumbling block," Kyle said, pointing with his extended tape measure. "The most elegant solution is to push the doors out so they're even with the front windows. Then I could build a common ramp that leads into both shops. That's also a very spendy solution, even with the friends-and-family discount. The ZZ Twins are talking about selling the building if they need to put Dale in care. Dropping big reno money into this place won't necessarily get a better price, so…" When he noticed the arch in my eyebrow he added, "That's what everyone called them in high school."

"They're thinking of selling?" Oh no. "Because of the meeting with Dale's specialist yesterday?"

"They've actually been going back and forth on selling since Tammy died. Dale wanted to hang on to the shop out of nostalgia. They didn't fight him because it got him out of the house and kept him busy. For years, he did most of the work, but now…" He shrugged. "Zara has never wanted it. Zak might feel differently now that he's decided to stay, but—"

He had?

The bell resounded as Zak walked in holding an upside-down toddler. The kid had sandy blond hair and blue eyes like Kyle's.

"Dada!"

"Hey, champ. Is it time to get Lance to soccer already?" Kyle checked his phone.

"Not yet," Zak said. "But this kid is a tornado. At least nothing in here is breakable."

"Only my marriage if your sister finds out you brought him in here. I'm almost finished. Let me see what needs doing in the can." Kyle slipped into the bathroom and I could hear the metallic whisper of the tape measure.

"What do you think of this, Ollie?" Zak set the boy stomach-down on the sex swing. "That's fun, right?"

"That is every colour of wrong," I said with a pained wince.

"At least he's smart enough to use a spotter." Zak spun the swing, then stepped back so he wouldn't be struck by Oliver's kicking feet as it unwound.

I bit my lip, not letting him see he'd made me laugh.

"How did it go yesterday? How's it going today?" I asked.

"Today is fine. Yesterday was okay. When he got up, Dad asked Zara why she was there instead of me. We went to the specialist, and we're going to tour some facilities next week. If and when it comes to that, we'll at least know which one Dad liked. Some of them have day programs for caregiver respite, so we're going to try putting him in some of those, but it's fu—" His gaze flicked to the toddler. "Fundamentally brutal."

"I bet."

He probably didn't hear me. Oliver was yelling, "Ahhhhh!" as he slowly spun.

The toddler was cute and lively and all I could think was that there was not enough money in the world to make me start having kids again. I wasn't ready for Shelby *or* Rod to turn me into a grandmother yet, either.

"Okay, champ, we gotta go." Kyle came out of the bathroom. "Say bye to Uncle Zak and Ms. Meg."

"No." Oliver clenched his fists in the straps of the swing and kicked against the floor.

Amateurs. "Oliver, come see this toy I have for you." I moved to the desk.

"Um..." Kyle cringed with worry.

"Relax," I assured him. I found a fuzzy chick Mom had set aside for the Easter display she was planning. I hid it in the cup of my hands. "Come see," I crouched down. "You can take this with you, if you want to."

Oliver ran straight at me. I braced myself for impact, but he braked in time. I made a big deal of slowly revealing it in my cupped hands.

"Why don't you show your grandpa? Be gentle. It's just a baby." I carefully transferred it into his cupped hands.

He was so enthralled, he hardly noticed as Kyle scooped him up. "Thanks."

"Impressive." Zak held the door for them but hung back as they crossed into the antique shop. "Once Lance sees Ollie got a toy from here, though…"

"Can open, worms everywhere." I plucked out a chick for the older boy.

"And Jade." Zak kept his hand out.

"Good grief, Mom will charge me." I forked over the last chick.

"What are you doing this weekend?" he asked, still holding the door.

The way his gaze flickered over me with speculation lit all sorts of unruly sparks of thought.

"I'm bringing Roddie to you so you can help him refinish his dresser."

"Right. I didn't forget. I was testing you." He winced. He had definitely forgotten.

"After I take him home, I have to come back here to host a workshop. Perimenopause. Uterus owners only. Shelby should be at Mom's by the time I get home from that."

I tried to contain my excitement, but it was radiating from my smile. I couldn't wait to spend time with my kids.

"That's cool. You gonna bring her in here? Will I meet her?" He nodded toward the store.

"It's spring break. She'll be here all week, so yeah, I imagine she'll want to see it."

I glanced over my shoulder, suddenly apprehensive.

There was no good reason for me to be nervous. I wholeheartedly supported my daughter having complete agency over her sexuality. I'd told her how tampons worked and how to avoid STIs. This was just another angle on that same topic, but…

Whatever expression was on my face made Zak chuckle.

"Uncle Zak—" The door to Twice Is Nice opened with its typical squeak and chime.

"And there he is. Talk to you later." Zak slipped out to head off the eight-year-old before the boy could barge into this den of iniquity.

CHAPTER THIRTY-SIX

MEG

Shelby stayed an extra night in Kelowna. She'd made it there safely on Friday night but wanted to hang out with her friend until Sunday.

What could I say? She was an adult. I swallowed my disappointment and texted her to let me know when she was on the road again, adding, *Drive safe.*

Roddie was up early Sunday morning, planning to play video games online with friends in Toronto. Mom was having lunch with an old neighbour who happened to be in town. I should have cleaned the garage, but I only washed my sheets, hid my sex toys since Shelby would be sleeping with me, then ran out to see Georgia.

Her recovery was coming along well. She'd started physiotherapy, but she was working so hard to get back to full strength, she didn't have much pep left after her exercises.

"You want me to leave so you can nap?" I asked when she yawned yet again.

"Do you mind? I still nap a lot, but less resentfully. It's not the drugs making me sleepy, it's healing and that's okay. Oh, hey, take these back to the store before one of Gail's kids gets into them."

"Gail doesn't want any?" I asked, taking the bag of sample toys I'd left a couple of weeks ago.

"She says her husband gives her all she needs." She shrugged. "I kept the one I opened and put a list in there of the ones I think you should stock. Try some yourself. See what you think."

"I might."

"You should."

"I have," I confessed.

"Yeah?" That caught her attention. "Like what?"

I told her which toys I'd brought home.

"That's a good start. See if your daughter wants any of these." She motioned toward the bag.

"I'll give Mom first dibs." I wasn't being facetious. "She hasn't let me pay her for the work she's done. She's earned a few perks."

"Sure." She spoke around another yawn.

"I'll let you sleep." I said goodbye and went out to my car. Shelby was probably on the road and getting close to the ferry, but still a few hours away. Mom was out. Roddie was busy.

I looked at the bag of goodies and had a sudden, outrageous idea. I scrolled for Zak's number and placed the call as I backed out of Gail's driveway.

"Joe's Rescue Service." His voice filled the interior of my vehicle. "What is the nature of your emergency?"

"Treed cougar. This is actually pre-emptive. I was thinking about getting stuck in the Dogwood. That's the motel on Seventeen, halfway to Sidney. I have a bag full of toys and a couple of hours to kill if—"

"I'll be right there."

"Wait what about—"

He had already ended the call.

CHAPTER THIRTY-SEVEN

MEG

I had second thoughts. Then third and fourth. But I pulled into the parking lot of the Dogwood and was relieved to see the budget motel had been updated in recent years. It wasn't a total dive.

Zak came out of the lobby and veered toward my SUV. I lowered the passenger window.

"Lucky number seven." He pointed and moved onto the walkway so he was at the door when I nosed into the spot in front of our room. He opened my car door and took the bag I handed him. "I didn't bring wine or anything. I did bring condoms, if that's something you're interested in knowing."

"I'm very interested in that information." I stepped onto the pavement, my heart beating intensely.

He kept me hemmed in at the V of the door.

"Are you waiting for a kiss?" I asked, feeling as though I'd taken some of Georgia's meds and was slipping into a hallucinogenic state.

"I'm drinking in the moment." His gaze tracked all over my face, making me self-conscious enough to blush.

"I'm trying to hide my stark-raving panic," I joked. Kind of.

"Don't be nervous," he said gently. "I don't have any expectations beyond hanging out on a bed with you and looking at toys. Clothing optional."

"So you don't want a kiss? Because I do."

He dropped a brief kiss on my mouth, then said, "That tasted like another," and inched closer, one arm on the open door, the other sliding behind my waist to pull me into him.

We kissed properly, lips parted and hungry, tongues tangling, until a moan escaped my throat.

His eyelids were low and smug when he stepped back, giving me space to move by him before he closed the door. I locked it and followed him into the motel room, my heart still thudding.

I had all the same adolescent emotions as my eighteen-year-old self—excitement, worry that it wouldn't be as great as I hoped, insecurity, and a thrill at doing something I probably shouldn't. Also a stupid amount of happiness at just locking myself in a room with this funny, sexy, incredibly attractive man.

He glanced around as he took off his jacket.

I slipped off mine along with my shoes, ignoring the faint smell of air freshener. The room was clean and bright and had the basics—table, chair, television, alarm clock. Queen-sized bed.

"I was surprised you were able to get away on such short notice. Your dad isn't alone, is he?" I set my purse on the table.

"Kyle was at the house, putting chimes on all the doors. I told him I had a chance to get lucky and he agreed to stay on the condition that I take their kids next weekend, so he might have a chance at the same. Yes, I realize that's my sister we're talking about. These are battle conditions, Meg."

"Did he know you were meeting me?"

"I didn't mention your name, but he's not stupid." He set the bag in the middle of the bed and flopped onto his side beside it, propped up on an elbow. He gave the bag a poke. "What's in here?"

"Samples. But I've been dying to ask whether you liked my surprise."

I curled my leg under me as I sat on the other side of the mattress.

"The beads? I'm not sure." His shrug lacked enthusiasm.

"You didn't try them?"

"I did, in the shower. It was okay, but not as good as I'd hoped."

"Huh. I liked them."

"*You've* tried them?" He lifted his gaze from peering into the bag. "In the shower?"

"Doesn't the shower wash the lube off?"

"You're supposed to use lube?"

"I gave you lube. It was in the bag."

"I thought you were restocking me. Is it better with lube?"

"I haven't tried them without. You tell me."

"Homework *again*? There'll be nothing left of me." He tipped out the bag. "What's on the menu today?"

I explained how I'd gotten this as swag. We took turns reading the notes Georgia had stuck to each item.

Nice variety for penis owners. This company's chargers never work.

"You never played with toys with your husband?" he asked.

"I was afraid to have them in the house, in case we died and the kids had to go through our things. I didn't want to put them through something as traumatic as discovering their father's affinity for seventies porn."

"Your dad had good taste."

"He was a doctor. I'm pretty sure he was studying the anatomy."

"Sure." He grinned.

"Would you try a butt plug?" I showed him the box. It reminded me of tampons with its size chart printed on the side. This was the smallest one, made of blue silicone. It had a ring on its base for easy removal.

"I'd rather see it in you, but sure. I'll try it if you want me to."

"Really?" I didn't know what turned me on more—the lusty way he eyed the butt plug or his casual willingness to try anything. I only knew that wicked tingles of anticipation began swirling in my pelvis. "If—I don't know how to do this." My face was hot, my words coming out as half-chokes and giggles. "What do you want to *do*?"

"Today? Right now? With you? I am *very* open to suggestion." He lifted his brows.

"But, like, what's your fantasy?"

"This whole thing is doing it for me." He gestured to the littered toys between us. "Meeting you in a hotel room, looking at toys, talking about putting one of them up your ass? This is fulfilling fantasy numbers six through eleventy-hundred. I'm already hard as a rock." He waved at his fly where a distinct bulge was pressing against denim.

I was blushing so hot my face hurt, but some of it was the ache in my cheeks from smiling and laughing.

"That seems like a lot of fantasies. How do you keep them all straight?"

"They're not straight. They're bent as hell, same as me." He removed a coupon for a UV sterilization box from a satin pouch meant to store sex toys. "I didn't know that about myself until I met you. You're a bad influence, Meg."

"You have no idea how long I've waited for someone to call me that." I fluttered my lashes as though I was about to cry, but I was genuinely flattered. "I think you're a bad influence, too."

His grin flashed, and his gaze dropped to the box I held. His expression grew more speculative.

"What—" I cleared my throat. "If I wore this, then what? Because I'm intrigued." I was wet already, just sitting here fondling toys on a bed with him. "But once it's there…" *In*. "Then what? We have sex? I can see how that's a new experience for me, but what does that do for you?"

"Is this a safe space, Meg?" He let all his humour fall away. "Because we talk about sex a lot, and we make a lot of jokes, and I love it. It's the most fun I've had in a long time. It's the kind of fun I need right now."

"But you don't want the doing of the sex?" I was more disappointed than relieved. "That's okay."

"No. I definitely want the doing. I really, really want the doing," he assured me with a steady look that I felt in the pit of my belly. "But it doesn't have to be bells and whistles. You can hold this in your *hand* while I fuck you. It would still be some of the hottest sex I've ever experienced."

"Yeah?" I was trying not to laugh. This *was* a safe space. And he'd just revealed that his level of experimentation was about as wide as my own. "Why don't you tell me what you want? If I don't like your idea, I'll say 'no thanks,' and we'll figure out something else."

"Okay." He bit the edge of his bottom lip, studying me. Then he said, "I want to put that up your ass so I can put my finger through the ring and force you to stay still while I eat you. After you come, I want to fuck you while it's still inside you. Maybe turn you over so I can see it while we're fucking."

A punch of nervous, helpless, eager lust contracted every muscle from my navel down to my knees. I swallowed—kind of intimidated, but also turned on by how direct he'd been.

"I went too far, didn't I?"

"No," I said weakly. My pussy was clenching with eagerness. I swore my clit was standing up like an erect penis. My labia felt heavy and hot. I was so wet, I was starting to worry I would seep through my jeans.

I couldn't hold his gaze, so I picked at the top of the box, trying to find the edge of the cellophane that wrapped it. The packaging was tricky, with hidden seals and a blister pack inside, offering plenty of time for second thoughts.

"I should warn you that I've never been with anyone except Joel."

"Is that why you're so nervous?"

"Do I seem nervous?" I let my voice go high with exaggerated anxiety.

He didn't laugh. He looked at me all gentle and tender, making me feel like a virgin all over again.

"I thought about, you know, finding someone online to break the seal." I finally got the cellophane off with a crinkle. "But I don't want a stranger to see my forty-year-old fanny."

"You're not forty."

"Almost. And you're only thirty-two, aren't you? I didn't know I was into age-gap kink, but—"

"For God's sake, if you can't open that, give it to me. There's teasing, and then there's teasing, Meg. This is not the good kind."

"I've got it." I freed it from its clamshell of plastic and took it to the bathroom to wash it, discovering I was shaking with nerves.

While I was in there, I gave myself a wash. I'd finally gotten around to getting a wax, hoping something like this would happen, but now I was wondering if I was really going through with it. I could say no if I chickened out. I knew I could. We could have straight vanilla sex or just neck for a while. Zak wouldn't make me do anything I didn't want to.

But I really wanted this. I wanted sex, and him, and yes, a little adventure. I wanted to know how it felt to have sex while my butt was full, and I really, really wanted to know how his cock fit inside me.

Even so, I was anxious. Horny-worried. My stomach was in knots.

I brought a towel when I came back, knowing we'd use a lot of lube.

Zak had closed the drapes and turned on a lamp. He'd shoved everything back into the bag except the lube and a strip of condoms. I set the toy on the night table beside them and accepted the invitation of his arms, lying half over him on the bed.

"What about you?" I asked.

"What about me?" He twisted so I was beside him on the mattress. Our legs laced together.

"How many have you been with?"

"Women?"

"Partners. I don't judge."

"You judge," he accused with good humour.

"Not about that."

"You'll be..." He looked across the room, calculating. "Number six."

"Really?" I asked skeptically.

"I thought you didn't judge?"

"You're a good-looking guy. I thought you'd be a chick magnet."

"I am *such* a babe magnet," he pronounced with deadpan irony. "Is this the kind of foreplay your ex enjoyed? Because I have notes if you want to give me his number."

"I want to know what I'm up against."

"Me." He rolled closer, shifting his hand to my lower back as he dragged me tighter to his warm body. I felt his erection against my abdomen.

"But you might compare me to someone in your vast experience," I complained.

"Let it go." He shifted down the bed so the ridge of his cock was against the seam of my jeans between my thighs. "I'm here with you and I find you very attractive."

"Were any of them funny? Those other women?"

"Every single one."

"You *bastard*. You knew that would hurt me."

He chuckled and rolled me beneath him.

"They weren't *as* funny," he assured me. "And not a single one of them ever brought me a butt plug." His lips nuzzled into my neck. "None got herself off behind a door, leaving me to think about that for days and days and days." His breath bathed my ear. "I think about it all the time, Meg. I'm going to need to see that today. I hope you don't mind." He slid his hand between us to possessively cup my mound.

I whimpered, going molten under the weight of his touch. I searched for his nibbling lips with my own.

We both groaned as we kissed the way we'd been building up to—wet and uninhibited, with suction and lots of tongue, deeply involved. I liked how he kissed: hungry and demanding, like I was something he wanted to devour. It turned me on, along with the weight of him half on me and the way he smelled of wood and wind and laundry soap. I liked how his hand rubbed between my thighs, then roamed up and down my side, getting to know my shape while I learned the planes of his back, the shallow valley of his spine, the bristles at the nape of his neck, and the strength of his shoulders.

We started to loosen clothing. I got my hands under his shirt and explored his chest, finding a light mat of hair and his pebbled nipples.

He lifted his head and looked at me through slitted eyes. His hand popped the button on my jeans, then slid the zipper down.

"Too fast?" he asked.

I shook my head. "It's cold. Maybe we should undress and get under the covers."

It wasn't that cold. I was actually very hot, but we rolled away and pulled our clothes off. My nipples stung as they tightened under his appreciative glance. I took in an eyeful of his nude form—winter-pale but neatly muscled. His cock stood out proudly from a tidy shave.

I self-consciously slid under the blankets.

"I suggest you pace yourself on your shyness," he teased, joining me beneath the sheets. Our cool skin brushed and warmed, and we kissed again.

This time, when our hands cruised and searched, it was against bare skin, making it that much more powerful. More pleasurable.

"This feels really good, Meg." He pushed his elbows into the mattress on either side of me, surging so his body slid along mine. The damp tip of his erection painted my upper thigh, then my stomach. "Better than I imagined."

"It does," I agreed, taking hold of his cock, fondling and exploring the heft of him, the textures of his shaft and the velvety tip. When I closed my hand around him, he pumped into my fist, eyes closed.

"I'm not going to last if you keep doing that," he said shakily, pulling from my grip. He guided my hand between my own thighs. "Show me."

I might have hesitated if I hadn't been so horny. He had the gall to shift away, throw the covers back, and push my leg open so he could see better. But I wanted to turn him on as much as I wanted to ease the ache building inside me. I toyed between my lips, gathering and spreading my juices, then slowly and deliberately penetrated myself with a finger, watching his intent expression as I did.

He stuck his finger in his mouth, wetting it, then pushed it in with mine, covering my hand and trapping it tight against my body. He swept his head down to kiss me, deep and messy. Our hands could barely move. I was full, very aware of his finger inside me alongside mine, causing that extra stretch, sparking renewed flushes of wetness that made the shifting of our fingers slippery and delicious.

Slowly, he eased his finger out of me and drew wet circles around each of my nipples, then tasted them with sloppy, wet sounds. When his eyes met mine, my hand was still over my pussy, my fingers half inside me. I felt drunk with lust.

"Are you ready for some ass play?" he asked in a deep, sexy voice.

I nodded. I really was.

He rolled away for the lube and plug, then shifted to a spot farther down the bed.

"I'd empty this all over you, but I want to taste you when I go down on you." He squeezed a generous line of lube onto the plug like toothpaste onto a brush, then spread it to coat the silicone. He set the cool tube of lube on my belly, startling me into sucking in my stomach. I was so distracted by that, I didn't protest when he folded my thigh up against my boob, exposing my ass and pussy.

"Play with yourself again," he said.

I did, running two fingertips on either side of my clit while he teased my taint and asshole with the slippery tip of the butt plug. I appreciated that he wasn't just jamming it in. He rimmed and rolled, giving light presses, each time with a little more insistence.

I was growing goopy around my asshole while my pussy didn't know whether to clench or relax and let this happen.

"I should've fingered you here first." The tip pressed a little more insistently against my hole. He rubbed lube around and around my sphincter, relaxing it with gentle pulses of the plug, easing it deeper and deeper. "You think you'd ever want my cock in your ass, Meg?"

The plug was pushing and pinching, making me start to think it was too much. Too big. As I drew a breath to say so, the stretch stopped. Relief washed over me as the ring of my asshole pursed around the narrow neck of the plug. The sensation inside me was dark and foreign and taboo. Filthy in the best possible way.

"Okay?" he asked, tracing and soothing where the plug was inserted. The motion tapped and twisted the ring, sending erotic vibrations through my pelvis.

"It feels really good," I breathed, rolling my fingertip across my swollen clit. When I clenched internally, I felt the firmness of the butt plug. Orgasm hovered, threatening to break.

"This is really fucking hot, Meg." He caught my hand, lifting it off my spread, pulsing pussy lips. "But this is mine now. You can rub your nipples if you want to, but I get this."

He stole a pillow and slid off the bed to kneel on it. Then he dragged my hips into position and pushed my thigh back up to my chest, leaving his hand behind my knee to hold it there. The butt plug shifted inside me as he worked his finger into the ring on its base.

I wanted that finger inside my pussy like I'd never wanted anything else, but this was exciting, too. When the back of his hand was flush against the bottom of my buttocks, I tested how much I could move. There wasn't pain, exactly. More like a zing of intense sensation that made my pussy flood with need.

"This is my best day ever, Meg. I hope you know that." The pad of his thumb rubbed against my taint, teasing my vagina. He dropped his head and lazily ran his tongue into the furrows of my inner lips, taking his time as he got to know every nook and fold.

Each time I started to wiggle in impatience or encouragement, that weight inside me shifted, and my sensitized anus stung against the protruding shape. My pussy clenched, and I nearly died of yearning.

"Fuck, Zak," I moaned, wanting to move, wanting to come, wanting to ride his face and feel his cock inside me. "Suck my clit. *Please.*"

He groaned and tongued my hole, making me squirm and take those delightfully soft stabs in my ass before he finally worked his way to my clit.

That's when I understood nuclear fusion. Points of pleasure folded in upon themselves like molecules being compressed into too small a space. It became impossible to contain the intensity. The power.

I said things I couldn't hear. I was trying not to move, but I was moving enough to make the plug shift in small thrusts. I was so wet. So tense. So ready and so close.

Then he sucked on my clit, and the explosion happened.

I think I screamed. I know my thighs clamped onto his head. It was too much. Too good. Contractions struck like gongs inside me, emanating huge waves of pleasure. It went on for a really long time, almost a punishment, but so fucking *good.*

He hugged my thighs and sucked my clit, and I had another quick little orgasm before the waves finally began to fade.

When I was spent and my thighs weakly fell open, he rose and went to the bathroom to wash his face. He returned, picked up a condom, and rolled it on, watching me as he did.

"I don't know if I can wait for you to come again," he said, his voice thick with lust. "I can barely touch myself right now."

I liked hearing that. I wanted to ride his hips and come again, but I didn't think I had the energy.

Instead, I let him roll me onto my stomach over a pillow and groaned as I welcomed the slide of his heavy cock into my aching, needy pussy. The plug made the penetration feel different. The angle was new and every part of my insides were being touched.

Maybe it was just him.

"Oh, fuck," Zak said, gripping my hips and giving a testing stroke. "Okay, Meg? Because—" He groaned and thrust a little harder.

I'd been afraid I'd feel the silicone of the ring—that it might hurt. But it was soft enough that the ring collapsed between us as he moved, so I was only vaguely aware of it. Mostly, I was caught in a vise of electric sensations. Currents ran through me as his cock slid in and out, his hips retreating and slamming into my ass.

I pushed up onto my arms, holding still for the impact, moaning out my ecstasy as every single nerve ending in my pelvis sang.

"Oh, fuck, Meg."

"Don't stop," I begged. His hard thrusts were pushing me toward the edge at breakneck speed. "I'm going to come. Don't stop. I am. I am. Oh, God—"

Orgasm struck, and he was only two strokes behind me. He clamped one hand on my hip, the other on my shoulder, and held himself deep and hard inside me, throbbing powerfully while his ragged shouts were probably heard all the way across town.

CHAPTER THIRTY-EIGHT

ZAK

We showered together, and Meg washed the plug while we were in there. We didn't talk much, but we used a lot of soap on each other and necked a lot. I couldn't keep my hands or mouth off her.

Afterward, as we dressed, I asked if she wanted to get a drink.

"Yes," she said in a voice that held a very large but. "But Shelby will be here soon."

She was excited to see her. I already knew that. I had my own family to get back to.

I really wanted to stay in this room with her, though. Possibly forever.

She picked up the gift bag and dropped the lube into it, looking pensive.

"Regret?" I asked, bracing myself.

"Not at all."

I was in the chair, tying my sneakers, but looped an arm out to pull her into my lap, needing to hold her a little longer.

"Thank you for this," I said. "It was amazing."

"It was." She petted my beard, her eyes level with mine, wearing the same smug, sex-baked glow I probably had.

"Would you do it again?" I asked.

"The butt plug? Or you?" God, her smile was pretty.

"Both."

Her lips parted. I expected something light and witty, maybe a bit snarky, but her expression turned serious. She kept petting my beard, and my stomach dropped into my untied shoes.

"I like you, Zak. I'd definitely keep meeting you like this, with or without the toys, but… I don't know." Her gaze flicked from my eyes to my mouth and back. "We should be careful. You need a distraction, and I'm okay being that because I'm not looking for anything serious either. I'm going back to Toronto when Georgia is better. You know that, right?"

I stopped massaging her waist, resting my hand on her thigh. I nodded. I did know. I just didn't like it.

"Do you feel differently about what this is?" she asked, dipping her head to make eye contact.

I tried to avoid her gaze. I didn't want her to see how disappointed I was.

"I don't know. No, you're right." I drew a hot, dry breath—like desert air, all heat and grit. "In some ways, I'm numb and just going through the motions. When I'm with you, I quit thinking about all the hard stuff. I feel happy. I like you, too." So much. A dangerous amount. "I'm not using you, Meg. I hope I'm not using you."

Was I?

No. I liked her. Genuinely. She was funny, honest, and had a generous heart.

A really big heart.

I swore, suddenly exhausted. The full weight of Dad's condition settled across my shoulders, but it was mine to carry, not hers.

"Am I using you?" I asked, pretty sure I was and hating myself for it.

"Maybe a little. But it's okay. It really is." She curled her arm around my neck and kissed the corner of my mouth. "I consent to being someone you talk to about sex and sometimes kiss and force mind-bending orgasms out of."

I winced. It sounded very one-sided. "You don't want more for yourself than that?"

"What I've got right now is pretty freaking great. I just made you wait to come until I got dessert."

"You did." The sheer glory of eating her until her thighs threatened to crack my skull rushed back. When I was inside her, I came so hard my balls still felt inside out. "I could seriously die happy right now. You know that?"

Her lashes cut down to a saucy angle. "You're welcome."

I kissed her grin, and we lingered a little longer before parting with a casual promise to "see you Monday."

But I sat in my car an extra minute after she drove away, thinking, *Am I using her?*

No. I wanted more with her. The problem was, my life didn't have any room in it for dating, living together, or planning a future. It didn't matter what I wanted. I couldn't have it.

I couldn't have her.

So it was good that she was fine with keeping it casual.

It just didn't feel good to me. Not at all.

CHAPTER THIRTY-NINE

MEG

Shelby was there when I came in the door.

"Finally!" She got up from the kitchen table to hug me.

I closed my eyes as I wrapped my arms around her, drinking in the feel of her. She was no longer a midge, but a fully grown woman with blue hair and a new eyebrow piercing. She'd gotten a stud in her nose back in high school, much to Joel's disgust. He didn't know about the navel ring she'd gotten with some of her graduation money. For all I knew, she had even more private places pierced.

"Is Georgia all right? You've been gone all day." Mom was tossing a salad, and the kitchen smelled like she'd already put the scalloped potatoes in the oven. "Did you wash your face? I thought you were wearing makeup this morning." She gave me a penetrating look that said, *I know you've been up to something.*

Only letting myself turn into teenage Meg, the one who let a boy dominate her world to the detriment of her own priorities. That's all.

"You were already gone when I left," I reminded her, instead of lying outright about showering with Zak. "Georgia is recovering well, but she got tired and kicked me out so I met up with Zak." I mumbled that detail into my purse as I made a point of stowing my keys.

"Did something happen with Dale again?"

"No. Just offering a friendly ear." I poured myself a glass of wine.

"The antique guy?" Shelby slipped back into her seat at the table, sipping from her own glass of pinot gris.

"Mom's boyfriend," Roddie said out of the side of his mouth. He was drinking something blue that was pure sugar and caffeine, making it a toss-up as to which one of them was stunting their growth.

"Really?" Shelby's curiosity sharpened.

"We're just friends," I insisted into the refrigerator.

"It's okay, you know. If you have a boyfriend," Shelby said. "I mean, Dad's got Wanda and Freddie. We're not going to freak out if you go on a date."

"Funny. I just said the same thing to *my* mother the other day." It was a deliberate deflection, and it worked.

"Grandma! Are you dating?" Shelby asked. "Are you on any apps?"

"I am not meeting a man online." Mom brought the salad to the table. "If I want a romantic prospect, I'll put an ad in the paper, the way my father did when he thought it was time I found a husband."

"Really?" Roddie started to giggle, very tickled by that.

"Of course not," Mom said with exasperation. "I met your grandfather when I started working for him. I wasn't even living at home. I'd been to college and was sharing an apartment with a fellow student from my office administration course. We were hot commodities because we had learned how to use a *computer*."

"Oooh," we all sing-songed while Mom buried her self-deprecating smirk against the rim of her wineglass.

"Turn it off and turn it on again," Mom said pithily. "That's all you needed to know back then."

"If you're such a computer pioneer, why are you afraid to use one for dating?" Shelby prodded. "There are sites for seniors." She picked up her phone.

"Careful. You might find Mom on one," Rod joked.

"Ouch." I bent to hook my arm around his neck in a loose headlock and made kissy noises against his hair until he shrugged me off.

"How's Weston?" I asked Shelby. "Since we're talking about dating."

"Good." She set aside her phone. "That's actually why I stayed an extra day in Kelowna."

"He's the friend in Kelowna?"

"Yeah." She wrinkled her nose. "He has family there, and his parents were coming to visit. He wanted me to meet them. He would have come here to meet you, but they were there for a funeral. I said he could come back to Toronto with me for the summer and meet all of you there."

I'd bought a condo with a bedroom and a den so I could have both kids over, but I had a moment of, *Do I want that*? It wasn't about Shelby having a boyfriend or sleeping with him under my roof. I knew when she'd become sexually active and with whom because she'd asked me to take her to the clinic for birth control before they did it. It had been distressing, because I'd had to reckon with the fact that she was growing up and making decisions about her own body, but also comforting, because she'd been willing to talk to me about it. I had always struggled—I still struggled—to talk about sex with my own mother. She had gotten pregnant, and that had been wrong, according to her mother. Thus, when I got pregnant the first time, outside the sanctity of marriage, that was also wrong.

We were both still trying to compensate for that, which was silly because, come on. How was Shelby a mistake? How was I?

No, this moment of hesitation was about Toronto. About going back to where I didn't even have a job anymore.

"What about you?" Shelby was asking Rod. "Are there any cute guys at your new school?"

"Mmm." His mouth squinched up toward his nose, but I suspected it was more reluctance to talk about it than dissatisfaction with the options.

"We are collectively setting back feminism by a hundred years, talking about our 'prospects,'" I pointed out as I peeked at the scalloped potatoes to see if it was time to start cooking the steaks, both beef and cauliflower.

"Yeah, but talking about boys is fun," Shelby said. "Or it would be, if you three found yourself some prospects to talk about. What else are we going to talk about? School?"

"Let's talk about helping Grandma with Grandpa's things," I suggested. "You kids have to tell Grandma if there are things you want, but you can also take stuff to the second-hand store and maybe sell Dad's fishing gear online. I'll buy you a day at the ski hill," I added, sweetening the deal.

"You don't have to bribe us, Mom. But thanks. We accept." Shelby sent a bright smile to Rod.

"The ski hill is closed for the season," Roddie informed her. "You walked right into that one. Good job."

Shelby made a face at me while Mom sighed wearily.

"Don't you want to come live with us in Toronto, Grandma?" Shelby asked.

"*You* don't live there," Mom pointed out.

"Not right now, but I will. Everyone else is there." She shrugged.

"Roddie will leave in a few years. Then it'll be me and your mother in a place I don't know. At least I have friends here. And your mother has suggested I start a window display service. What would I do? Pack up my whole craft room and ship it across the country to start fresh there? I don't know. It sounds too complicated."

"Are you thinking seriously about that, Mom?" I asked her.

"Were you not serious when you suggested it?"

"I was," I assured her.

"Grandma's been doing the displays at the sex shop. They're actually pretty funny. In a good way," Roddie told Shelby. "I was in the coffee shop across the street and some people came in laughing about it, but it made some other people walk over to see it, so you're good at it, Grandma."

"Sex gets everyone's attention. I don't know that I'd be as successful with a clothing store. But I do keep wondering what I'll do with my time once you've gone home. I can't keep rattling around this house, but…

I suppose that's why women my age remarry, so they have someone to look after and don't have to think about how empty their life is."

Oof. "Mom. If you want something to fix up, this house is begging for it."

"Yeah, Grandma. Start with looking after yourself. See? Feminism is alive and well here," Shelby said.

"Then why isn't Roddie doing the cooking?" I asked.

"Because you never let us in the kitchen! I'll barbecue if you want me to," he said.

I really was my mother. I peered outside. The rain had stopped.

"Fine. Go fire it up."

CHAPTER FORTY

MEG

When I left for the shop on Monday morning, Mom was letting Shelby load Dad's clothes into her car so she could take them to a thrift store in Langford. It was a "good" one, Mom had said.

It was bittersweet. It was a big step for Mom. I was glad Shelby was there as an extra emotional cushion, and to allow me more time to focus on running the business. I pushed down the guilt I felt leaving the wrangling of Mom to my kids and headed to work.

The workshop strategy had been effective; two women from the perimenopause meeting on Saturday came in, looking for lube. One stuck around to browse the books and ended up adding one to her purchases.

I finally heard back from my contact on senior sexuality, too. They had some names and numbers for caregiver support groups. I forwarded some details to Zak and reached out to one that also offered grief support, thinking Mom might find it helpful.

Coffee? Zak texted when it was getting close to lunch.

And split a sandwich? I replied.

He sent a thumbs-up.

I watched him come back across the street a few minutes later with a tray of four cups and a takeout bag. He went into Twice Is Nice first, which made me curious.

"Zara's here with my aunt," he said when he came into my shop. "Dad's sister. She hasn't seen him in months and needs to know what we're up against. Zara kicked me out for the afternoon. Told me to take a hike, literally, but I thought I'd come say hi first. Hi." He dropped a kiss on me that was light but lingered like the finish of a good wine.

"Hi."

"Any chance you can take a hike with me?"

"I prefer rappelling, as you know. Missed opportunity. You're losing your touch."

"Low blood sugar," was his excuse. "I got you your own sandwich. I'm hungry enough for a whole one." He sat down on the stool and started to unwrap his turkey with cranberry. His phone dinged. He glanced at it. "Your kid is killing me today."

"Which one?"

"Right. That's another reason I wanted to see you. I was hoping to meet your daughter." He scrolled his screen. "Rod has been texting all day. He asked if he could play the dead-grandfather card when selling your dad's things? I said, of course."

"Of course," I agreed wryly.

"He sent me some photos, and I gave him some ballpark prices to ask." His thumb moved across the screen. "Then we punched up his pitch. 'After losing her husband of forty years, Grandma had to let go of Grandpa's favourite gear. He loved to fish on his days off. He always had the biggest fish stories, like the time he caught one that was being eaten by another.'"

"That one's true. At least, it's true that Dad told that story every chance he got. Maybe it *was* a fish tale."

"Doesn't matter. That's not even the good part." Zak continued quoting. "'I miss Grandpa every day and really want his rods and flies to go to someone who will love them as much as he did. I don't know how much to ask, but maybe two hundred for each rod and another hundred for the box of flies?'"

"What are they worth?"

"Not that. *Maybe* four hundred for the works. I bet he gets at least six. Kid's a natural. He wanted to post all your dad's tools, but I sent Kyle over. Apprentices are always breaking or losing their own. He likes to have spares on hand."

"Thanks, big guy. That's a huge help."

He shrugged it off. "I dread the day we have to do that with Dad's stuff. His house is still full of Mom's things. I keep thinking I should start sorting through it, but—"

"Zak. You're doing enough."

He bit into his sandwich and chewed, nodding, but he seemed glum.

"Hey. I could have started on the garage at Mom's yesterday. I played hooky with you instead. I don't feel guilty. It's okay to take time for self-care."

"Is that what we're calling it?" His expression brightened. "When can we self-care again?"

"I don't know. The shop is pretty quiet. I could put a note on the door." I was only half-joking.

"Yeah?" He started to shove his sandwich back into its paper bag and stood. "Can we try the swing?"

"That is a suspension bridge too far," I said with a chuckle. "But I like your enthusiasm." I found a pad of sticky notes and wrote, "Back in five."

"Also, given your history, we could wind up having to call the fire department." He crowded me against the desk. His hand found my waist. "Maybe we should pre-order the jaws of life."

There was a flicker of light at the window. I glanced over to see Shelby cupping her face against the glass to look at the display.

"Oh." Guilt dropped into my belly like a stone. I stepped away from Zak. "Good news. Shelby's here."

"Oh." His mouth kicked sideways in a rueful grin. "Is this going to be awk—"

The door opened. "Mom?"

"Hi," I said in a voice that was an octave too cheerful.

"Thanks for this," Zak said as he whipped the sticky note off the pad. "I'll call them later." He folded it and stuck it in his shirt pocket, then thrust out his hand to Shelby. "Judging from the resemblance to Meg and Vickie, you must be Shelby. I'm Zak."

"Hi." She gave him a thorough, curious look, her gaze flickering between us as she read the undercurrents. "I was going to ask if you wanted me to get you a sandwich, but it looks like you have one."

"I do. Want to share?" I reached for the bag I hadn't yet touched. "Zak was telling me he's helping Roddie sell Grandpa's fishing gear by brazenly tugging on heartstrings."

"Cast a line and reel 'em in." Zak threw an imaginary line into water and rolled his wrist.

"Grandma finally called that guy who gave her his number for Grandpa's car."

"Really?" My eyebrows nearly escaped my forehead.

"She said three cars in the driveway looks like she's running a hostel. She wants to park in the garage. Also, I found some boxes of taxes and stuff that are from before I was born. I said I'd take those to the shredder."

"You're a lifesaver." I gave her half my sandwich and pointed at the stool.

Shelby made herself comfortable and turned her attention to Zak. "Roddie said you live in Vancouver?"

"I've been there since I left for BCIT, yeah." He didn't so much as blink at the fact he was facing an interrogation. "My dad and sister are here, though, so Victoria has always felt like home."

"Zak is a tech bro," I stage-whispered.

"I prefer 'brogrammer,'" Zak said with a mock look of insult.

"Meaning you're used to being surrounded by dicks? Is that why this isn't weird for you?" Shelby nodded at the shelf of dildos and vibrators next to where he stood.

Zak snapped a look at me. "I like her. Which doesn't surprise me." He took a bite of his sandwich and motioned while he chewed and swallowed. "Roddie cracks me up. He said he wants to hide in the wardrobe so the next time Dad runs his magician spiel on a customer, he can pop out and claim he's the magician and that he's been stuck in there for years. Best coming-out story ever, he said."

"Oh, Rod." I couldn't help laughing while Shelby covered her mouth so she wouldn't lose the bite of sandwich she'd just taken.

Zak finished his and chased it with a gulp of coffee. "I know I should offer to help take boxes to the shredder or whatever, but I think I'll go home for a nap, then—I don't know—get an oil change? I'm not sure what to do with a day off. I haven't had a real one in a long time."

"When I had a break from helping Mom with Dad, I used to drive out to Sooke and have lunch at the pub. It's long enough to clear your head, but close enough you can be back quickly if you have to."

"Maybe." He nodded. "Good to meet you, Shelby. I'm sure I'll see more of you later this week. If you guys need the van for anything…"

"We'll figure it out. Go," I insisted. "Take a break. You need it."

"Yeah. Going." He took his coffee and left.

Shelby turned wide eyes on me. "Rod told me he's hot, but he's *hot*."

"He's cute," I agreed, setting down my sandwich to flip the record that was playing.

"Cute? Mom. I saw you guys through the window. What's going on between you?"

"Nothing." That was a blatant lie, considering where Zak's face had been yesterday. "I like him, but we both have a lot going on. And he's too young for me."

"Oh, is he still in high school? Is that why he and Roddie are friends?"

"I mean life stages." I came back for my sandwich. "He'll want kids, and I am *not* starting over."

"Are you sure of that? Have you asked him?"

I thought of Zak's wistful what-if when he had talked about Roddie.

"Whether he does or doesn't isn't the point. We've both got a lot going on. I don't live here. Your dad is putting up with Roddie being here because it's only a semester and they've got a new baby. Eventually, he'll want Roddie living in the same city, if not in their house. I've already spent too much time here. If Roddie's in Toronto, I need to be there for him."

"Mom." A mix of perplexity and scoff flickered across her face.

"What?" I braced myself.

Her mouth opened, shut, then she gusted out a breath that meant she was giving up any attempt at being careful.

"Grandpa was sick. You had to be here. We know that. We came out and saw him and we know how awful and hard it was for Grandma. And for you." She waved emphatically at me. "We never thought, 'Oh, Mom's forgotten all about us.' Maybe you weren't there, but you always answered if we called. You checked in all the time and you always knew what was going on with us. You know who wasn't there? *Dad*."

I made a strangled noise, but Shelby wasn't finished.

"I mean, I love him and everything." She rolled her eyes. "He gives me money if I need it and says, 'Good job,' or whatever when I get an A. But Roddie and I don't talk to him about anything important. Roddie didn't want to come out to Dad at all. He thought if you were there it would be okay, but he also thought you had enough to deal with, so he put it off."

"I didn't know that." My heart sank. "Now I feel like shit for making him hold on to it."

"Same here," she said, surprising me. "I felt awful when I left for school because you were still helping Grandma and started going into work again, and Dad kept going away for his 'conferences.'" She put bunny ears around that word.

Yeah, I had known about Wanda before I really acknowledged that I knew.

"But you and Roddie told me to go, so I did. Then Wanda got pregnant, so Dad had to tell you about her and you left. Roddie stayed with Dad because of school and everything, but when I asked him why he came here to stay with you, he said, 'I honestly thought that if you and Mom weren't there, Dad would notice me and act like a parent, but he never will.' Dad's a complete dick to Wanda. He doesn't do anything for Freddie. So, like, we both want a relationship with our baby brother, but if Dad wants a relationship with us, he could start acting like it."

I ran my tongue over my teeth, considering how to react. I don't trash-talk Joel to our kids, but I don't lie to them, either. I wasn't prepared to defend him when he was reaping what he'd sown.

"Anyway, we know you're here for us," Shelby said, tone easing. "We've never felt like you weren't. So don't move back to Toronto because *Dad* expects it. Ask Roddie if that's what he wants. And, like, post a photo of you and Zak so Dad sees it. Preferably with that wall of dildos behind you. How do you work here every day, staring at those things?"

"They're like cans of soup."

"Size-wise or…?"

"You're dying to look around, aren't you? Go for it." I waved in invitation.

"I had to wait for your secret boyfriend to leave, didn't I?" She brushed past me and began to explore.

CHAPTER FORTY-ONE

MEG

Zak was not my boyfriend, but he was a good friend. He came over Saturday evening to help me set up the garage sale. He brought Dale, who settled into a visit with Mom on the back patio, since the weather had turned warm.

Roddie was in the shower, and Shelby had left Friday. She had a long drive and was picking up Weston along the way. She and Roddie had made a ton of progress this week. They had turned the divestiture of junk into a game with intricate rules and scoring values based on the speed of removal, the weight and volume of whatever was removed, and whether it resulted in a sale or a disposal cost.

Mom trounced them both when the guy who bought Dad's Corvette came to pick it up. He had hurried over, worried she would change her mind or, now that she had made up her mind, that she'd be so impatient to get rid of it she'd sell it to someone else.

She had taken us all to dinner on Thursday to see Pretty Please again because Shelby hadn't seen the show. It was even more fun the second time, thanks to a catastrophic wardrobe malfunction that stopped the performance.

While the dancers crowded around their colleague, one joked, "Is there a doctor in the house?"

Mom popped out of her seat and said, "I'm a doctor's wife. I can sew."

That put the whole place into hysterics.

Nina Rhinestone waved her forward. "Yes, Vickie. Come help suture this up."

Mom disappeared backstage, and the show went on. She returned twenty minutes later, wonder in her eyes. "You should see the racks of costumes. It's like the Oscars."

After that, she was determined to offer her notions and craft supplies to the cast of Pretty Please, but she also agreed to let me hold this garage sale to unload various disused household items.

"Thanks for helping," I said to Zak as he affixed bits of masking tape to everything and wrote fire-sale prices on them. "It's really nice of you."

"You think I'm being nice? No. I'll be here bright and early with my sister's monsters. I'm on uncle duty all day tomorrow."

"Oh." I bit back my smirk, recalling the deal Zak had struck with Kyle last weekend when we'd met at the Dogwood. "With your dad, too? That's a lot." Oliver seemed like a handful all by himself.

"Dad's going to a respite group at one of the care homes we're considering."

"Oh." I sobered and stopped picking at the roll of tape. "How do you feel about that?"

"I don't know. It seems like a nice enough place, but..." He shrugged, expression guarded. "We'll see how it goes."

"I completely forgot that you were taking the kids or I would have scheduled this differently so I could help you with them." Sunday was my only day off, and I wanted to keep things moving, now that Mom was on board.

"We'll be fine." He shrugged again, this time more easily. "We'll swing by here so they can buy something from your box of knickknacks, then we're going to the trampoline park, the arcade, and the bug zoo. They each got to pick one."

"You're a glutton for punishment, aren't you?"

"I've taken the older two before. They're pretty low maintenance.

I've never been out with Ollie, though. He's mostly potty trained, or so my sister claims." He frowned at my fingers, once again exploring the roll of tape. "Did you seriously lose the end *again*? Stick to your skill set." He took it from me.

"You say that like you know what my skill set is."

"I do, actually." He sent me a heated look as the tape gave a satisfying rasp. "Dirty talk." He held my gaze as he cut off a strip with his teeth. "Spirit of adventure. Ability to give clear direction." He was looking at me the way he had when he lifted a hand outside Room Seven and watched me drive away. Sexy. Pleased.

"What about the consummate way I jump double Dutch?" I asked, referring to the swing.

"See, it's not the store. You make everything sound filthy." He smoothed the tape across the back of my hand, then pulled the fine-tipped marker from behind his ear. He wrote *Priceless* on it.

"I feel like you're being sarcastic."

"I'm not." He crowded closer, head dipping. His hand splayed against my waist, inviting me to press up against him.

Damn, he felt good.

I slid my arms around his neck and offered my mouth for the kiss we both wanted. It was lazy and thorough, sending swirls of arousal through me. My ears were open to Roddie or Mom or Dale coming into the garage, but no one interrupted us. We kissed until we were breathless, then drew apart, looking at each other with amusement and hunger, and the memory of last weekend in our eyes—and with want for another hour of privacy and debauchery.

"I should get Dad home for his game shows," Zak said reluctantly.

I nodded, wistful. I wanted more time with him. A lot more time. That wasn't in the cards for us, though.

Zak turned up at nine a.m. on the dot the next morning, along with Zara's three kids and all the early birds swooping in for first crack at our sale items.

I hadn't met his niece, Jade, yet. She was five and I could tell right away she was the little mom of the group. She kept Ollie's attention as she showed him all the toys in the box while Roddie tried to sell Lance his PS3. Lance was only curious because it was older than he was.

"Might as well take it to the antique shop," Roddie said in a disgusted aside to Zak.

"Kids these days," Zak commiserated.

"Right? My sister and I were really excited to get the 3 for Christmas, even though we had asked for the 4. Grandma got this one because it was on sale."

"That must've stung." Zak's show of empathy was deeply facetious. I expected an *Oh, Muffin* to follow.

I didn't hear any more because I was being fleeced on the table lamps. When I turned around again, Zak had struck a deal with Roddie to spend the day with him and the kids.

"Do you mind, Mom? You and Grandma don't need me, do you?"

"Poacher," I huffed at Zak.

"He offered," Zak defended. "I'll bring dinner when we come back."

"Fine." I wasn't really mad. More like jealous. I asked Roddie, "Do you need money?"

"I got it," Zak assured me. Then he handed over a fistful of fives for the things the kids had picked out. "See you later."

"'Kay." I shoved the bills into the fanny pack I was wearing and lifted my head just in time for Zak to drop a kiss on my mouth.

He did it so absently that we both froze in surprise. So did Mom, Roddie, and even Lance. Everyone stared.

"Um…" Zak pushed his mouth to the side in an exaggerated wince.

"Go," I urged him, catching his arm and steering him toward his car.

Mom contained herself until they were gone and the rush had died down. Then she pulled her lawn chair even with mine on the driveway.

"What…?"

"I promise I won't get pregnant this time."

"But what is your plan?"

"We don't have a plan, Mom. We're friends who kiss sometimes.

I swear, the minute it's more than that"—and yes, it was already more than that—"you'll be the first to know."

Thankfully, a woman walking her dog stopped to browse. Mom got up to answer her question about whether the bread machine still worked. She showed her that the recipe book and all the parts were there.

We had a few more small rushes before Mom went into the house to make sandwiches. That's when Negasi pulled up.

"Hi!" I called from the table of books. They'd been browsed to death but hadn't diminished at all. "Mom told me you were coming to look at her craft supplies. Did you get my email?"

I'd put together a package with a rough business plan that Negasi could plug figures into to get an idea of the costs he faced, and included a list of grants and other types of funding beyond simply going to the bank.

"I did, and I want to talk more about it, but today…" Negasi opened his passenger door and waved like he was presenting a game show prize.

"Georgia!" I grinned and hurried forward, arriving in time to take Georgia's other hand as she reached out for assistance. "I was going to come see you later," I reminded her.

"I know, but—" Her grip was strong. She stood and looked around. "It feels good to see someone else's front yard for a change."

"You look great," I told her.

She snorted with skepticism, but she really did look a million times better. She wore baggy sweats, a hoodie, and a scarf over her hair, but she was out of pajamas, and her eyes were bright, no longer glassy with pain or medication.

"You should have told me you were going stir crazy. I would have come to get you."

"It was an impulse. I was texting with Negasi. He said he was coming to see Vickie. I was kind of joking when I said I wanted to come, but…" She looked to Negasi.

"She said you can drive her home?" he asked me.

"For sure. Mom's making lunch. I'll tell her to make a couple more sandwiches."

"Not for me, thanks," Negasi said. "I'm taking a meeting about bringing in unfinished suits from Asia."

"That's cool. Help me to that chair before you go," Georgia said, holding on to both of us. "I know I can walk it alone, but I swear, if I trip and cause myself a setback…"

Mom came out then with two plates and a wide smile of surprise.

"Georgia! It's good to see you!" She stooped to kiss her cheek, then insisted Georgia take her sandwich. "I'll make more while I'm inside with Negasi."

"Let me know if you need help with anything," I said before sitting down next to Georgia. "You really do look so much better."

"I feel better. I'm barely taking any painkillers, and the physio feels good instead of, you know, like it'll kill me. Why is your mom leaving crusts on my sandwich like she doesn't even know me?" She frowned at the plate in her lap.

We snickered and ate, faces turned up to the spring sun.

"I thought I'd see your boy. Is he not here?"

"Which boy?" I said with a significant flutter of my lashes.

"What do you mean by that? You got a fuck boi? Zak?"

"Maybe." I gave her some smug side-eye, then wrinkled my nose with indecision. "I don't know what he is, but he kissed me in front of Mom this morning before he took Roddie to help babysit his niece and nephews."

"Oh. He's acting like he's your *boy*."

"Yeah, a little." I set my elbow on the arm of my chair and cupped my chin, cycling through all of Zak's most appealing qualities. He called me priceless. He showed up to help without being asked. He took kids to fun places and offered to bring dinner.

Good grief, my bar was low if he was clearing it that easily.

"I really like him, but Mom's finally looking ready to make a shift. You're getting better, so you'll be back at the shop soon. That means I have to make some of my own decisions. I just don't know what the right decision is."

"Good God, woman. Just pick something. If you don't like it, choose something else later. I love your commitment, Meg, I really do. But you don't have to devote the rest of your life to one thing. Especially not one guy. It's okay to keep it casual and see what happens."

"You're not wrong, but changing my mind later feels like I made a mistake in the first place. I prefer to know I'm right from the jump."

"And where would you get that from?" she teased.

As if on cue, Mom came back out with Negasi, each of them carrying a tub of craft supplies.

"I knew your theater friends would be able to use these," Mom was saying.

Georgia and I exchanged a look of laughter, then I left my plate on my chair and helped Mom and Negasi with the rest of it.

CHAPTER FORTY-TWO

ZAK

I glanced in the rearview mirror to see Ollie sacked out in his car seat. Jade was leaning against the side of it, also fast asleep. Lance had put up a good fight, but he'd lost, too. His head was tilted against the window.

Sorry, Zar. They'd be up late on a school night—but maybe not. We'd logged a lot of miles today. It had been fun, especially having Roddie along. He was good with Ollie, Jade adored him, and he'd played games with Lance at the arcade while I entertained the little ones.

"Mom is driving Georgia home. She says she'll pick up dinner," Roddie said after glancing at his phone.

"Tell her I'll get it next time, but that it'll just be you guys tonight. I have to get these brats home. They're all going to need a Silkwood shower."

"What's that?" Roddie asked.

"An old movie. My mom brought it home one time when Zara and I were kids. Fun fact: Brim Stokers used to be a video store."

"I've heard of those. They're like the antique store, but for movies, right?" Roddie joked.

"Yeah," I said dryly. "And we quit letting Mom go there alone after she brought home *Silkwood.* To be fair, it's an Oscar winner. Kurt Russell. Meryl Streep. Cher, too, I think."

"I've heard of Cher."

"You don't know Snake Plissken? I'm going to send you some homework. Anyway, this one's based on a true story. Streep works at a nuclear plant and becomes a whistleblower. At one point, she gets contaminated and has to shower while guys in hazmat suits scrub the hell out of her with long-handled brushes. It left an impression."

"I've seen parodies of that in cartoons. I didn't know what it was from."

"I would have blocked it out completely, but Zara brought it up a few days ago—" I realized where I was going with this and shut my mouth.

Zara had asked why Kyle had covered for me with Dad. When I admitted I'd had a date, she demanded, "With who? Meg?" I told her it was none of her business and she said, "If you hooked up with a stranger off Tinder, I suggest a Silkwood shower."

It was such an old reference to something that had scarred the two of us for life—and was such a typical thing for our mother to do, bringing home a movie we were too young to watch—that we had doubled over with tears in our eyes.

"Why did your mom think you'd like it? Or was it like a cautionary tale? 'You kids stay away from that radioactive waste.'" Roddie shook his finger.

I snorted. "Pretty much. She was always trying to elevate our taste. She sure as hell didn't want us watching *Dumb and Dumber* again." I glanced at his blank expression. "Jim Carrey? Ace Ventura? He's a Canadian icon. I'll add him to the list." Even though some of those movies hadn't aged well.

Roddie twisted to look at the sleeping kids, then said, "Speaking of moms…"

Right. After I'd kissed Meg the way my parents used to kiss before one of them left the house, he'd given me a few curious looks, but the kids were so excited, he spent most of the day answering their nonstop questions.

"We're friends," I said. Who sometimes kiss. And do other things. "I like her. A lot. I honestly don't know how I'd get through my days with

Dad if I didn't have your mom next door, making me laugh. But we both have a lot going on. I know you guys are going back to Toronto. I have to stay here. And… Remember when I said I was dumped? I was actually engaged."

I could feel his stare as he took that in. "To who?"

"Erica. She's a nurse. We bought a condo together a couple years ago, but when I said I had to move in with Dad, she didn't want any part of it. I don't blame her. I really don't. This is not the life she signed up for when we talked about getting married. But it also made me realize this isn't something any woman would want to tie herself to. It's brutal. And Alzheimer's can be hereditary. So your mom and I are keeping it light."

"Mom wouldn't care about something like that."

"No, it sounds like she's willing to put up with a lot of bullshit before she calls it quits." I said it before I remembered who I was talking to. Not cool, but Rod didn't flinch.

"She told you about Dad and Wanda?" There was a tinge of disgust in his tone.

"Yeah. And I don't want to be the guy who takes advantage of her just because she's nice."

"Hmph." Roddie looked out the side window.

"Thanks for helping out today," I said as I pulled into Vickie's driveway.

"It was fun." Roddie slid out of the passenger seat. He paused before shutting the door. "For the record, I'm not mad that you guys are seeing each other. I'm disappointed you thought you had to hide it from me."

The door slammed shut, leaving me chuckling—and suspecting I was falling in love with this whole silly family.

CHAPTER FORTY-THREE

MEG

That week, Zak texted me a few times, and I brought him and Dale lunch twice, but it sounded like Dale was out of sorts after his day at the care home. They came to work late and left early, finally getting back into their regular routine on Thursday.

I was missing Zak and trying not to be bothered by it, so I concentrated instead on what Georgia had said—that there's no right answer. I understood Zak's situation and didn't expect more from him than he could give, but I was wired to think that if he wasn't in a position to make a commitment, then I shouldn't be either. And if I wasn't making a commitment and going all in, should I even pursue things at all?

I wished I could be more like Georgia and go with the flow. I'd learned to do that in some respects. As a mom, I had to make adjustments on the fly. Same when Dad had been in treatment. Best-laid plans had often gone out the window, so I ought to be able to do that with my love life, right? I mean my sex life.

Ugh. Maybe that's what was really bothering me. I was starting to really like Zak. Really, really.

My phone dinged as I was helping a customer. I patiently waited until they'd decided on a cock ring and bagged it up for them.

"Have a good day." I waved them out, then saw the text was from Roddie, telling me he was next door.

I'm hungry, I texted him. *Feel like running over for scones?*

It took a full minute before he answered.

Zak asked me to stay with Dale. His exit is here.

**ex*

"What?" I said aloud to the empty store.

CHAPTER FORTY-FOUR

ZAK

When I heard the shop door chime, I figured it was Roddie. This was about the time he usually arrived from school, but I stopped sanding to listen.

Out on the floor, Dad said, "You came back for the steamer trunk! I knew you would. I saved it for you."

It continued to amaze me that he couldn't remember how to flush a toilet but knew how to draw in a customer like a seasoned carny.

"We're not actually together. I'm Roddie. I help you and Zak after school," Roddie said, then seemed to speak to someone else. "I'll put my backpack away, then I'll come help you. I'll just be a sec."

"I'm actually here to see Zak," a woman replied. "Is he here?"

A jolt of recognition went through me. My limbs went numb and I dropped the sanding block. I quickly began stowing things in the cupboard, thoughts jumping all over the place. Why was she here?

"He's probably in the back," Roddie said, his voice getting closer. "I'll get him."

I could hear Erica saying, "Hi, Dale. I'm Erica. I haven't seen you since Thanksgiving last year. How are you feeling?"

"Erica. Of course. You look well." I could hear the vagueness in Dad's voice as he tried to place her. He had asked me a few times about her, but he mostly lived in the summer I'd been home from college before Mom died. People he'd met after that either remained strangers or became a version of someone he remembered from the early years—like how he often mistook Roddie for a teenaged Kyle.

As I locked the cupboard, Roddie came to the door, brows raised in question.

"I heard," I said and stepped into the bathroom to wash my hands.

When I came out, Roddie was still at the door. "I'm gonna go across the street. Mom wants a scone."

"I'll get it. Can you stay with Dad for a few minutes?"

"Sure." He glowered at me like I'd kicked his dog.

I was just as surprised as he was, but I couldn't keep an eye on Dad and have any kind of serious conversation with Erica. Maybe she brought papers for me to sign?

"Hi." I came out to find her admiring the Royal Doulton figurine Dad was trying to sell her.

"Hi." She smiled warmly, her eyes searching mine. She was pretty, with round cheeks and a few freckles that were downplayed by makeup. That wasn't something she usually wore. Her loose hair was held back by her sunglasses, and her blue slacks matched her blazer. She looked breezy and businesslike.

"Dad, this is Erica. We were living together in Vancouver before I moved back here."

Her smile dimmed, and Dad winced.

"Of course. My memory isn't what it used to be," he said. "How are you, Erica? How are your parents?"

She wasn't on speaking terms with her mom, but she smiled and murmured, "Good, thank you."

Dad took back the figurine and set it inside the cabinet.

"Did I miss a text?" I asked her.

"No. I, um… I came over for a job interview, actually. I wanted to see you before I drove home."

"Oh. That's big news." It landed like a kick in the stomach. I was reaching for thoughts and coming up empty. Was this how Dad felt all the time? "Lemme buy you a coffee. Dad, I'll be across the street, but Roddie is here."

Roddie was standing in the office doorway, pretending to read his phone while shamelessly eavesdropping.

I opened the door for Erica.

"I should have called first," she said as we walked to the corner to cross. I usually dodged traffic like a bolting deer, but I didn't expect her to risk her life like that.

"It's fine. You're not interrupting anything." My shoulders tingled as I said that. I wondered if Meg was watching us.

"How is he?"

"Dad?" I shrugged. "Zara took him to a day group on Sunday. She said it was tough because he didn't really want to be there, and a lot of the people were a lot further along." This glimpse into Dad's future had upset them both. "He's still pretty independent, so I'm mostly here to turn off the stove when he forgets. We have our moments, but we have some laughs."

I thought of our road trip to Leavenworth, which had been entertaining in its low-key way. We'd talked and joked about that old trip that had been such a disappointment after Disneyland.

"I've been thinking about you a lot." Erica paused outside the coffee shop door. "Feeling terrible for the way things ended."

"I don't blame you for setting boundaries." Her ability to do so was hard-earned. She had reasons for not speaking to her mother. "It's okay. We're okay."

"Are we?"

For some reason, the way she was looking at me had my chest feeling chewed by thousands of ants. I opened the door to the coffee shop and waved her in.

It was quiet, just a pair of women at a window table. One was pushing a stroller back and forth while the other showed her something on her phone.

"Hi, Zak." Ali paused in her scrubbing to greet me with a smile. "The usual?"

"Just mine. And a scone to go."

"We only have cranberry muffins left."

"That'll do. And…?" I looked to Erica.

"A latte with an extra shot, half oat, half almond milk, and a shake of cinnamon."

Meg would be appalled.

I paid, and we sat down in the back corner where there was a hint of privacy.

"Tell me about the job interview." *Why are you here?*

"I've been watching for something since you left. This one is in maternity. The interview went well. Decent salary and benefits package. No nights." She widened her eyes to emphasize what a bonus that was. "I thought I'd see if I could picture living here. And see…" Her shoulder hitched. "…Where we stood."

Where did she think we stood? I still paid my half of the mortgage, but we'd closed our joint accounts.

The sensation in my chest grew itchier and more compressed.

"Nothing has changed on my side. I still have to live with Dad."

"I know, but if I was living and working here, we could see each other at least." She leaned forward a little. "I know we rushed into living together, but we also rushed into breaking up. I really miss you, Zak."

I should have said I missed her too. I could sense her trying to pull those words from me.

The truth was, our ability to cohabit peacefully had more to do with the fact that we'd had demanding jobs, and less to do with our compatibility. We hadn't weathered much in the way of life's inevitable storms, but the minute the waves had picked up, we'd fallen apart.

If I had missed her, I would have been texting her all this time. I would have been happy to see her. Instead, I was surprised and a little dismayed. I felt guilty for buying her a coffee, like this was a date when I was promised elsewhere.

"I'm not sure what to say. If you want to move here—if you like the island and the job—then do it. But for me, things are all-consuming with Dad. I don't have the bandwidth for a relationship."

"Here's your coffee." Ali set them down. "I assume this is for Meg?" She set the bag with the muffin on the edge of the table. "I gave her extra butter."

Erica stiffened. "Who's Meg?"

CHAPTER FORTY-FIVE

MEG

She came for a job interview. They're going for coffee, Roddie texted.

I positioned myself so I was hidden by shelving but could still see out the window.

Zak walked across the street with a pretty woman in her early thirties. At least, she looked pretty from behind—tall and slim, wearing a chic blue blazer and matching trousers. She used her sunglasses to push her long dark hair off her face as Zak held the door to the coffee shop for her.

I heard a whimper and realized it was me.

Gross.

I put on Aretha Franklin and checked the online orders, only to find that Georgia had already filled the ones that could be shipped directly from our suppliers. She'd also written a few posts thanking everyone for their support while she was off work and promised to be back soon.

I wasn't mad or even disappointed, but I did feel superfluous.

Thankfully, a couple came in with questions about one of the upcoming workshops, which distracted me.

I didn't see Zak and Erica come back, but the door jangled, and Zak stepped in far enough to say, "Roddie said you were hungry. They only had cranberry muffins." He offered the bag.

"Oh." I came forward. "Thanks." I looked past him, but didn't see anyone else.

"I have to get back to Dad. You got time later? I'll see if I can find someone to sit with him. Buy you dinner?"

"I thought you just did," I said lamely, lifting the bag.

My stomach felt as though I'd swallowed curdled milk. There was no way I'd be able to choke down this muffin. I wanted to ask if we were going on a date or breaking up, but we weren't really together so all I said was, "Text me."

CHAPTER FORTY-SIX

MEG

We met at a bistro downtown near the water, one with comfortable chairs and a date-night ambiance. The tables held candles and fresh flowers, and the menus came in leather folders. Zak held my chair.

My hands were cold and clammy. My pulse pounded in my ears.

"Who's with your dad?" I asked, trying to break the ice.

"Zara," he said in a clipped tone. His movements were stiff as he sat across from me. He wasn't his usual flippant self. When the server asked if we wanted drinks, he looked at me like it was one decision too many.

"Wine? House red?" I suggested.

"Sure."

The server walked away.

"So. Erica was here. You know that," he said flatly.

"Roddie told me." I busied myself pretending the cutlery needed straightening. My stomach was full of acid.

"I wasn't expecting her." Zak ran a hand over his beard. "She came for a job interview and stopped in to talk. I didn't want to be an asshole, so I bought her a coffee, but I feel like one anyway." His mouth twisted.

"Why? We're fine. Even if you've decided to get back together with her, you and I are fine." *Just tell me.*

"We're not getting back together." His sharp gaze pierced mine before he looked away. "But are you so used to being treated like shit that you'd say it's fine if I did?"

"Ouch." I scowled. "Where did that come from?"

"Everything you've ever said about your marriage? When I got back to the shop, Roddie said to me, 'You know my dad cheated on her twice? *That we know of.*' Christ, Meg. I know you're not mad at your ex because you don't fucking care about him anymore, but I'd rather you were a little pissed with me." He gave the back of his neck a disgruntled squeeze. "So I know I matter."

Our wine arrived, giving me a few seconds to react while we ordered crab cakes and ravioli.

"She's very pretty," I said once we were alone again. "Young." *Fertile.*

"Oh, fuck off. You're not old." Zak sipped and studied me, still radiating charged energy. Then he scowled and looked away. "I don't mean to keep swearing at you. I'll stop."

"Are you really upset that I'm not in a jealous rage? Or is something else bothering you?"

He chewed the inside of his cheek while he considered his words.

"She floated the idea of getting back together," he admitted. "When I left Vancouver, it was an all-hands situation with Dad. Zara was at the end of her rope. I didn't give Erica a lot of warning—just told her I needed to do this and didn't know when I'd be back. She didn't want to quit her job and take her chances with what she might find here, so we took a break. I was hurt that she didn't want to come with me, but I understood. And I've come to see that Dad was a convenient excuse. We were never strong enough to stay together."

"She feels differently?" I asked.

"I guess." He rubbed his beard again. "She said she's been watching for something to come up here and that the interview went well. She wanted to see what I thought about her moving so we could keep seeing each other. What's that face for?" he added, catching my expression.

I straightened it. "I don't know. It sounds like she made sure she was interested in the job before she told you she was in town. That doesn't scream *I can't live without this guy*."

"I know, but..." He looked like he was going to scrub his beard right off. "Maybe she wanted to see how things were with Dad. She's a nurse. She has a better understanding of what we're in for than we do. I think she was worried that if she came with me without her own life in place, I'd shift all of Dad's care onto her."

Been there, I thought.

"Anyway, I told her to take the job if she wanted it, but not to do it for me because I don't have room in my life for a relationship. Then Ali brought your muffin and said, 'Is that for Meg?' and Erica said, 'Who's Meg?' Ali looked like she'd stepped in shit, and all I could think was that you would be gutting yourself over how awkward it was."

I bit my lips, nostrils flaring as I fought a bubble of laughter.

Our crab cakes arrived. Zak's must have been made of sawdust because he looked disgusted as he ate.

"I *don't* have anything in the tank for anyone but Dad," he said in a low voice, poking at his food. "I'm exhausted. Just leaving him with Roddie while I was across the street with Erica stressed me out. I'm not a catch, Meg. You're starting fresh and you want to build a life that works for you. I know that. You deserve that. But that's why I'm angry. I'm really fucking lonely, and that made the idea of getting back with Erica tempting for a short minute. It would be comfortable, you know?" His gaze came up, shadowed with compunction. "But I don't want to be with Erica. I want to be with you. Which doesn't feel possible. That makes me sad."

"Oh, Zak." I pushed my plate and the candle to the side and offered my hands.

He moved his plate and pinched my fingers in his tight grip.

"I married Joel because I was pregnant with Shelby. I moved to Montreal because that's where he was going to school. I stayed with him when he cheated because I'd just had Roddie. I've made a lot of concessions in my life for other people. I can't move back here for you. Or even for Mom. It needs to be something that *I* want. And I don't know what I want."

"It's not me, it's you. I know." He was aiming for a light tone, but his voice cracked, and there was injury in his eyes.

"I need to ask you something." I squeezed his hands. "No, I need to *tell* you something. I'm never having another baby. I have no plans to be the parent of any kids except the two I've already got. I'm sure you and Erica were planning to have kids, though. Weren't you?"

"That was before Dad," he said firmly. "Kids are the last thing on my mind right now."

"Understandable, but you have lots of time to change your mind. And you can't keep your own life on hold indefinitely." I gently pulled my hands from his, trying not to let the compression in my heart show on my face. "At some point, you're going to realize that and start moving forward again. If you want kids, you need to be with someone who wants to start a family. I don't."

He shook his head, mouth flat.

"Zak." Now I was a little angry. I clenched my hands in my lap, nails digging into my skin. "I can't be complacent about this. My ex-husband blew up the family we had by starting a new one with someone else. A family I had fought and sacrificed for. I put a brave face on, but he threw me away for a baby he didn't even *want*. Do you really think I'm prepared to go all-in with you, knowing that deep down you *do* want a baby? I *can't*."

Zak would be a more hands-on dad than Joel ever tried to be. I could tell, but I couldn't go back to midnight feedings and living my life by the needs of my child. I just couldn't.

"And fuck you for making me think I should," I said with soft anguish, unable to hold it back. "I was really hurt when I saw you go across the street with her. Not because I thought you were throwing me over, but because you two looked so good together. You looked *right*. Maybe I'm not old, but we're at completely different life stages. I'm mad that you're tempting me to fall back into all my most self-eroding habits, just so we can be together." I shifted the heels of my palms into my eye sockets. It was my fatal weakness that I wanted to be whatever he needed: vessel, therapist, instrument of comfort.

"Meg." He touched my shoulder.

I lifted my head to see he was standing next to me.

"Did I make you cry? I didn't mean to. C'mere."

He opened his arms.

Somehow, I was standing and letting him gather me against his big body where I felt very sheltered.

I was aware that people were probably staring, but I kept my face hidden in Zak's warm, hard chest. I tried not to sniffle because I'd cried enough over Joel, but I was deep in the ache of loss. It wasn't only the future I'd planned with Joel that was gone, but the memories that had become tainted once I realized how little he'd valued them. It was the thousands of opportunities I'd missed when I could have made different choices that benefited me—choices that would have meant I'd be somewhere else entirely right now.

Zak's hand tracked up and down my spine, soothing.

But this was exactly where I wanted to be, I acknowledged. If all those other things had had to happen to bring me to this point, maybe that was okay.

The ache in my chest altered, still there, but shifting into something I could bear.

"I'm not crying," I said, drawing back a little. "I'm just feeling sorry for myself."

"You throw a truly pitiful pity party. No balloons. No clowns."

"Just you." I poked his chest, but he held firm, trapping my arm between us.

We were both fighting our unsteady emotions with a wavering smile.

"I know you have to protect yourself, Meg. I want you to." His brow furrowed with agony. "Otherwise, I will take everything you're willing to give me." He cupped the side of my neck in his hand and touched his lips to my forehead. "Thank you for pretending to be devastated about Erica. I needed that."

I wasn't pretending. We both knew that.

He held my chair.

I sat and looked at his self-deprecating expression as he settled across from me.

"How much time do you have?" I asked. "Do you want to finish dinner or go somewhere for make-up sex?"

"Check!" he shouted, silencing the entire restaurant.

I hid my eyes behind my hand, shoulders shaking with laughter.

CHAPTER FORTY-SEVEN

MEG

We walked to the nearest hotel so we didn't have to move our cars. It was a five-star place with a four-poster king-size bed and a balcony overlooking the harbor. I wanted to stay the weekend, or at least the night, but he only had an hour. He even set his phone alarm in case we fell asleep.

"You can stay," he said, peeling off his shirt. "One of us should use it for the night."

"I'm not staying without you." I closed the blackout drapes and came to slide my hands over his bare chest.

He sucked in a breath, hollowing his stomach, then dipped his head to give me a rough, hungry kiss.

"Want to get super kinky and do it missionary?" he asked.

"If you say you want to look into my eyes, you'll hit my hard limit."

"Ha," he barked, then patted his jeans. "I have condoms, but I don't have lube. The condoms weren't on purpose. I've taken to carrying them in case of emergency."

"This feels like an emergency. Way to be a Boy Scout. I can run down to the shop in the lobby, see if they have lube."

"No, I'll go down. On you, I mean."

"I thought we just negotiated that I would lie still and act like I'm doing you a favour."

"I'm really turned on by that, actually. Why are you still dressed?"

I took off my boots and pulled off my pullover, not giving myself time to catch a case of nerves as I asked, "What if I want to go down?"

"On me? Have at it. My cock is your cock. That's how the saying goes, doesn't it?"

"Not quite, but I meant together. At the same time." Joel and I had tried a sixty-nine in the early years, but mostly stuck to straight screwing. I was invariably on top because he had literally expected me to do everything for him.

Zak dropped his hands to his naked hips, cock thickening, black socks still on his feet. "Exactly how much do you want to corrupt this missionary, Megan?"

"Excuse me, sir, but Meg is short for Margaret." I straightened from kicking off my jeans, now down to my bra and underwear. When I saw the shock on his face, I started sputtering with laughter. "Is this really news to you? You didn't know my *name*?"

"Are you messing with me? I genuinely thought Meg was short for Megan."

"How dare you. Megan is a pretty cheerleader with perky tits and an ass you can bounce quarters off. I'm named for my mom's maiden aunt who never had children. By choice. She worked for a company that printed women's magazines and wrote articles about feminism. She was built like a rectangle." I waved at my figure, which was as square as my personality.

"We've established that I like magazines with women in them, so I think we would have gotten along great." He dragged me close and kissed me, fingers working to drop my bra straps off my shoulders. His erection pressed into my belly, the tip leaking against my skin. His hand slipped into the back of my underwear, palming my ass.

I released my bra and pulled back enough to drag it out from between us, then went back to sucking the tongue that was invading my mouth.

I rubbed my breasts against his chest, loving the feel of him. In the last few years, sex had become a touch-and-go thing for me. I hadn't been all that interested for a long time. I'd blamed stress and a stale marriage and perimenopause, but now I was feeling the want again. That horny need to fool around and enjoy the process, not just get 'er done.

I shifted so I could fondle and stroke his cock, loving the feel of it—sleek and hot and hard.

"Babe." He lifted his head, eyelids heavy, cheeks flushed, lips shiny. "You know I'm going to come down your throat if you sit on my face and suck my cock? I'm ready to come right now."

I circled my thumb over his frenulum, making him twitch and pulse in my grip. "I can live with that."

He groaned and pulled me onto the bed.

It was awkward at first as we bumped around trying to get into position, but he groaned again when I closed my mouth over his tip. I moaned as his tongue began sliding between my lips, searching out my clit.

His hands never stopped moving and neither did his tongue. It was kind of distracting in the best possible way, but I didn't have the mental capacity to be creative. I just sucked, and he seemed fine with that, pulsing his hips as I rocked mine against his face.

I wasn't planning to swallow, but when I was getting close, he stuck two fingers in my pussy and sucked hard on my clit. A sharp twist of pleasure went through my uterus, radiating waves of sensation that reached all the way to my nipples. I came hard all over his face, moaning and writhing, completely lost to the moment. When his come hit the back of my throat, I didn't mind at all.

Seconds later, I rolled off him and felt smug and close to him as we lay top to toe, sweaty and salty and still trying to catch our breath.

"I have to get in the shower or I'll fall asleep," Zak said into the silence. "But that was incredible, Meg. I would've been happy if you had just let me cry on your tits, but that…" He rolled to set a kiss against my thigh, beard still damp. "Shower with me?"

"Sure."

He was the king of afterplay—necking and washing me, fingering me until I had another little orgasm in the shower.

"So conceited," I accused, catching his self-congratulatory grin as we dried off.

"That was a thank-you for riding my face like a bar bull."

"Anytime, Sailor." I slid my arms around his neck, and we kissed once more. But as we drew back, we got tangled in a stare full of all sorts of things—sensual memory, yes, but also the heavier things. The knowledge of how transitory this was. How thin a future we had.

He sighed, sounding so weary my heart broke for him. I'd been on a similar journey, the kind where you stepped off the train once in a while to stretch your legs and breathe some fresh air, but you always had to get back on even though there was no sign of your destination. Not one that you really wanted to reach, anyway.

Dementia was a particularly long and gruelling track. I had a friend in Toronto who'd gone through it with her mom. At least with my dad, he'd had bouts of better health, and until the final few days, he'd retained enough of his faculties to make decisions about his own care.

With Dale, Zak and Zara would have to make decisions for him, like when to take his car keys or when caring for him was more than they could manage at home.

We parted a few minutes later, but I texted Zak when I got home to say good night. In the morning, I texted again, asking if he wanted anything from Brim Stokers.

Nothing.

He didn't come into the store at the usual time, either.

I did get a text from Georgia saying that Gail was coming to pick up a few things from Tap That. Apparently, one of the yacht owners had a special request.

Can you pull the stock for the online orders? I'll send them while we're out.

I sent Georgia a thumbs-up, then texted Zak again.

Everything okay?

Crickets.

I didn't feel ghosted so much as worried. He finally popped his head in at lunchtime.

"I couldn't find my phone," he said. "Dad put it in the dishwasher. I didn't notice until I was putting the clean dishes away. That was after I spent all morning looking for it. Then I had to run to the mall to get a new one."

"Good times."

"So fun. Now he's mad because I was mad. I have to get back." He nodded toward the antique shop.

"Text me later, once you've got the new phone set up. Is it a new number?"

"Nope. Text me something filthy. Cheer me up."

I was positioning sex toys in comical poses and sending him snapshots when Georgia walked in. I had forgotten she was coming and felt as though she'd caught me disrespecting her merchandise, seeing as I'd pulled the plush bunny from the front window and tangled him upside down in the swing ropes. He wore a bright purple strap-on around his middle.

"Um…" I scratched my upper lip and told her why Zak needed a pick-me-up. "You look great," I added.

"Thanks."

She really did. She was moving around without holding on to anything. Her sandals, flowing skirt, and low-cut top were breezy and bright. Her hair was growing out into a thicker cap of tight curls. She wasn't wearing a lot of makeup, but she'd put on some lashes and a mauve lipstick.

"This came up well." She ran her hand over the lid of the polished wood of the stereo cabinet. From inside it, Peaches and Herb were murmuring about being "Reunited."

A pang of loss hit me.

This was what I'd wanted—for Georgia to walk back into her store and absently straighten a book on the rack and take in Mom's latest table display with a cocked eyebrow. The theme was Tiptoe Through the Tulips. There was a vase of silk tulips in yellow and pink, but the rest was an array of flavoured, lip-shaped cock rings, lip-shaped ball gags, and an oral-simulating masturbation sleeve. She'd left a couple of tubes of lipstick open amid flavoured lube and condoms. There was even a double-headed dildo with a small sign tented over it that read: "When your lips meet mine..."

"*Vickie* did this?" Georgia gave me a skeptical side-eye.

"What can I say? She has a gift."

"Sure does," she said with a chuckle. "Is this the stuff to go out today?" She nodded at the box of products I'd pulled and left on the cash desk.

"It is. Do you want me to carry it to the car for you?"

She gave the edge of the box a lift and shook her head. "I can manage." She left her hand on the box while she looked around. "I can't wait to be back."

"And change everything to the way you like it?"

"A little," she admitted ruefully. "Are you offended?"

"No. But when do you think you'll start coming in?"

"I'll try some half-days next week. See how it goes. I was talking to Gail's neighbour. She's looking for part-time work. She volunteered at a teen clinic for years so nothing really fazes her."

"That's good."

Georgia had known me too long not to read the forced sincerity in my tone. Her brows pulled into a frown.

"I'm happy you're coming back. I am. It's just…" I squinched up my nose and tilted my head toward the common wall between this shop and Twice Is Nice. "I really like having an excuse to see him every day."

"Girl, if you want to see him every day, see him every day. Don't put that on me."

I curled my lip at her tough love, then shot back with, "Meaning you're going upstairs to see Bruno while you're here?"

"We're having breakfast tomorrow morning, after he gets off work."

"Really? That's nice." I was genuinely pleased to hear it.

She lifted one shoulder. "I don't know if we can make it work with his shifts and all the rest, but we'll see."

"I hope you can. He seems great. From all the one times I've met him."

"I haven't even met yours. After I put this in the car, I'm going next door to introduce myself." She gathered up the box of toys. "Since he's my landlord and all."

I had a very adolescent urge to ask her what she was going to say, but I held the door for her and pretended I was completely unbothered.

A customer came in, taking up my attention for the next while so I didn't see Georgia leave, only noticed her car was gone from outside.

The ping of a text took me to the desk to check my phone. It was from Zak:

Georgia caught me putting this together. She said we're made for each other.

The photo showed a twelve-inch blue ceramic rooster with a pair of snow globes on either side.

A cock and balls.

I texted back, *Pervert.* Then added a heart.

CHAPTER FORTY-EIGHT

MEG

Roddie was making dinner when I got home. It was only spaghetti with jarred sauce and a Caesar salad kit that needed to be used up, but I appreciated his initiative. I handed him the garlic bread he'd asked me to pick up on the way home, and he tossed it in the oven.

"Do you want some pop, Roddie?" Mom hovered anxiously, acting like he'd been in the kitchen all day preparing a Thanksgiving turkey with all the trimmings.

"What's the occasion?" I asked him as I poured myself a glass of wine.

"Nothing. I was talking to Bethany, and this is what she was having for dinner. Made me want it too."

"You and Bethany are talking? That's good. Is she still seeing Tyson?"

"Tyson dumped her for someone else. A guy he met in a coffee shop."

"Oof. Sounds like Tyson doesn't know what he wants."

"You think?" He used a fork to fish a noodle from the bubbling water.

"Do *not* throw that at the wall."

"Grandma's the one who taught me that's how you test it."

"That was your grandfather," Mom said, "and it's the reason he's six feet underground."

"Mom."

"Grandma." Roddie spoke at the same time I did.

We both laughed while Mom looked pleased at having caught us off guard.

Roddie ate the noodle, then set the colander in the sink.

"Bethany wanted to know when I'm coming back," he said once we sat down to eat.

A small wrenching sensation twisted in my heart, but I made myself say, "Georgia is going to start coming into the store next week. I was thinking April first, but you can go back sooner if you want to. You can stay with your dad."

"Maybe? I don't know. I want to see Freddie. I kind of miss him. And Dad. I mean, he's never going to be like other dads, but I'm never going to be like other sons, so…"

"Roddie." Mom spoke before I could. She reached across the table and set her hand on his. "You're perfect exactly as you are. I hope you know that."

"Thanks, Grandma." He ducked his head, shy but pleased, then looked at me. "But once you're home, I'll probably live with you if that's okay?"

"Absolutely." I nodded, but the hook in my heart tugged harder, tearing it open. I wasn't ready to leave Zak.

"What about you, Grandma?" Roddie asked.

"I don't know." Mom sent a pensive frown toward the living room and the picture window that overlooked the cul-de-sac. "That's a lot to decide by the end of the month."

My conscience gave me another pinch.

"Mom, it's okay. I've been pushing you. I know I have. But now that we've cleared out so much clutter, I think you could list the house as is, whenever you feel ready. Maybe bring in some painters, maybe not. People like to choose their own colours. This house will appeal to a young family looking for something affordable, with good bones they can update over time. You don't even need professional stagers. Put a few things in storage, then put your own talent to work. Maybe borrow a few key pieces from the antique shop."

"Not Georgia's?" Mom said with dry sarcasm, earning a snicker from Roddie.

"You said it yourself, sex sells. If you want to turn the basement into a dungeon, that's up to you."

She sniffed but looked around again, her gaze introspective.

"It's hard to say goodbye," she said wistfully, "but it's also hard to stay. I've wanted to paint and redecorate for years, but then your father got sick. After he was gone, I couldn't face the chaos, so I put things off. It's been nice having you two here, but it's too much house when I'm alone. I don't know the neighbours anymore… but I wouldn't know anyone in Toronto, either."

"It's okay, Mom. You have lots of options. Think about it as long as you need."

She nodded, then changed the subject, and I zoned out to brood about leaving Zak.

CHAPTER FORTY-NINE

MEG

On Sunday, Mom asked me to go with her to Barbara's. Her neighbour was donating some small furniture items to the thrift store, but they were too big for either of their sedans.

Barbara's apartment was only ten minutes from Mom's, but I'd never been there. Mom directed me to visitor parking beneath an L-shaped condo building.

"This is a nice place. Have you thought about moving here?" I asked.

"Barbara asks me that me every time a unit becomes available. Your father and I looked at some of them when he first got sick. He wanted us to downsize while he was still alive so I wouldn't be stuck with all the work of moving. I was letting go of enough at the time, so I told him I wanted to stay in the house. I'm glad we did."

I bit my tongue, accepting that Mom would have to make her own decision when she was ready.

Barbara buzzed us up to her third-floor condo. The living room opened onto a large balcony brimming with flowerpots and had a lovely view of the communal garden where colourful tulips were blooming.

"Bill is golfing, otherwise he'd be here to help us. It's nice to see you again, Meg. How, um… how are things at the shop?" Barbara met my eyes with a brave refusal to be embarrassed.

The furry handcuffs. Right.

"Georgia is going to start coming back to work this week, so I'll be leaving soon."

"That's good news for her, but…" Barbara sent Mom a concerned frown. "I'll be sorry if Vickie follows you. My ulterior motive in asking you here today is to show you an apartment."

"Barbara," Mom protested.

"You've met Isabella. She's expecting us. It will only take a minute." Barbara was unrepentant as she led us into the hall and called over her shoulder. "Her condo is a mirror of mine. She's moving to be closer to her sister in Kelowna. You already know half the people here. Last year, you did nothing but complain about the lawn service and house maintenance. All of that's taken care of here."

Mom gave a beleaguered sigh but managed a pleasant smile for the woman who opened the door to us.

Isabella pulled an oxygen canister behind her as she showed us into her spare bedroom, which was tidy and well-dusted. She pointed out the bench and night tables that we'd be taking off her hands.

"There's no rush to take them. My grandson and his wife are expecting a baby, so I'm here through the summer. But Barbara said you might be interested in buying this unit?" She directed the question at Mom. "I'd expect market value, but it would be a tremendous load off my mind if I didn't have to fuss with showings."

Rather than protest that she wasn't ready to move, Mom said, "Is this real hardwood?"

"I can't have carpet." Isabella gestured toward her oxygen. "The spring pollen bothers me too, which is why I bought the unit with the sunroom instead of the balcony." She pointed out the full bath as she walked us back to the living area and the jut of space surrounded by windows, offering a view of treetops and a small park with a pond.

"It's cozy to read here in the winter," Isabella continued. "Lots of morning sun, but as you can see, the direct sun is already gone for the day now. That's good in the summer. Otherwise, it would be too hot."

She led us through the rest of the unit, pointing out her high-end appliances and quartz countertop.

"I was a pastry chef for twenty years. I still enjoy cooking and baking, but I don't do much of it these days." This time she patted the canister she'd been pulling behind her. "It's a lot to be on my feet."

"Do you want to sit down?" I offered.

"I'll show you my bedroom first."

The bright, spacious room was at the end of the hall. It had a walk-in closet full of neatly organized shelves. The view was just as nice, and the ensuite bathroom was huge.

"I like the walk-in shower separate from the tub. That's a big help for me." Isabella had a plastic bench in the shower so she could sit while washing. Like the rest of the apartment, the bathroom was immaculate—no doubt because mold and dust were as bad for her lungs as everything else.

We sat down and chatted a little more. I tried to steer the conversation so Mom didn't feel put on the spot, asking Isabella where she'd worked as a chef and how many grandchildren she had.

"Do all those windows open? In the summer, I mean," Mom asked, glancing back at the sunroom.

"They do, but I use the air conditioning," Isabella said.

"Of course," Mom murmured.

"Where in Kelowna—" I began.

"Do you get complaints about the hardwood from people below? When you walk around, I mean," Mom interrupted.

"No. Never." Isabella's brows lifted in surprise. "I wear slippers, and the wood doesn't creak."

"You could also put down area rugs," Barbara suggested.

Mom nodded thoughtfully.

"Will this baby be your first great-grand—" I tried again.

"There wouldn't be enough room for you and Roddie," Mom said with concern. "Unless you sleep with me. If Shelby visits at the same time, it's definitely too small."

"There's a guest suite on the first floor," Barbara said. "It's a studio with a kitchenette. You have to book early if you want it for Christmas or summer months, but it's very affordable. Bill and I have a spare bedroom too. We'd always be happy to have company."

"How much are the monthly fees?" Mom asked Isabella.

I gave up trying to change the subject and let Mom run with it.

By the time we left thirty minutes later, Mom and Isabella had a handshake deal that gave Mom the right of first refusal.

CHAPTER FIFTY

ZAK

Busy? Meg texted on Sunday. *Feel like a visitor?*

I feel like I'm stranded on an alien planet, I replied. *Sure. Drop by.*

I was in the front yard when she pulled up twenty minutes later and parked at the edge of the lawn. She brought a six-pack from Tap That and fish tacos from a food truck we both liked.

"I was hungry," she explained as I popped open a couple of lawn chairs and gave her a brief kiss. "I should have asked if Dale can drink alcohol, though."

"I'll open a beer for him. He doesn't usually finish it." It was great to be outside on such a nice day. I'd already mowed the lawn and washed the car. Dad was in the open garage, poking around on the shelves.

"Hello." Dad came out with a pair of pliers in his hands. He smiled politely at Meg. "Are you selling cookies? Run get my wallet, Zak."

"This is Meg, Dad. She works in the shop that used to be Debra's. You've met her a few times. Meg brought tacos and beer. You want some?"

Dale looked at me with confusion. "Where has Debra gone?"

"Retired," I reminded him.

"Oh, that's right. Debra's a good friend." He resisted when I tried to guide him into a chair. "I should call her. See how she's getting on."

"You can eat first, Dad. We'll do that later." I got him seated and opened a bottle by tilting one against another, then handed it to him.

"We can share," Meg said to me. "I don't want a whole one. I'm driving."

"I'll get the opener. It's on the fridge." Dad rose again.

I let him go, thinking of all the times I'd silently judged parents who couldn't keep their kids in line. It wasn't that simple. Sometimes you just didn't have any fight left. He'd eat later, while watching his game shows.

I shifted my chair so I could keep an eye on Dad in the garage. It also brought me closer to Meg—not exactly a hardship.

"He's kind of wound up today. Doesn't want to sit still. That's why the mower and buckets are still out. We always used to wash the car and mow the lawn on Sundays if the weather cooperated. When he sees the bucket and mitt, he remembers it's Sunday and doesn't ask if we're going to the shop. How's your day?"

"Well, my mother basically agreed to buy a condo today."

"Wow. And Georgia's coming back to work, so..." My heart sank to the soles of my grass-stained sneakers. I bit into a taco and lifted it. "Is this a breakup dinner? Because I took you to a nicer place when I thought that's what was going to happen."

"How—oh. Right. Georgia came into your shop the other day. I forgot." She took a bite of her own taco and glanced toward Dad, who was now engrossed in rearranging the shelves. "I wanted to see you. But yes, I also wanted to tell you I'll probably leave at the end of the month."

Eleven days.

We each took a pull from the beer we were sharing.

"Something I haven't told you is that I feel like a shitty mother," she said, still watching Dad.

"Why?" It was inconceivable. "You're a great mom."

"Not in the last few years. Not for Roddie—or even Shelby. She basically got herself through her last year of high school and accepted into U of C, all while getting Roddie to school and doing Joel's laundry. Roddie didn't tell me he was gay because he thought it would be too much for me on top of everything I was going through with my dad and the divorce. How awful is that?" She turned to me, eyes full of regret.

"That's not abuse or neglect, Meg. That's life."

"I know. But divorcing Joel still felt like something I did to them. I made Roddie pick between staying in his home near his friends with his dad—who might be a dick, but he's there—or the mom who parents via text. If Roddie was thriving with Joel and Wanda, I'd move here. But he's not. He wants to live with me there. He wants to be back at the school where his friends are. I feel like I owe him that."

"I understand." I did. "But it sucks." I took another swig. "You'll come see your mom, though? When does Roddie graduate?"

"I'm not going to ask you to wait four years, Zak. Everything I said the other night still stands."

"About me wanting kids? I've got one." I nodded toward the garage.

She didn't say anything.

I thought about Erica saying nothing lasts forever. About how she was willing to accept scraps until things changed. I wanted more for Meg.

We finished eating in silence.

"Do you want me to go?" she asked, balling up her napkin.

"No," I said sullenly.

"I meant right now."

"I know what you meant. I don't want you to leave now or ever. Especially not now." I felt like a child saying it, but it was the truth.

She stood and cradled my head against her stomach. I wrapped my arm around the backs of her thighs and let myself enjoy the sift of her fingers through my hair.

I never wanted to let her go. That was the bald truth. But I had to.

"Nothing is going to change in four years, Meg. Except Dad'll be worse." And I would still love her.

I loved her so damned much it was tearing me up, but saying it would be selfish. She'd think I was laying a guilt trip on her.

So I said, "I guess once Georgia is next door, I can flirt with h— Ouch."

Her closed fist in my hair pulled my head back. Her mouth was tight with outrage, her eyes spitting green venom.

"Thanks, babe." I grinned and fondled her ass. "I needed that."

CHAPTER FIFTY-ONE

MEG

Between Georgia and her new hire, I was only needed at the shop on and off the following week. Mostly off, which gave me time to finish up at Mom's and hang around the antique shop with Zak.

I'd never really paid attention to his woodworking projects before. Sometimes I heard him banging around in the back, or caught a whiff of paint stripper, but now I had time to perch on the rickety stool and watch him sand, fiddle with a drawer pull, or repair decorative molding on a shelf.

Zak relaxed back here because Dale was comfortable in the store and loved to busy himself with rearranging things to "give them more appeal." In here, Dale rolled with the inconsistencies because it felt like everything stayed the same.

"Did you sell the model train set?" Dale popped his head in to ask.

"Last week," Zak said.

"Candace," Dale said, assigning me yet another random name—usually one of Zara's friends from high school. "You've changed your hair."

"This is Meg, Dad. You've met her a few times. She's been working at the shop next door, the one that took over from Debra."

"The toy store. Right." He tapped his nose. "Got that one mixed up, didn't I?" He seemed to be having a good day. "What'd you get for the train set?"

"Not much. They were cheapskates."

"Typical. I'm going to move the clocks onto that table."

"Sounds good." Zak leaned to watch him as he retreated.

The bells on the front door were loud, and Kyle had installed a second chime that rang in the back room. Whenever Zak heard it, he'd hurry out to make sure his father wasn't leaving the store. If customers had come in, he checked on them, letting his dad run some of his patter if they seemed patient enough for it.

"How much do you actually sell?" I asked.

"What do you mean? The train set? That was bullshit. It's been gone for years." Zak returned to his sanding block. "Zara hates that I lie and say Mom's at an estate sale or whatever, but I don't see the point in upsetting him."

"I meant the actual business. Is it profitable?"

"Hell, no. But we own the building. The rentals upstairs and the shop next door give us enough to keep the lights on. Why? You want to work your magic here, now that Georgia's fired you? We don't really care whether it turns a profit. It's a day camp for Dad that we don't have to pay for."

Zak was paying in time, though. And in ways no one else saw. These were his top earning years. That didn't even touch the emotional toll this was taking on him.

"I was just being nosy, wondering how many people actually buy antiques."

"Fewer and fewer as the boomers die off. Millennials don't have the same nostalgia for old crap like this. Ironically, we've been selling a lot online. Roddie's been adding photos to our website, so we're moving stuff that way, but shipping is a pain in the ass. I prefer when people wander in and throw whatever they buy into the back of their car."

"You like this, though?" I nodded toward the short bookshelf he was sanding, prepping it for staining. "Woodworking?"

"It's something to do while I keep an eye on Dad." He paused and straightened. "Why?"

"I don't know. I just worry that you've got a lot to deal with—"

"I do," he agreed curtly. "So what? It's my problem to work through, not yours."

I blinked. "I'm not trying to pick a fight."

"I'm not mad at you. I'm mad at the situation. I'm mad that you're leaving in three days. Not because I want you to stay here and fix my life. I'm not your son, Meg. You don't have to solve my problems for me. I'm an adult. I'll figure it out."

He wasn't yelling, or even being mean, but his words landed like lawn darts in my chest.

"I just worry you don't have enough emotional support," I said defensively.

"You know you're not my only friend, right?"

"Wow." I glared at him.

"I'm not trying to be an asshole."

"Apparently you don't have to *try*."

"I'm saying you should go do the thing you keep telling me you need to do. Go fix your life. Quit worrying about mine."

"It feels like you're throwing rocks to make me go. I don't want to end on bad terms, Zak."

"We're not *ending*, Meg. I'm going to keep texting you stupid shit until you block me. When you come back in September, I'm going to help you move your mom and hopefully fuck your brains out at least once. I *love* you. I wasn't going to say it because it sounds like I'm only saying it to keep you here, but I do. Now you know. So go figure out what that does for you. I'll be here when you get back."

He bent over the sanding block, putting his weight into it while I sat there with my lip quivering.

I loved him, too. And if I said it, if I made it real, then I really would stay.

"Zak?" Dale called out. "Did you sell the model train set?"

"Last week, yeah," Zak called back.

"Did you get a good price?"

"Sure did."

"That's good. I'm going to put the clocks on this table."

"Let me know if you want help."

He looked at me and probably saw that my eyes were too bright. Maybe his were, too. I couldn't see very well anymore.

"Can you just go for now?" he asked, his voice thick.

I swallowed the ache in my throat and nodded, slipping off the stool and out the back way. I knocked on Georgia's shop door until she let me in. Then I cried on her shoulder.

I didn't see Zak again until I was leaving. Roddie and I stopped by the shop to say goodbye. It was short. It was painful.

Zak promised to text, but I wasn't convinced he would.

CHAPTER FIFTY-TWO

MEG

Georgia was having a May Day sale. Your mom was setting up the window. Please let me show her this. #MayDay

Zak had added the photo of me tangled in the swing.

I looked ridiculous, but I was laughing, which made me chuckle. The sheer glow of attraction and joy on my face made me wistful. I missed him in a way that was nearly unbearable.

Tell Mom she should wrap one of the monster dildos like a maypole.

I wouldn't dare. Your mother is a creative genius. She'll get there on her own.

"That must be your man again. No one else makes you smile like that in the middle of the day," my new boss, Folami, said.

"Sorry." I set aside my phone.

"I wasn't scolding. Life is short. I just wonder why you're not there with him if he makes you happy."

"Mostly because I've got this brand-new job I'm trying to keep," I said wryly.

"Pssh," she dismissed. "But you're right not to let a man hold you back, career-wise. I learned that the hard way. I'm running out for coffee. You want anything?"

"I'm trying to cut back. Sleep better, eat better. Be more boring."

"You're nailing it." She slung her purse strap over her shoulder, flicked her braids over the opposite one, and flashed me a cheeky grin as she headed for the door.

I was still just getting to know Folami, but I liked her. She'd joined the small business division at Peterson, Londale, and Funk when I was switching to remote work back when I needed to be in Victoria more often with Dad. At the time, I mostly interacted with her through online meetings and chat. She was always pleasant but stuck to business, which I appreciated. She was ruthlessly efficient, too—another quality I liked.

The only time I'd been miffed with her was when she called in sick for a week during tax season. It was made worse by the fact that the rest of our division was a pile of listless potatoes who didn't pick up the slack like I did.

When Folami returned from her week off sick, the photo of her with her husband—who looked like he'd been ordered from the L.L. Bean catalogue—had disappeared from the shelf behind her. She'd replaced it with a photo of her dimpled twins in Sunday dresses, standing next to an elderly woman in a wheelchair.

Soon after, I left Joel. We didn't talk about it, but I felt a kinship with her. I had quietly envied the way she navigated her divorce and tried to emulate her. Anytime I saw her, she was in full makeup, with hair and nails impeccable, outfits always professional yet colourful, giving her a cheerful, approachable vibe.

Her unspoken better-off-without-him message had kept me washing my hair and making an effort. I'd started going back into the office, hadn't I?

She left for another firm without any fanfare and that's where I thought she'd stayed, so I was surprised to learn she'd opened a boutique accounting office last year, one that specialized in small businesses. Since I was looking for work, I impulsively messaged her to congratulate her—and to ask if she was hiring. I added, *Or we could just get a drink and bitch about exes and PLF.*

Two drinks and a shared plate of nachos later, I had a job. Folami already had an associate and more clients than she could handle. Within days of my posting online about my new job, four of my best clients from Peterson, Londale, and Funk reached out, asking to make the switch.

I felt good about bringing fresh clients into Folami's office, but it was scary, too. It meant I was putting down new roots here in Toronto.

Which was okay, because Roddie seemed to be thriving. He was back at his old school, staying at Joel's a couple of nights midweek, but officially, he lived with me, eating his weight in groceries and leaving his shoes in the middle of the floor like old times.

Actually, he was staying with Joel tonight, wasn't he? I grabbed my phone again and texted Zak.

Want to have phone sex tonight?

Hi Meg, it's Zara. I have Zak's phone.

Oh, he thought he was funny?

Offer's still open, I replied.

I hate you. What time?

God, I loved him.

Thankfully, I was alone in the office so no one heard the whimper that caught in my throat. I really did. I loved Zak with my whole entire being, in a way I had never loved Joel.

And I had loved Joel in many ways. There'd been the sexual crush and teenaged romantic idealism, along with a co-dependent's love of being needed. There was the love built on shared years and fond memories. I mean, yes, he was a self-involved dickhead, but he had a decent sense of humour and could tell a good story. He made great kids, and he'd never been afraid to spend money on what he wanted. We'd taken some amazing vacations, like taking the kids to see gorillas in Rwanda. I'd call it a trip of a lifetime, but we also took them to all the Disney properties, snorkelling on the Great Barrier Reef, and we once watched a space shuttle launch.

When we went to counselling after his first affair, Joel shared some things about his dad's alcoholism that helped me understand him better.

He'd missed out on a lot in his own childhood, which led him to indulge himself as an adult, sometimes in ways that weren't entirely healthy.

So, even though I had a lot of mixed feelings about Joel, I loved him in the way you love a place that you know is gone. He was that copse of trees at the end of the street that's now a shopping mall, or my grandmother's attic after the house was torn down. The special thing we had no longer existed. I accepted that. I was okay with only having the memory of it.

But I didn't have enough memories with Zak to sustain me. I didn't want the safari, either. I wanted to roll over in the dark and feel him beside me. I wanted to wash the car while he mowed the lawn, then drink beer and debate ale versus pilsner. I wanted to feel his arms draw around me while I washed the dishes, and have him rub my feet while we watched TV.

I wanted *him.*

So I made do by texting Georgia, asking her to bag up one of the remote-controlled masturbation sleeves with some lube and walk it over to him.

Fifteen minutes later, she texted: *I said that's from Meg. He said, For Dad? He's such a weirdo.*

I know. Isn't he great?

We texted a little more about how she was feeling—*Great!*—and how the store's sales were picking up thanks to some videos she was posting. Then she sent me a photo of Mom wrapping ribbons around a double-headed dildo to make it look like a Maypole.

Zak had called it; Mom was a genius.

I stopped at a local store on my way home, picking up a new vibrator that worked with the same app as the masturbation sleeve. While waiting for Zak, I figured out how to connect it and texted him which app to load on his phone.

Time zones were another piece of the long-distance relationship puzzle that people didn't always talk about. By the time Zak was home and had Dale tucked in for the night, I was usually asleep.

I was eating take-out Thai I'd picked up on the way home, still browsing the instructions and figuring out how the chat function worked, when Roddie walked in.

I leapt to my feet and swept my arm across the table, brushing the vibrator and its packaging onto a chair, but he caught me and knew what it was.

His brows came together. "Are you still working for Georgia?"

"This was something I was texting with her about, yeah." It wasn't a complete lie. I finished tucking it out of sight. "What are you doing home? I thought you were staying at your dad's tonight?"

"I forgot my good shirt for band. Dress rehearsal is tomorrow. Can you drive me in the morning?"

"Sure."

"Is there any more of that?" He pointed at my plate.

"In the fridge. Help yourself." I picked up my phone and texted Zak: *Roddie's home. Rain check?*

A few minutes later, Zak sent a photo of the blue rooster with a stack of wooden children's blocks beside it. Cock-blocks. He added a snorting-face emoji puffing out clouds of outrage.

I chuckled and replied with a GIF of a girl with her mascara running: *I'm sorry.*

"Who's that?" Roddie asked as he put his filled plate into the microwave.

"Zak." My tone said, *Do you even need to ask?* I set my phone aside.

"Oh, Mom." His voice dropped several octaves. "Did you guys have a date?" His appalled gaze slid to the end of the table where I'd hidden all the evidence.

"What?" I wanted to die. I wanted to *lie*. But I also wanted to be an adult about it. Model healthy sexuality, right? But also: *Nooo.*

"I'm really sorry. I'll go to my room." He looked that way, clearly calculating the fastest escape route, then glanced at the still-humming microwave. "Actually, I'll grab my shirt and catch the train back to Dad's."

"No, Roddie. It's fine. Zak has plans anyway."

"I thought you guys broke up," he said defensively. "I didn't know you were still…" His hands floated through the air, searching for an appropriate term.

"We're still friends. We text."

"That's actually called sexting." He put on his best dad voice. "Are you aware of the dangers of sending nudes online?"

"Are you being serious right now?"

"I don't know. You haven't dated since before they invented the telephone." He shut off the microwave before it finished and brought his plate to the table. "Dad hasn't figured out how to have safe sex. Maybe you need a refresher too."

"Wait, wait, wait." I pushed my half-finished plate aside to lean forward as Roddie sat down. "Please tell me you're not saying what I think you're saying."

"Yeah." Roddie let his jaw drop dramatically, eyebrows lifted like he was preparing to release a nuclear bomb. "Wanda's cookin' another one."

"I'm speechless." I was. "On *purpose*?"

"I don't think so. That's the real reason I came home tonight. They had a huge fight last night." He grimaced at the memory. "I had to watch Freddie while Dad ran after Wanda 'cause she walked out."

"Without Freddie?"

"Yeah. But they came back a couple of hours later. She'd calmed down a lot. I guess Dad was being Dad and wouldn't set a wedding date. They've got one now. June fifteenth."

"Oh. That's good." I guess. I mean, I kind of wanted to host a small intervention and ask Wanda if she really knew what she was doing, but… "Were you okay by yourself with Freddie? You could've called me."

"I'm sure Wanda would've loved to come home and find you giving Freddie his bath," Roddie said, grinning as he shovelled rice into his mouth. "It was fine. There was a thing of breastmilk in the freezer and Shelby texted me, so I fed him and talked to her until they got back."

"She told you she's not coming back this summer?" Shelby had called me the other night to say she'd been accepted into a work-study program that would keep her in Alberta.

"Yeah. It sounds cool. Hopefully she can still come to the wedding."

That was very much for Joel to work out with his daughter. I was super proud of myself for acknowledging that.

"Grandma will probably be here then. She's getting a couple of rooms painted, then staging the house. I told her once she lists it, she should come stay here so she doesn't have to worry about keeping it clean for viewings."

"That's a good idea. What about when she moves? Zak has that big truck."

"I've already booked movers, but yeah, he offered to help." And had promised to fuck my brains out while I was in town, which I was planning to encourage.

"If—" Roddie started, then paused, fork down, silent as he looked at his nearly empty plate.

"What?" I prompted. "This?" I passed my plate to him. "Sure."

"No." He scraped my leftover rice onto his plate, though. "I was just wondering…" He rolled his eyes to the ceiling in a long-suffering way. "I'm trying to respect your privacy, but I'm also wondering why you didn't tell me that you and Zak are still together. I like him. I'm wondering why you left if… Is it because of Dale?"

"No. Not really. Obviously, Zak needs to stay with Dale and I live here, so in that way, yes, it's a little bit about Dale."

"But you don't have to." He frowned. "Live here, I mean."

"I'm sure you'd love to have this place to yourself, but—"

"No. Mom." He was sounding very adult and borderline patronizing.

"No. Rod," I said more firmly. "*You* live here. You're my kid, and we've had a lot to adjust to over the last few years." Losing Dad. Shelby leaving for university. The divorce. Him coming out. "Now your dad is having *another* baby. I'm not going to drop you into that without a safety net. You need stability. Something you can count on. I'm trying to find the same thing for myself, to be honest. And—" I drew a breath, choosing my words carefully. "When I married your dad, I loved him. I have no regrets about the life we made with you kids, but I cannot move across the country for a boy again. Whatever life I build now has to be one that works for *me*."

"I get that, but…" He chased a few grains of rice with the edge of his fork. "You know how you were obsessed with getting Grandma out of her funk and into a better place? I feel the same way about you. I mean, I thought you'd had a full psychotic break with reality when you quit your job and started working for Georgia—"

I sputtered a laugh, but he didn't crack even the tiniest smile.

"Oh God, you're serious."

"It wasn't *you*. Or, I didn't think it was. Then I talked to Zak about it, and he made me see that you really were just trying to help Georgia. He said grief is hard, and that divorce is a type of loss, and that for you, making everyone around you feel safe and happy is your painkiller of choice. He said I couldn't really do anything except wait for you to deal with it in your own way."

"He said all that?" I lifted my head. "Did I really worry you? I'm so sorry."

"Whatever. I mean, one of the reasons I stayed with Dad was because I thought you had enough on your hands with Grandma being super sad and everything. And, honestly? I couldn't take you asking me if I was okay every ten minutes. It was too much."

"Oh," I groaned, cradling my head. "I didn't mean to. Grandma turns into a helicopter-mom with me too. It drives me nuts."

"You're still doing it, by the way. You don't have to text me twenty times a day. I can get myself to school and find my own lunch. At least now I know *why* you do it. It's because you miss Zak, isn't it?"

I felt absolutely transparent. Kicked in the stomach. *Heartbroken*.

"Don't cry," he said with distress.

"I'm not," I lied, touching the edge of my cuff to the brimming corners of my eyes.

Roddie got up and brought the box of tissues from the counter. "Do you want more wine?"

"Sure," I choked, and he topped me up.

"You and Dad getting divorced sucks," he said, returning the bottle to the fridge. "But I'm over it. Dad having another baby with Wanda? That's not something you can fix for me. I mean, I'd rather live with you and just visit them, if that's okay."

"Always." My voice was strained by the tears gathering in my throat.

"Thanks. I feel bad about not really liking Wanda, but I honestly can't tell if Dad likes her either. That's what makes it so uncomfortable. I did think you and Zak made each other happy, though. Like, if he was going for coffee, I'd offer to do it and he'd say, 'I want to say hi to your mom.' And you always talk about him like he's the funniest guy in the world."

"He is."

Roddie shook his head and rolled his eyes. "If you think that, and you want to move to Victoria to be with him, I'd try living there with you. I could always come back and stay with Dad if I didn't like it. It's only four more years, then I'll leave anyway."

"Roddie—"

"*Mom.* You just said you don't want to move across the country for a boy. Don't do it for this one, either." He pointed at himself.

"That is bullshit," I said fiercely, rising to hug him. "You can tell me how to parent once you become one. And that better be *at least* twenty years from now."

"I don't know if you understand how gay sex works, Boomer, but accidental pregnancy is almost never a problem."

I squeezed him harder.

CHAPTER FIFTY-THREE

MEG

I thought about what Roddie had said. I thought about it a lot. I thought about Negasi, and how satisfying it had been to work with him, moving one step at a time, building his business plan. He wasn't there yet, but his vision was taking shape. That helped me start to see my own vision.

I took Folami out for drinks and laid all my cards on the table.

"I wouldn't leave you in the lurch. I could work remotely. But I think my long-term goal is to do something like what you're doing. I like this client base you're cultivating, but I want to lean into the launching side."

Working with small businesses and entrepreneurs wasn't as lucrative as corporate clients, but the work was more personal. More challenging and more rewarding.

"Victoria isn't Toronto. Whatever I build will be slow. It'd be at least a year before I could even think about striking out on my own."

"Maybe we should talk about a partnership," Folami suggested.

"Yeah?"

"Maybe." She shrugged. "If only we knew a good accountant who could explain the tax implications."

"I'll call PLF. See if Cameron's available."

We shared a snicker over that one. God, I was happy to be out of that place.

"You really like this guy, huh?"

"Zak? I do. But he's the first and only person I've dated since the divorce, so I'm trying not to rush into anything. I miss him *so much*, though." I was pining. Eating my heart out.

"How'd you meet him?"

"Bit of a funny story. You really want to know?"

"I do."

She ordered another round, and I started spilling the tea.

CHAPTER FIFTY-FOUR

MEG

When I thought about what anchored me to Toronto, Roddie was it. Most of my real friends had been made when we were still in Montreal, when I'd been a young mom and Shelby was starting play group. I kept in touch with them online, but I didn't see them in person much anymore. I had a few friends in Toronto, but those connections had fallen stale through Dad's illness and the divorce. None were so precious to me that I would take over *their* adult toy shop if they asked me to.

As I considered leaving, I made myself look at all my options. For instance, I could move to Calgary to be closer to Shelby. Roddie might like that, but the thing that drew me to Victoria was the familiarity. It had grown up and grown busier through the years, but compared to Toronto, it felt quaint and laid-back. It felt like home.

I waited until Shelby came for Joel's wedding before I told anyone that I was secretly shopping real estate in Victoria. Mom had taken me up on my offer to have her stay with us while her house was being shown, so she was there when I took the kids out to dinner.

"This is fancy, Mom. What's the occasion?" Shelby asked.

We were in the rotating restaurant atop the CN Tower with a window seat overlooking the city lights.

"The occasion is that I work ten minutes from this place and I've never been. There are a ton of things to do here and I never do them. That leads me to wonder why I live here. And now that I've got you all together, there's something I want to tell you."

Roddie slapped the menu closed. Shelby's eyes widened. Mom picked up her drink and seemed to hold her breath.

Oof. I really had set some rough precedents.

"I've decided to move to Victoria."

"You and Zak are getting back together?" Shelby clapped her hands in excitement.

"Spoiler alert, they never broke up," Roddie said.

"Oh, I like Zak," Mom said warmly. "Are you going to marry or—"

"Mom. Everyone calm down." I held up a hand. "I don't know what will happen with Zak. I haven't told him because I don't want to put any pressure on him. This move is something I want to do. And hopefully Roddie? Do you still think you would come with me?"

"I told Bethany I might. She said, 'What would you even do there?' I said, 'I don't know. I can't learn to fish 'cause I sold all of Grandpa's gear.' She laughed so hard, but she said she'd visit. And I'll see her when I visit Dad. I can come back if I don't like it. Right?"

"Exactly."

"Then, yeah." He shrugged and opened his menu again.

"I wish you'd said something before I listed the house," Mom said with mild annoyance. "I'll call in the morning, see if I can back out…"

"No. Mom. I love you and I want to be closer to you, but not that close. This is a fresh start for both of us."

"Aren't you excited about the condo, Grandma?" Shelby asked.

"It will be convenient. Did your mother tell you I've started doing the window display for the pro shop at the golf course? Let me show you the photos. They're paying me in store credit, but I buy enough there that it works out well for me."

She showed us a photo of three large stuffed teddy bears propping up golf clubs. The mannequin in the middle wore a wig of long gold curls and was teeing up. The whiteboard next to her said, "Ask us about custom clubs. We'll make sure they're just right."

"That's so cute!" Shelby said. "Where did you get the bears?"

"Zak. He and Dale went to an estate sale. The wig is from Negasi. I've been talking to him about helping with financing his business, once the house sells, as an investment. I had forgotten that. Of course I can't back out on listing it," she murmured.

The next day, the kids went to Joel's wedding and Mom was getting a mani-pedi at a salon she liked to visit when she was in town. I had planned it this way because Dale almost always went to his respite group on Saturdays now.

Any chance you're free for an hour? I texted to Zak. *I'm home alone.*

I was looking forward to driving to Sooke and chucking bread at seagulls, but…

A few minutes later, his voice was in my ear.

"Can you hear me?" he asked.

"Yup."

"Cool. What happens if I push this button?"

"It vibrates in my hand."

"What's it doing in your hand? Put it in your pussy," he said crossly.

"Where's yours?"

"In the drawer."

"Zak!"

"Babe, I'm so hard and so horny I'm going to come just hearing your voice."

"You really don't want to do this together?"

"Okay, I will. Just a sec."

I heard some huffs and rustles while I lubed my toy and slid it between my thighs, accepting the small pinch as I inserted it.

"How are you?" he asked. "I'm kissing your neck as I ask that."

"Thanks. I'm good. Are you—Oh!" A low vibration rumbled deep in my vagina.

"Too much? I'll dial it down."

"No, I was just surprised. I didn't realize we were starting."

"Did you hear the part where I came twice because you texted me? I'm—Oh, fuck."

"Feels good?" I smiled as I increased the suction on his toy one degree.

"Really good. Fuck, I miss you, Meg. I—"

I didn't hear him. I groaned, pinching my thighs together as the buzzing inside me began sending waves of pleasure through the rest of my body.

"Is that a good noise?" he asked in a strained voice.

"It feels really good, but not enough."

"More?"

"No. I just really wish it was you. Your cock. Oh, fuck, Zak."

"Rub your clit. I wish I was sucking your nipples right now."

I pushed my hand between my thighs and it was over. I was gasping into the phone, coming hard. His sexy, ragged noises followed in seconds.

I touched the button to stop his toy, and the rumbles inside me ceased. We both sighed and lay there, not talking.

"I miss you, too," I confessed.

No response.

"Zak?"

"Hmm? Oh, fuck," he said in a drowsy tone of discovery. "I gotta clean up. Can I call you after I shower?"

"You don't have to. Get some sleep. It sounds like you need it."

"I do." He yawned. "Dad's been getting up at night. He keeps thinking the TV is on." I had the sense he was moving, then I heard the thrum of the shower starting. "But thanks for this. Let's do it again soon."

"Sure. Um, maybe we could do it in person. I might, um…" Why was I so nervous? "I'm hoping to fly out with Mom when she goes home. I'll let you know. Hopefully, you could get away for a few hours."

"I'll make it happen."

I smiled. "Okay. Bye, Zak."

"Bye, Meg."

CHAPTER FIFTY-FIVE

ZAK

"Is there any chance you can hang out with Dad for a few hours on Wednesday?" I asked Zara when we were having dinner at her place on Sunday night. "Meg is coming in late Tuesday. She was hoping we could have lunch Wednesday."

Meg wanted to talk, and I was kind of nervous about it. The phone sex was great, we texted all the time, but long distance wasn't ideal. I kept thinking she ought to want more from me. To get more.

"I'll see what I can figure out." Zara glanced out at the empty driveway.

Kyle was picking up Jade from a playdate. Lance was in the living room, flipping through old hot rod magazines with Dad. Ollie was doing his best to take me down, tackling my leg. One day he would. For now, I could still pick him up and dangle him by his ankles, which he seemed to love.

"I know—" Zara paused in setting the table. She sent a miserable look toward the living room, then back to me. "I know you really miss her. I know I should say you should go to Toronto."

"We're not having this conversation again. I'm here."

"I know. But I feel like one of us should be happy." She brushed the back of her wrist beneath her eye.

"*What's* going on with you two?" It was killing me.

"Nothing. But everything." She waved her hand in frustration. "We're seeing a counsellor. Kyle's business is being audited. It's routine, but it's a nightmare. And—" She lowered her voice so she mostly mouthed, "I'm pregnant."

"*What?*"

"That was Kyle's reaction too." She clattered the rest of the cutlery into place.

"I'm sorry. That's... a surprise. I didn't know you guys were trying."

"We're not. We were definitely trying *not to*." She blinked fast to hold back her tears. "He kept promising me he'd get a vasectomy."

There were too many words in my mouth to find any good ones. All I could think was that Zara was the one who was leaving. Not really. Not on purpose. But how the hell would she manage another baby on top of everything else she was juggling?

"I really need you here, Zak," she said with a sniff.

"I know. You don't have to keep saying it." Meg was coming to town, and I couldn't wait to see her, but she was starting to feel farther away than ever. I ached with missing her and lived for our texts and chats, but it wasn't enough. I wanted more.

I was starting to see I couldn't have more, though. There was no room for her in my life.

"I like Meg. I really do. But she makes me feel so freaking threatened." Zara took the roast out of the oven. "Just knowing she's coming back makes me happy for you. You've barely smiled since she's been gone, but I'm also terrified she'll talk you into leaving with her."

"She won't." That's why I loved her. She understood what I was up against. And yes, I had fantasies of running away with Meg every damned day, usually to a hotel room where we did dirty things to each other, but I knew where I needed to be. I'd accepted it. And being here wasn't just about Dad.

"Zara, listen to me. Remember that time I came home for spring break, and you said I needed to start looking after myself because I looked like death and you were worried about me?"

"Hey," she said with a frown of hurt.

"You look fine," I amended, even though she had dark circles under her eyes and her hair could use a wash. "But you sound like I sounded then." Completely overwhelmed. "Quit worrying about me and Dad, okay? I'm here. I'm doing it. And I'm going to ask Meg what she can do to help with the audit. Don't argue." I lowered Ollie to the floor and pinned him with my socked foot. "You need a breather. See a doctor and make sure there's nothing else going on, because *I* need *you* here. We all do. So start looking after yourself. Okay? Promise?"

Her mouth trembled. She looked like she wanted to push back, then she flickered her gaze out the window.

"There's Kyle with Jade. She'll be hungry. I'll get Dad to the table."

I took Ollie to wash his hands, but my heart twisted with guilt that I'd asked Zara for Wednesday when she was so close to snapping.

I didn't want to cancel on Meg, but I had to.

CHAPTER FIFTY-SIX

MEG

Zak told me he couldn't get away until Saturday, when Dale was in his respite group.

Our conversation had been awkward. He said Zara was struggling and asked me for advice on helping with Kyle's audit. I could tell he was reluctant to ask, though. I sensed a withdrawal of sorts. It was subtle, but it was there and it scared me. It *hurt.*

I almost told him I was planning to move there, but I had second thoughts. Was I, yet again, trying to rush in and fix things for other people? Was I trying to be needed to prove to myself that I was lovable? Did I want the reassurance of knowing he wanted me before I made such a big move?

I did want to be a support for him, though. That's what love was. And, in the end, I channelled my inner Georgia. If Victoria didn't work out, I would move somewhere else. It was okay to try something and change my mind later.

I flew west with Mom on Tuesday. Roddie had gone on Joel's honeymoon with him. He and Wanda were visiting an all-inclusive in Aruba with Joel's brother, his wife, and all the kids. School was finished for the year and Roddie would have fun with his cousins. I had no qualms about him leaving the country with his father.

Having said that, my mommy radar went on high alert when Joel called me as I was putting on my shoes to meet the real estate agent on Wednesday.

"What's wrong? Is Roddie okay?" I asked Joel.

"Totally fine," he said briskly. "But he told me you're taking him to Victoria?"

"I'm not taking him. I'm moving here—"

"You're there now? With that guy?"

"His name is Zak, and he's not here, but what if he was?" Did he remember the wedding last week when he married someone else?

"You're not taking our son across the fucking country."

"It's his choice, Joel. He wants to try it, and if he doesn't like it, he'll come live with you. It's right there in our custody agreement that Roddie is old enough to decide who he lives with. But go ahead and run up the lawyer fees if it makes you feel better."

Joel hissed out an impatient breath. "Wanda is taking it personally that he doesn't want to live with us."

"Oh. I'll stay in Toronto then. I couldn't bear for Wanda's feelings to be hurt."

"Why are you even doing this? It's the fucking *Island*. We both couldn't wait to get away from there. How well do you even know this Zak?"

"How well did I know you, Joel?" I sat down on the stairs and listened to the silence ripen with twenty-plus years of history that had to be rewritten after clerical errors had been discovered.

Was that what this was really about, though? I wondered if the reason Wanda was stung was because Roddie *liked* Zak.

"Joel, this isn't about you," I said as gently as I could. "You and I had a good run. Now we're doing different things. Roddie's caught in the middle, but I swear I'm not trying to pull him away from you. If he decides to live with you, I will accept that." I would *hate* it, but I would suck it up.

"No—" He swore under his breath. "It's probably better that he lives with you. Things are really complicated right now. I think Wanda's mom is going to come live with us."

"Is she sick? Oh Joel, I'm so sorry." My sympathy receptors went to max level.

"No, her mom's fine. Everyone's fine. But yeah, uh… Wanda's having twins, so…"

She was. Not *we*. Oh, Wanda.

I bit my lip and actually had to cover my mouth to hold back my laughter. It was mean. I know it was. Babies are a blessing, not a joke, but come on. That was some serious karma.

"I'll be there in a sec," Joel said to someone, then sighed. "Either we have to move so Wanda's mom has her own suite, or she has to take Roddie's room. Wanda thinks I'm blaming her for him not living with us. At least if he was with you in Toronto, it wouldn't be as bad."

"Joel." I strained for my kindest possible tone. "I'm not going to fix this for you. Talk to your son. Talk to your *wife*. Figure it out. I'm late for an appointment. But congratulations."

I meant it, but he took it as sarcasm and choked out a cynical, "Fine. Bye."

He ended the call.

I rolled my eyes and dropped my phone in my purse, then yelled, "Mom! Guess *what*?"

CHAPTER FIFTY-SEVEN

MEG

Mom was due for her shift at the thrift store, so she couldn't come with me to the viewing. I didn't mind. I had a lot to think about as I drove into downtown, then across the bridge.

Old parts of me were wondering if maybe I should stay in Toronto. I was taking Roddie away from his new half-siblings. Being close to Mom would be nice, but what did I really have here in Victoria if things didn't work out with Zak?

I pulled into the parking lot of the condo building and nosed into the visitor stall. As I left my SUV, a man popped out of the alcove entrance to the building.

"Meg? Hi. I'm Greg. It's nice to put a face to a name." The realtor offered his hand to shake and held my gaze. I sensed I was being assessed and that he liked what he saw.

"Nice to meet you, too." We'd only talked on the phone.

He was taller than I expected and even more of a silver fox in person than his headshot. I didn't hate what I saw, but—

"Meg."

My heart leapt as I turned to see Zak striding toward us. He wore jeans and a T-shirt. His hair was tousled and shaggy, his beard scruffy and in need of cleaning up. God, he was gorgeous.

I threw myself at him. "What are you doing here? I thought you couldn't make it?"

"Zara came into the shop and told me to go have lunch with you." He hugged me, but briefly. His attention was pinned over my head at Greg. His hands shifted to my shoulders, both holding me off and keeping me close. "I tried calling. You didn't pick up, but your Mom sent me the address. What are *you* doing?"

"Meeting strange men behind your back. What do you think?"

His gaze clashed into mine.

"I'm jok—"

"Oh, fuck it," he growled and kissed me. Hard.

His arms wrapped around me so tightly I could hardly breathe. His mouth smothered mine, and his hand came to the back of my skull. His lips seared across mine, forcing them apart, and he hungrily dragged me into the deep end of passion.

I kissed him back with all the longing that had been consuming my soul. I slid my arms around his neck and pulled myself higher and closer, sweeping my tongue into his mouth, encouraging him to kiss the ever-loving daylights out of me—because I needed this man. Desperately.

From a distance, I heard a male voice say, "This is Greg returning your call."

Greg. Right.

I pulled back from Zak, panting and breathless, and looked over my shoulder. Greg had walked away to make a call, pointedly giving us privacy.

"Who is he? Never mind. Get rid of him. I was planning to tell you we should cool things off," Zak said, making my heart lurch. "But I can't. I love you too much. And I don't know what to do about it."

"I do."

I smiled, cupped his beard, and kissed him once more, this one a tender peck. I tucked myself under his arm and slid mine around his waist as I turned to face Greg.

He came back toward us with an expression somewhere between

bemused and rueful, politely pretending we hadn't been groping like oversexed teenagers.

"This is Greg. He's showing me a condo. This is Zak. My, um, friend."

Zak jolted at the word condo, then gave me a pithy look down his nose. "Friend?" He reached out to shake the other man's hand. "Hello, Greg. I guess I don't hate you after all."

"Nice to meet you, Zak. Shall we go in?" Greg was grinning with amusement as he led us to the entrance.

Zak kept his arm around me. "This is the kind of thing I'd expect friends to tell each other sooner."

"You're mad?"

"I haven't decided yet."

He didn't let go of me as we entered the bright foyer, then the elevator.

Moments later, Greg let us into an empty unit, making our footsteps seem overloud on the hardwood.

I'd studied the photos extensively and liked the floor plan. It was wedge-shaped with a small bedroom and full bathroom on the right of the entryway and a den on the left. Those would be Roddie's domain, with a pull-out sofa in the den for when Shelby visited.

The sliding doors off the den led into the galley kitchen, which connected to the dining and living room. Here, a wall of windows offered a stellar view of the inner harbor. We all halted to silently appreciate the glitter of sunshine on the water.

The covered balcony ran across the entire width of the unit, including the primary bedroom, which shared the same expansive windows and views. The ensuite was a luxurious five-piece, with a walk-in closet behind it. That meant that if Zak and I decided to boink ourselves silly in my bedroom, we'd be well-insulated from Roddie hearing us.

"This is really nice." Zak went back to eye up the granite countertops and what looked like new appliances.

"The floors are heated. You also have the fitness resort, which includes a gym, sauna, pool, and hot tub. There's an owners' lounge with patio seating. Two parking spots."

"Do you mind giving us a minute?" I asked him and slid my gaze to the patio.

He took the hint. "No problem. I'll make a few calls. Take your time."

He stepped outside and closed the doors behind him.

"I didn't mean to spring this on you," I said to Zak.

"I kind of think you did."

He walked into the hall to open a door and glance at the stacked washer and dryer, then walked into the primary suite, which could easily accommodate a king-size bed and a small desk.

"What are you thinking?" I asked warily.

"Is this an investment?"

"No. I'm selling my condo in Toronto. Roddie wants to live with me here. Oh my God, I have the funniest story about Joel—"

"Fuck Joel. I don't care about him. Are you being serious, Meg? You're moving here?"

My mouth opened, but my voice got caught behind my breastbone.

"Yes?"

I couldn't tell if he thought this was good news or bad. He had just told me he loved me, but he seemed angry.

"I don't want you to feel pressured, though," I rushed to say. "I'm doing this for me. I mean, I hope you want us to keep seeing each other." I clenched my arms across my middle, hugging myself. "I love you, Zak. A *lot.* The whole time I've been thinking about this move, I've been thinking I should be able to live without you, but I don't want—"

He had his arms wrapped around me before I realized he'd moved. I had to wiggle to get mine up around his neck. I expected him to kiss me, but instead, he picked me up so we were eye to eye.

"Yes," he said, in such a strong, steady tone it made my heart quiver. "Whatever this is, I'm in."

"But what if…" I petted his beard and searched his eyes.

He waited patiently.

"What if you want babies?" I asked in a whisper.

"What if you can't take how bad it gets with Dad?" He let me slide down his body until my feet met the floor, then kept his arms around me. "You know it could be hereditary, right?"

"I know there are going to be hard times." I shifted my arms to hug his waist. "I'd rather be with you through them than not."

His arms tightened around me. "I've thought a lot about kids since we talked. And yeah, if I had some, I'd love 'em to death, but I don't want them badly enough to give you up just so I could make them with someone else."

"Really?" I pressed my face against his chest, eyes closed and stinging with emotion.

"Really," he assured me. "And honestly, I love my sister's kids, but they're exhausting. Also, she needs me to help her where I can. That means I need you to be the independent badass that you are, Meg. I couldn't add the life of a goldfish to my plate of responsibility right now. I love the idea of skipping making our own kids and letting Shelby or Roddie turn us into sexy grandparents."

"Not just grandparents. The sexy kind." I tilted my head back.

"Very sexy. Why not?"

My eyes were filling up, which was making me laugh at myself—at us—but I was shaking, I was so happy. "I do love you, you know."

"I had a feeling."

"So smug." I went up on tiptoe to kiss the whiskers on his chin. "I guess if it doesn't work out, we'll always have the Dogwood."

"That was a really great afternoon," he said throatily.

"Delightful, even."

"Go sign whatever you need to sign." He nudged me out of his arms. "Then let's go do that again."

EPILOGUE

FOUR YEARS LATER...

I was not quite the magnanimous taker of the high road that my mother was. I did not invite Joel and his family into my home for Roddie's high school graduation party. Instead, I had Mom book the multi-function room at her condo and arranged for the event to be catered.

Thankfully, the weather was great. The younger kids ran out onto the small lawn. Zara's older kids hovered around Gail's teenagers. Ollie and Freddie played tag, while Jade mothered Joel's twins and Zara's youngest, Ester, at the bubble station Mom had set up.

Zak and I loved to pretend Ester was ours for an hour here and there, along with the rest of Zara's brood, but we had never felt moved to try making one of our own.

Zak sat at a table near the door with Dale in the chair beside him. I hadn't seen Shelby arrive with her boyfriend, Aaron, so I was surprised when I glanced over and saw her sitting with them.

"We all deserve fireworks in the bedroom," I overheard Mom say in a tone I recognized as her not-to-be-messed-with voice. "Why would I be ashamed to convey that in a creative way?"

I paused while filling the plates I was making for Zak and Dale, thinking we were about to get a display of fireworks right here and now.

When I met Georgia's gaze across the room, she set her hand on Bruno's wrist—a silent request he pause what he was saying so she could listen and come to Mom's defense if necessary.

Negasi had taken note, too. He had made a special trip over from Vancouver where he had a tiny, profitable, and very beloved shop in the West End, yet still found time to perform weekly in a drag murder mystery show. Negasi and Roddie still bonded over music and theatre, but Negasi was also here to see Mom. She picked up the slack on mending and sewing tasks whenever his shop needed an extra hand. He would definitely throw down if he thought she was being attacked.

"Well, you always had your own way of doing things, didn't you?" Aunt Linda said before walking away in a huff.

"She never changes," Mom hissed as she sidled up beside me.

"Did you expect her to?"

"No," she grumbled, then broke into a smile as she looked past me. "Oh. Hiram is here."

Hiram was her new beau. He was a short, heavyset man who had lost his wife ten years ago and lived in Nanaimo. He and Mom had met at a golf tournament at the end of last year and took a cruise together in January to get away from winter. He'd been golfing this morning, so we weren't sure he'd make it.

Did he give Mom fireworks in the bedroom? I refused to ask, but they smiled a lot when they were together, so I liked him. I left them saying hello and went to Zak's table.

"Hi." I set down the plates, then gave Shelby a hug from behind, kissing her cheek while I was there. "When did you get here?"

"Just now. I think you were outside. Where's Roddie?"

"Working the crowd." Zak shifted some things on Dale's plate and set it in front of him, then handed him a spoon. "I told him to make a point of saying hello to all the relatives so they'll slip him some cash. That's how you get beer money your first year."

Drinking age in B.C. was nineteen, but I wasn't naive.

"Where were you when *I* graduated high school?" Aaron asked. "I skipped out on the family dinner, went to the rock quarry for an all-nighter, and wound up getting my stomach pumped."

"Maybe don't tell that story when I introduce you to Nanna and Pop," Shelby said wryly, referring to Joel's parents. "Oh, there he is! C'mere." She stood and waved Roddie over. "Where's Brian? I want to introduce my boyfriend to yours."

"He's got his own family thing. We're meeting at the party later, but he said he'll come to the hotel for Nanna's brunch tomorrow, to meet everyone. Nanna just asked me when you would get here, so you should probably go say hi to them."

"Okay." Shelby rose with Aaron and said to Zak, "We're at the hotel with Dad and his family tonight, but then we'll be at Mom's for the rest of the week. We'll see you there? You're mostly living with Mom now, aren't you?"

"I've been waiting for Rod to move out so I can have my own room."

Shelby and Roddie looked at each other with long-suffering amusement. They adored Zak as much as I did.

He *was* mostly living with me, and much as I wished he was fully living with me, he was torn up about the ways he was having to say goodbye to his dad. He and Zara had closed the antique shop, mostly because it had become more of an anxiety than a comfort for any of them.

They hadn't sold the building yet but Georgia and Bruno had first refusal when they did. Dale's care was becoming expensive. They had a pair of care aides who did three twelve-hour night shifts a week, allowing Zak to spend those evenings at my place, but he spent his days at the house. He took some programming contracts here and there, but most of his waking hours were spent caring for his father while slowly preparing his childhood home for its eventual sale. Dale had nearly started a fire with the toaster a few weeks ago and had cut his hand the other day because he forgot how scissors worked. He would need a safer environment soon, which meant a facility. Zak and Zara were still coming to terms with it.

None of that anguish showed on Zak's face when he spoke to Dale, though.

"Try some of this, Dad. You like macaroni salad. And you—" Zak pointed at Roddie. "Call me if you need me to pick you up later. I don't care what time."

"I will. Thanks."

Shelby set a gentle hand on Dale's shoulder. "It was good to see you, Dale. We're here for vacation, so we'll see you again really soon, okay?"

Dale gave her a distracted glance, but he was more interested in the salad.

"More coffee?" I peered into Zak's cup as the kids walked away.

"I've had enough, thanks. We'll go soon." Outings with Dale were a nice break, but they also disrupted his routine so Zak kept them short.

"Thanks for coming. And I can pick up my own kid in the middle of the night, you know. You don't have to do it." I reached over to press Dale's napkin into his hand. Usually, that was enough of a signal for him to remember to dab his mouth with it.

He looked up at me with a vague smile, always his very sweet self, but he had never really learned my name. These days he seemed to think I was a nice stranger who showed up at unexpected times. It broke my heart, especially since I was so deeply in love with his son. I wished Dale had some memory of us being together, but c'est la vie.

Zak guided Dale's hand to wipe his mouth, then looped his arm around my hips, looking up at me to say quietly, "I was planning to get you drunk and have my way with you tonight, since we'll have an empty apartment, but go ahead and stay sober if you want to."

"What exactly are you planning that I need to be drunk for?"

"I don't know." He wore that look that made my stomach flutter and my heart melt. "Sometimes I think about asking you to marry me."

"You kinky bastard. Are you really proposing over macaroni salad, on the day I'm losing my son to adulthood, with my ex-in-laws judging me from the other side of the buffet?" I had zero qualms about his hand on my ass. I cupped the whiskers on his cheek, loving the silky feel of them against my palm.

"That depends. If the answer is no, then I'm definitely joking."

"If the answer is yes?"

"Then I'll do a way better job of asking, so we have a way better story."

"You'd better get started on that better story, then."

"Yeah?"

I nodded, smiling so hard my cheeks hurt.

He stood, wrapped me in his arms, and kissed me.

Then the fool—the absolute thunder-stealing *clown*—lifted his head and shouted, "She said yes!"

I hope you enjoyed *Afternoon Delight!* Would you like to read Georgia and Bruno's romance? Download *After Hours Rendezvous,* the prequel novella to *Afternoon Delight*, at danicollins.com/afternoon-delight-prequel.

You will also find new-release info, sneak peeks at my future books, and other insider gossip. Happy reading!

Dani